Ends of the Earth

ENDS OF THE EARTH

BY KEIRA ANDREWS

Ends of the Earth
Written and published by Keira Andrews
Cover by Dar Albert

Copyright © 2019 by Keira Andrews
Second Edition. Originally published as *Road to the Sun* copyright © 2017 by
Keira Andrews

ISBN: 978-1-988260-43-3
Print Edition

Acknowledgements

Thanks as ever to Anara, Anne-Marie, Becky, Jules, and Mary for their support, friendship, and excellent beta reading. Profound gratitude as well to Leta Blake for the superb developmental editing that made this book so much stronger. Couldn't do it without you! Thanks also to Annabeth Albert for suggesting the new title of this story!

Author's Note

While Glacier National Park is a real (and gorgeous!) place, some aspects of the park and ranger details have been fictionalized for plot purposes.

PROLOGUE

HARLAN DIDN'T HAVE to turn around to know it was her—he'd recognize Mary Beth's nauseating giggle anywhere. In the week since she'd walked out, he hadn't missed her at all. He was better off without that bitch nagging him all the time and sticking her big nose in his business.

The fluorescent light above the bank of refrigerators flickered restlessly, a low rattle echoing through the back of the roadside store. Harlan curled his fingers into the plastic holder of a six-pack of Bud cans. After a moment of debate in the snack aisle, he grabbed a bag of corn chips, a smirk curving his lips as he heard Mary Beth ask the cashier for a pack of smokes.

She'd come crawling back soon. She always did.

Turning toward the cash register, he stopped dead, staring at Dwayne. Dwayne had been his buddy since high school, when they used to pump iron and camp out in the woods, living off the land, practicing for when the world finally went completely to shit.

Now here was good ol' Dwayne, with his shock of red hair and ugly freckles—and his arm around Harlan's woman.

Mary Beth had been Harlan's since they were kids, and Dwayne knew she was off limits. But here they were, giggling and whispering with their heads real close.

Just who in the hell did they think they were? They were making a fool of him. No one made a fool of Harlan Brown.

No one.

Ears buzzing with a hot rush of blood, Harlan watched them slide open the ice cream cooler by the counter. Why, they hadn't even *noticed* him standing there. Like he was *nothing*. That little whore had gotten all she could out of him, and now she was making a spectacle of herself with Dwayne, of all people. Digging around for popsicles and laughing like they didn't have a care in the fucking world.

The steel was cool in Harlan's hand, trigger smooth against his finger. He'd carried the same pistol in his belt going on twenty years, and ain't never used it for more than shooting cans off fence posts and putting the fear of God into anyone who sorely needed it.

Mary Beth rubbed herself against Dwayne, her peroxide curls bobbing. When the bullet slammed into her back, she wailed like a calf being branded, staggering against Dwayne and toppling him over. They collapsed on the floor in a heap, Mary Beth's blood pouring out onto the dirty tile.

Dwayne stared at Harlan, his mouth open but no sound coming out, like a fish flopping on the bottom of a boat, eyes bugging. He shoved at Mary Beth as Harlan approached. Then he started to cry and beg—a sorry sight if ever there was one. Harlan put the bullet through Dwayne's forehead to save the man's dignity.

No one should go out crying like a little bitch.

From the corner of Harlan's eye, he saw the cashier raise the rifle. Harlan was faster, and the man went down hard behind the counter. It was a damn shame—Harlan had no argument with him. Why did people have to go and make him do things he didn't want to?

With his six-pack of beer under his arm, he returned to his Mustang and tore open the corn chips. The salty crunch was just what he'd been craving, but he belatedly wished he'd picked up some beef jerky too.

As he drove away down route five, distant sirens already echoed. Damn cashier must have tripped the silent alarm. Stupid fucker deserved to die.

Harlan sighed. They'd have his license plate from the surveillance camera before he could make it back to his trailer. Fucking technology. Good thing he always kept his gear in the car. He was prepared.

Harlan drove to his favorite spot out by the old quarry and finished his chips and beer, listening to the CB radio frequencies. Sure enough, soon they were talking about him, although they didn't know his name yet.

Then a trucker with the call sign Big Papa piped up into a conversation. "My buddy's a cop out there in Whitefish. The dead woman's uncle is on the force and they're out for blood. Said the unofficial order is shoot to kill the bastard. Apparently he was her ex, a loser by the name of Brown."

As strangers chimed in with enthusiasm for this idea, Harlan crushed his last can. He'd just wanted a fucking quiet night.

He drove the car off the dirt road and hid it in a stand of thick trees. His rusty Mustang had been a good friend over the years. A man couldn't ask for better. He ran his palm over the trunk and swallowed the lump in his throat. Bitterness roiled in his gut. God damn Mary Beth and Dwayne. Look at what they'd gone and done to him.

Harlan slung his bug-out bag over his shoulders and disappeared into the forest.

CHAPTER ONE

ALTHOUGH HE TRIED to burrow deeper into his sleeping bag, Jason Kellerman couldn't escape the finger poking his side. He mumbled, "Five more minutes."

"Dad, are you going to sleep all day?"

He pried open his eyes and peered up at his daughter's round face and clear hazel eyes, her bobbed, golden hair grazing her chin. Groaning, he asked, "What time is it?"

She grabbed his phone from beside his sleeping bag and checked the screen. "It's already six thirty-five."

Jason groaned again. "Mags, this is supposed to be a vacation."

"The sun has been up for almost a whole hour. I let you sleep in."

"Oh, what a kind and generous daughter I've been blessed with." He wasn't sure how Maggie had ended up a morning person, but she'd woken with the sun since she was a toddler, and at eight years old, it didn't seem likely to change anytime soon.

"I'll make you breakfast. But you have to start a fire first."

"Why did I ever agree to go camping?" Jason rubbed his face and yawned, the air mattress wobbling as he stretched out.

She put on a sing-songy voice. "Because you're the bestest daddy in the whole wide world." With that, Maggie pressed a kiss to his cheek and darted out of the tent, the flap left hanging open in her wake.

Jason smiled despite himself. Her sleeping bag was tidily zipped on her side of the small tent, her pillow tucked inside. He supposed she got her neatness and early bird enthusiasm from her mother, since it certainly hadn't come from his genes. At the thought of Amy, the familiar twinge of guilt rippled through him.

Brushing it off as he did every day, he traded his plaid pajama bottoms and ratty T-shirt for jeans and a sweatshirt and crawled through the opening in their little tent. The sky was a clear blue above the treetops, white-capped mountains soaring high on the horizon. They called it Big Sky Country, and compared to Philly, Montana was a different *planet*. He breathed the clean air deeply.

"The wood's ready, Dad." Maggie fidgeted by the stack of logs and kindling she'd carefully piled, tugging on the hem of her purple hoodie. Her skinny legs stuck out of her too-short capri pants. At the rate she was growing, she'd need a whole new wardrobe to go back to school in September.

Jason's stomach clenched. He'd spent too much money already on this trip, even with redeeming years of Air Miles. How was he going to afford more clothes and shoes? Maybe he should have put off the vacation until next summer and saved more first. But by the time he'd been eight, he'd already been to Europe, and Maggie hadn't even been outside Pennsylvania. He had to give her everything she deserved—everything a good father would.

Looking at Maggie's sweet face, he pushed the worry aside for later. "Good work, sweetheart. Where did you get the kindling?"

"Just from right there." She pointed to the brush on one side of the campsite. The campground was fairly secluded, and neighboring sites were separated by fifty yards of trees. "Don't worry, I know I'm not allowed to go off by myself. But I had to pee."

Jason's heart skipped a beat as he peered into the dense bush. "Why didn't you wake me up? It could have been dangerous." Why *had* he agreed to go camping? In nature, there were so many variables.

Maggie rolled her eyes artfully. "Dad, we're in the middle of the woods."

"I'm painfully aware of that."

She ignored him as she added, "No one was here. The people next door were still in their tents. Besides, I'm not a baby."

"So you keep reminding me. But you know we're in grizzly country. Tomorrow, wake me up when you have to go to the bathroom and I'll take you over to the outhouse. Okay?"

"Okay, okay. Now will you light the fire?" She held out the box of matches.

"Gladly." Jason took the box, shivering. He was surprised by how low the temperature dropped at night, and it was still too early for the sun to have had much effect.

Jason boiled a can of water for coffee, missing the old machine in their kitchen that whined alarmingly but still produced a delicious brew every morning. He grimaced as he swallowed the instant crap, but it was better than nothing.

"Dad, where's the ketchup?"

"I think it's still in the trunk." Jason fished the keys out of his small backpack and pressed the button on the fob as Maggie raced over. He was continually amazed at the way she rushed into even the most mundane task with enthusiasm.

"Make sure you seal up the cooler."

"I *know*." Her voice was muffled as she rooted around in the trunk of their Toyota rental car. "Always keep food and toothpaste and shampoo and deodorant or anything that smells locked away or hung up in a tree. I taught *you* that."

Jason had to smile. "My deepest apologies." Bacon sizzled in the pan, the salty aroma wafting through the air. Jason glanced around at the encroaching wilderness and fished their can of bear spray out of the tent, keeping it close by.

As Maggie cracked eggs into the pan, Jason grabbed his

sketchpad and pencils from the tent. It was silly of him to always keep his pad by the bed at home and stash one in his car—and even bring it all the way to the middle of nowhere. He knew that. He was never going to art school, and he'd never be a real artist.

Standing under the rising Montana sun with pine needles beneath his sneakers, he let himself think of what it would have been like to go to Parsons or CalArts or the Rhode Island School of Design. He imagined being immersed in art, making real friends who understood him, living on campus and going to parties and all the stupid stuff he'd dreamed of since he was a kid.

His prep school friends had gone off to college and careers and forgotten him, especially after he left home and moved across town. He could still remember the gape-mouthed horror on Colin Nason and Richard Wong's faces when he'd told them he was keeping Maggie and getting his own place, even if it was only a tiny studio apartment. They couldn't fathom why he wouldn't let his parents take her, saying the same thing everyone else did.

"But you're too young."

Even now that he was twenty-five and an official adult, people still didn't think he was old enough to be a father. Didn't think he was *good* enough. He'd prove them all wrong. He'd made the right choice, even if it had meant no art school.

Shaking his head, Jason snorted to himself. As if his parents would have let him go to art school anyway. No, it would have been an Ivy League business degree for him. A suit and tie and shiny leather loafers in a soulless high-rise. No smudges of charcoal on his fingers, no pencils flying across paper.

He ran his fingertips over the smooth edges of his sketchpad. It was only a cheap one from Staples, although a little voice hissed that he could get them for even less at the Dollartown in the strip mall. Guilt slithered through him. He shouldn't spend a penny on himself before Maggie had everything she needed and more.

It was ridiculous anyway. He was never going to create story illustrations or comic books like the ones he'd loved to read since he was a kid. His art was never going to be anything. Yet the lure of pencils and paper called to him, and he opened his pad, knowing he should be a better father.

He sat on a fallen log and sketched a few pages of the campsite and mountains rising across the wide horizon beyond the looming trees. Then he knocked off a drawing of Maggie by the fire, optimism and happiness shining from her wide eyes as she lived her dream of coming to Montana. He'd given her that, at least.

After breakfast—mercifully free of any animal visitors save for two little chipmunks that Maggie scared off with her delighted shrieks—they headed to the visitors' center for a guided nature walk. Jason glanced in the rearview mirror at a stop sign and grimaced as he ran a hand through his messy blondish hair, which was due a wash. Ah, the many joys of camping.

It was also due a cut, and he could imagine his parents' pinched expressions at seeing him in worn jeans with stubble on his cheeks and his hair shaggy. His mother's golden hair had always been perfect, even if it was just in a ponytail for yoga. Even on weekends, his dad had worn button-up shirts and his Rolex.

If Jason had chosen differently all those years ago, he'd probably be sitting behind a desk at his father's firm in a bespoke suit, calling clients and monitoring the stock exchange.

With a pang, he thought of his younger brother, Tim, who'd just graduated Waltham Prep and was going to Harvard according to his Instagram. Jason would love to talk to him and discover the man he was becoming, but that door had closed when their parents made their ultimatum.

Maybe now that Tim was going to college, he'd reach out. *And maybe Tim doesn't want anything to do with me.* If he did, surely he'd have tried to contact Jason before now?

Jason gave his head a mental shake as he turned into the lot and parked. He shouldn't hold his breath for Tim to try and contact him. They were strangers now. Maggie was his family. He'd learned long ago not to dwell.

"Dad? You coming?"

Jason jumped. Maggie had already clambered out of the back seat and now peered in through Jason's window, hopping a little in place, a grin lighting up her face. He returned the smile and said, "Right behind you," as he closed the windows.

Every day, he knew in his heart that his little girl had been the only choice. Maggie was all he needed.

She skipped all the way from the parking lot to the trailhead, where about ten people gathered. Jason made small talk with a few other campers as they waited for the guide.

Maggie's eyes lit up as she tugged on his arm. "Look, Dad. A real park ranger."

Jason glanced over at the man walking toward them in a green uniform. His short-sleeved shirt under a darker green vest stretched over broad shoulders, with a gold badge on his chest and leather belt snug around lean hips, green uniform pants hugging long legs. Probably in his late thirties or so, he was about Jason's height—six feet—but likely had an extra twenty pounds of muscle compared to Jason's lanky frame.

"'Dad'? My goodness." An older woman blinked at Jason and Maggie, an incredulous smile tugging at her lips. "I thought this must be your kid sister."

Maggie ignored the woman with a clenched jaw, and Jason smiled thinly. "No. Maggie's my daughter." Given that his baby face made him look even younger than he was, they were used to this reaction, but familiarity didn't make it any less damn annoying. He turned away from the woman and watched the ranger near.

The ranger adjusted his tan hat over his short, thick, dark hair. The hat was almost like a Stetson but more round, with a brown leather band around it stamped with *USNPS*, which Jason assumed stood for U.S. National Parks Service.

The man cleared his throat and spoke in a low baritone. "Hi, everyone. I'm Ben Hettler, and I'll be your guide today. Welcome to Glacier National Park." He told them a bit about the history of the area as they headed out onto the trail.

"Does anyone know which variety this is?" He stopped by a gnarled tree with pine needles.

Maggie's hand shot into the air. When Ben motioned to her, she said, "Whitebark pine."

His cheeks creased. "The young lady knows her stuff. What kind of bird really likes to eat this tree's seeds?"

"Clark's Nutcracker," Maggie answered without hesitation.

Ben rose his eyebrows and led them farther down the trail. "I see I'm going to have to step up my game here. What's your name, kiddo?"

The other campers on the hike didn't seem to mind that Maggie had most of the answers and even more questions, so Jason didn't try to hold her back. Every so often, Ben would stop and point out certain trees, bushes, or rock formations. He described the various indigenous animals, and gave them the same warning they'd heard everywhere about the potential danger of grizzly bears. Jason certainly didn't need convincing.

Maggie hiked alongside a game Ben, hanging on his every word. She was in her element, and Jason buzzed with pride. Montana was her dream come true, and it was worth every hour of overtime at the factory to see his baby this happy.

Behind Maggie and Ben as they followed the twisting trail, Jason's gaze wandered. He noticed Ben was in great shape. The green ranger uniform clung to his butt and powerful thighs, and his cardio fitness was probably excellent with all the hiking and outdoors work he did.

Sometimes Jason found himself admiring other men's muscles, but there was never time to bulk up himself. He wished his job on the assembly line involved more heavy lifting instead of standing there inspecting cookies. Although his co-worker Ryan was in amazing shape. Jason watched him sometimes, wondering just how much time Ryan spent getting sweaty at the gym.

The day grew warmer with each passing minute, and Jason peeled off his sweatshirt and wrapped it around his waist, glad he'd worn a tee underneath. He gave his bare arms a critical glance before eyeing Ben's lean, sculpted muscles.

He refocused on what Ben was saying about wolverines being close to reaching endangered status, and Maggie piped up with some information she'd learned doing a book report. Ben surely knew everything she was saying, but he listened avidly as Maggie chattered away, and Jason gave him a grateful smile. Some people were impatient with Maggie's tendency to talk a lot—loudly and rapidly—about things that excited her.

After the tour ended back near the parking lot, Maggie continued to pepper Ben with questions until Jason intervened to let the guy off the hook. "Mags, I'm sure Mr. Hettler has other work to do."

Her shoulders slumped. "Oh. I'm sorry."

Ben smiled down at her. "Don't be. I have some time, so fire away."

"Are you sure?" Jason asked. "We don't want to keep you."

"Positive. Most of the people on my nature walks nod and smile with glazed expressions. It's a pleasure to talk to someone as passionate as your sister." Ben smiled again, this time at Jason. His white teeth were dazzling next to his tanned skin, and Jason found himself grinning back.

"Maggie's my daughter, actually. I'm Jason Kellerman, by the way." He extended his hand, and Ben shook it firmly. Ben's palm was slightly callused, and a strange, tingly warmth skittered up Jason's arm.

"Nice to meet you both. My apologies for the assumption."

His brow had furrowed, but he didn't stare at them with disdain or judgement the way some people did.

Jason waved his hand. "It's okay, we get that a lot. Maggie, what did you want to ask?"

She bounced on her toes. "Okay, so if we see a grizzly bear, will it try and eat us?"

Ben looked thoughtful. "Well, little girls do taste awfully good."

Maggie giggled. "Be serious. Would it *really* try and eat me?"

Ben dropped the teasing tone. "The simple answer is: maybe. But remember that bear attacks are extremely rare. If you're sensible and take precautions, you'll be just fine. Most bears want nothing to do with us."

She persisted. "But what if you do everything right and still run into a bear?"

"If you see a bear in the wild, the first thing to remember is not to run. It'll go against all your instincts, but if you run, the bear will follow, and believe me—bears can outrun anyone."

Jason tried to laugh. "Gee, that's a comforting thought."

Ben smiled at him. "Don't worry, grizzly attacks really are rare. So if you see one, first you assess the situation. How far away is the bear? Has it spotted you? If it hasn't, back away slowly. Remember, *don't run*. Now, if the bear does see you, just stay still, and talk to it in a calm voice. Bears don't see very well, so it could help to let it know you're a human by talking."

"*Could* help?" Jason asked.

Ben spread his hands wide. "I'm afraid there are no guarantees when dealing with the wild." He smiled again, and Jason's stomach flip-flopped oddly. Talk of bears always made him nervous.

"*Daaad*, stop interrupting!" Maggie eagerly waited for Ben to continue.

Jason made a zipping-his-lips motion as Ben said, "Okay, so

once it's clear that the bear's getting aggressive and not leaving, try and make yourself look as big and threatening as possible. Wave your coat over your head and shout, and hopefully the grizzly will decide you're not worth its while."

"Maggie, remind me why we came to Montana?" Jason teased. She shushed him.

"Like I said, no guarantees," Ben added. "If the bear charges, then spray it with bear repellent. Basically pepper spray. Much more effective in a bear attack than a gun."

Jason frowned. "Do many people here carry guns?"

"It's unfortunately legal now in national parks. We discourage it, but that doesn't mean visitors listen to us. You can be a great shot on the range, but it's a different story when a six-hundred pound grizzly is charging. Bear spray is far more effective."

"We have some!" Maggie proudly patted Jason's backpack.

"Excellent. And if the bear is still in the vicinity after you spray, it's time to curl up in a ball and play dead. Hug your knees to your chest and keep your head tucked in. If you have a pack on, you can lie on your stomach with your hands over the back of your neck. If you're lucky, the pack will take the brunt of any attack."

Maggie looked thoughtful. "How long do you play dead for?"

"For as long as you have to. Even after you think the bear's gone, wait a long while before you move. It's entirely possible that the bear's waiting nearby to make sure the threat—that's you—has been contained. And if playing dead doesn't dissuade it and the attack continues, you have to fight back."

"But the bears around here must be pretty used to people. They can't be that dangerous, right?" Jason asked hopefully.

"Actually that's when bears are the most deadly, and grizzlies are dangerous no matter what." Ben patted Jason's arm, fingers squeezing the bare skin just below Jason's T-shirt sleeve. "Don't worry. Like I said, attacks are really rare. Although to properly answer Maggie's initial question, there have been rare instances of bears stalking people with the sole purpose of eating them. In those cases, you'll probably never see the attack coming."

Jason shuddered. "'Stalking.' Wonderful."

Maggie bit her lip. "But that won't happen in the campground, right?"

Ben shook his head. "Don't worry, you'll be fine. You're locking up your food tightly?"

She nodded. "Yes! We're being very careful."

"Then I'm sure you don't have anything to worry about." Ben squeezed her shoulder.

Just then a group of kids nearby whooped with excitement, circled around something on the ground. Maggie switched gears effortlessly as she ran over to see what was going on, any worry over bears forgotten.

Jason laughed. "Sorry, she has an insatiable quest for knowledge. This is basically her Disneyland. She's obsessed with national parks and mountains. When she was little we rented a nature DVD from the library and I ended up buying her a copy. She pretty much wore it out and the interest never faded."

"That's terrific. I wish more kids were interested in wildlife and conservation." Ben took off his hat, his long fingers toying with the brim. "Where are you folks from?"

"Huh?" Jason jerked his gaze up from Ben's hands. "Oh, Pennsylvania. Philadelphia area."

"I've never been. What's it like?" Beneath long lashes, Ben's sea-blue eyes were focused on him, and Jason went hot to the tips of his ears.

He stammered, "It—uh, well it, you know, it has its pros and cons." *So eloquent.* "Great museums and stuff." He winced internally. He sounded like a dumb kid, and turned the conversation back to Ben. "Philly feels like another universe compared to how wild it is Montana. Are you from around here?"

"I am. Born and raised in Kalispell."

"Population twenty-two thousand, right? First established at the end of the nineteenth century after the railway was built. There's a dragon boat festival in September."

Head tilting, Ben smiled quizzically. "Sounds about right."

Why am I being such a spaz? "Maggie did her term project on Montana last year and couldn't stop talking about it. Guess some of the info sunk in." He jammed his hands into his jeans pockets.

"Nice to have visitors who've done their research. Is Maggie's mom here too?"

Jason kept his tone even. He despised talking about this. Hated the pity and questions that followed, and the incredulity that *he* could possibly be raising a child alone. "No, her mother died when Maggie was a baby. It's just the two of us."

Ben blanched. "I'm so sorry. I shouldn't have…"

"No, no, it's okay. You didn't know. Obviously."

Ben scratched at his head, mussing his thick brown hair, and Jason had the insane urge to reach up and straighten it. Fortunately he kept his hands in his pockets as an awkward silence stretched out. He waited for Ben to ask the usual questions, but Ben only fiddled with his hat, those long fingers smoothing over the band of leather.

Finally, Jason blurted, "I like your hat."

"Thanks." Ben's low chuckle sent a shiver down Jason's spine. "Want to try it on?"

Maggie called, "Dad! Come see this!"

Feeling oddly guilty, Jason whipped around and squinted at where the kids were gathered over something in the dirt. "Apparently there's something I've got to see. I should let you get back to work anyway. I'm sure you have plenty of other…rangery things to do." He hesitated. "It uh, well… It was really cool to meet you." *Oh my God, I am so lame.* "We'll be sure to lock our food up tight. Thanks for the tour."

"Anytime. Which site did you pick?"

"Bear Creek. Not very reassuringly named, by the way."

Ben grinned. "That's one of the sites on my route. At night, I make sure everyone's food is locked and confiscate it if it's not. Maybe I'll see you around. And I'm doing another hike tomorrow morning on a different trail. I can change the focus and give Maggie some new info."

"Really? That would be great." Jason's voice rose excitedly, and he cleared his throat. "As long as it's not any trouble."

"No trouble at all. I like to mix things up anyway. So I'll catch you tomorrow? Nine o'clock. If I don't see you tonight first."

"Uh-huh. See ya." Jason waved and came alarmingly close to tripping over his own feet as he hurried off to make sure Maggie wasn't getting up to any trouble. She grabbed his hand and pulled him into the circle.

"Look, it's a fossil!"

Jason examined the strange-looking rock the kids had found. He was pretty sure it wasn't a fossil, but didn't want to burst their bubble. "That's awesome!"

Maggie looked back to where Ben was heading toward the ranger station. "He's nice. I like him."

Jason followed her gaze. "Yeah." Ben had stopped to talk to a young couple, smiling at them and pointing toward a trailhead. Obviously he was kind and helpful with everyone, and there was no reason whatsoever Jason should be feeling a ripple of...disappointment? Jason was just another camper Ben was being friendly to. It was the man's job, after all.

"Can we have lunch soon?"

He refocused on Maggie's hopeful face. "Lunch? It's barely ten o'clock! I don't know where you put it all."

She shrugged and skipped off toward the parking lot. Jason glanced over his shoulder and watched Ben disappear inside the ranger station. Ben was only being nice, but it would be cool to hang with him again. Jason didn't get the chance to have many grown-up conversations, and Ben was great with Maggie. Why shouldn't Jason want to see more of him?

As he followed Maggie to the car, Ben's baritone rumbled in a loop in Jason's mind.

"If I don't see you tonight first."

For some reason, it sounded like a promise.

CHAPTER TWO

B EN WATCHED MAGGIE AND JASON KELLERMAN through the window in the ranger station as they walked to their car. "Hey, Dee. Who's working the Bear Creek clean-up?"

Dee, nearing retirement but in better shape than most people half her age, picked up her wire-rimmed glasses and opened a folder. "That's Tyree's route."

"Think you can switch us for the rest of this week?"

"Why? What's wrong with Cloud Lake?" She raised an eyebrow.

Ben shrugged. "Nothing. Just feel like a change is all. If it's a big deal—"

"Did I say it was a big deal? Tyree's off this week anyway, so I'll just put his temp on your detail. Satisfied?" She tucked an errant strand of gray-blond hair behind her ear and tightened her ponytail.

"Thanks."

It could be slim pickings for a gay man living in the wilds of Montana, and Ben had an inkling that Jason Kellerman might provide a needed diversion. Sure, he had a kid and apparently a dead wife or girlfriend, but Ben's instincts were rarely wrong. Jason had definitely been checking out Ben's ass during the hike.

When the Kellermans drove away, Ben turned from the window and holed himself up in his little closet of an office in the rear of the station, flipping through a new accident report and rubber-stamping it.

His mind kept wandering back to Jason. Tall, slim, sandy blond hair that curled over the tops of his ears, and a killer smile with juicy lips. Hard to believe he had a kid Maggie's age since he didn't look a day over twenty. Ben wasn't usually into younger guys, but Jason Kellerman was clearly older than he appeared, so why the hell not?

As if on fucking cue, Brad's voice rang out from the main office. Groaning, Ben sat frozen at his desk. Should he go say hello? Be mature and rational like the forty-one-year-old man he was?

After all, Brad Cusack was the district manager and technically his boss. Ben couldn't avoid him. Shouldn't. It wasn't as if he were in love with Brad anymore. They hadn't been in love with each other for a long time, and that was part of the reason Brad had an affair and dumped Ben for a hot actor with a ranch near Great Falls. After just about two decades together—half their lives—their relationship had just…evaporated.

The usual swirl of shame and indignation churned Ben's gut. Since college in Missoula, he and Brad had been "B&B," openly gay and fighting for equality in the parks service, which they'd gotten since they were both dedicated to their jobs. Acceptance from colleagues had followed, and they'd eventually planned to marry and start a family.

But that had all been before Brad started moving up the parks food chain, more interested in administration than actually being out in the wild. Even after marriage equality was won by the Supreme Court's ruling, there had always been one reason or another why it wasn't a good time to plan a ceremony, let alone begin the difficult adoption process.

Then Brad met Tyson Lockwood.

In the outer office, a baby wailed, and Ben squeezed his eyes shut against the swell of resentment and longing.

Brad and Tyson Lockwood had married on horseback at Lockwood's ranch the year before, and had now adopted a little boy. *People Magazine* had featured glossy, breathless, five-page spreads on both events.

Ben flattened his hands on the smooth, worn wood of his desk, listening to the murmur of deep voices as the baby wept. Over the years as he and Brad had grown apart, Ben had thought they wanted different things. But as it turned out, Brad *did* want marriage and a family—just not with him.

Brad had even kept their house outside Kalispell, albeit with grand new wings jutting out on either side. One night in a particularly self-pitying mood, Ben had driven by, slowing his pickup to peer into the gloom at the home, so familiar after living there more than ten years, but utterly foreign at the same time, dwarfed by the wood and glass additions.

The windows had been dark, and Ben figured Brad and Tyson were at the ranch. He'd pulled into the driveway, thinking about getting out and actually peeking in the shadowy windows, when a stark motion-sensor light illuminated the night.

Blinking into the harsh white glow, he'd slammed the truck into reverse and sped back to his dad's old cabin, humiliation burning his cheeks.

That same shame flushed him now, and he shoved back his chair. No, he wasn't going to hide in his tiny office. He hadn't done anything wrong. He hadn't cheated or lied. Squaring his shoulders, he took a long breath and opened the door.

The baby—Lincoln—was cooing now, cradled in Dee's arms. She looked up, her face creasing guiltily. Ben put on a wide smile. "Hi, Brad. Tyson. Great to see you."

"Ben!" Brad was out of uniform, so apparently this was a social call. He was still stupidly handsome with his crooked smile and green eyes, fit and tall, cowboy boots heavy on the wooden floor as he strode over to shake Ben's hand and pull him into a back-slapping half hug as if they were fishing buddies.

Tyson was right behind him, taller and even more stupidly handsome with gleaming white teeth—too straight and perfect to be anything but veneers—and brown skin. He pumped Ben's hand, and they all pretended they were great old friends, and that Ben's heart hadn't been eviscerated, no matter how much he and Brad had grown apart.

Ben nodded at Lincoln, still being held by Dee, who kept her gaze down. "He's really growing."

"Every day we notice something new," Brad gushed. "It's incredible."

Tyson asked, "Would you like to hold him?"

In the beat of awkward silence, bile rose in Ben's throat. God, he did want to hold him. He'd always imagined fatherhood as a huge part of his life. Raising and shaping and loving his kids, guiding their first steps, bandaging scraped knees, reading stories before bed and giving in as they begged for just one more.

He wanted to explore the world with them, take them camping and hiking the way his dad had. Teach them to love the forests and lakes and mountains the way he did. He wanted more from life than he had. He wanted a family.

Now Brad had one with Tyson. How wonderful for them.

With all eyes on him, Ben managed a smile. "No, no. I've got work to do." But to prove it didn't bother him—nope, not him, not bothered at all—he went over and leaned close, ignoring Dee's sympathetic gaze. "Hey, little guy. He's beautiful."

Lincoln gurgled, and when Ben tapped his nose, Lincoln grabbed onto his index finger, his tiny, pudgy hand gripping with surprising strength. Ignoring a pang of wistful longing echoing dully in his chest, Ben stepped away and smiled brightly as he asked, "You guys on vacation?" He realized he was fisting his hands and forced his fingers to relax.

"Just for a few days," Tyson answered. "I'm going to New York next week to shoot a movie, so we wanted to make the rounds of all the offices and show off Lincoln like Brad promised everyone."

"Terrific," Ben said too forcefully.

Brad eyed him over a strained smile. "Great job on the proposal for the new guest services. I'm going to push for it with the board, but they're cutting back more and more. I can't make any promises."

You never could. "Sure, sure." The phone rang, and Ben practically lunged for his office. "Dee, I'll get it. Catch you guys later!" He shut the door behind him and stabbed at the blinking light on the phone to take what turned out to be a report of garbage dumped on the side of a road, which would draw bears.

A few minutes later, there was a tentative knock at his door, and he forced an even, pleasant tone. *Nothing wrong with me! Nope, not a thing.* "Come in."

Dee filled the doorway. "They're gone."

Ben glanced back at his paperwork. "Hmm? Oh, okay."

"Sorry about that." She jerked her thumb over her shoulder. "You know, with the kid."

Some of the tension loosened from Ben's shoulders, and his smile was real. "You're allowed to hold the cute baby, Dee."

She sighed. "Too bad his fathers are schmucks."

"Yeah, well. That's life, right? He can cry into his millions."

"Brad's got some nerve. If he wasn't the boss, I'd tell him exactly what I think." She crossed her arms. "You know you deserved that promotion to chief ranger. You're never going to get your due here, not with him in charge. He's afraid people will cry favoritism if he promotes you."

"Not much I can do about that."

"I mean, you shouldn't even be on nightly food patrol. With all your years of experience? You're way beyond that, and he knows it. We all know it."

Ben shrugged. "I don't mind that part, actually. It's peaceful at night, walking through the campgrounds." He loved strolling under the stars, spotting the campers around their fires, or knowing they were tucked away snug in their tents. It made him feel good to keep them safe.

Despite the many warnings, some visitors didn't take the threat of bears seriously, and while Ben didn't enjoy confiscating food, he was responsible for these people, and it brought him a sense of calm and satisfaction he couldn't really explain.

"Be that as it may, you know there *is* something you can do about the fact that you deserve more from this job." Dee raised an eyebrow. "I know Grand Teton wanted you to head up their program."

Shaking his head, Ben tapped his computer and pulled up a random file. "I'm happy here. This is my home."

"It is, but I'm calling a load of BS on the happy part. You mean to tell me you're really happy as pie living all alone in that ramshackle old cabin of your pa's?"

"I like the peace and quiet. Besides, it's temporary."

"You moved out of the house in Kalispell two years ago."

"I haven't found the right place." He jabbed at the keyboard. "But this *is* my home, Dee. I'll be damned if I let Brad and Tyson run me out."

Her lined face softened. "I know. I'm sorry. I just hate seeing you so miserable."

"I'm *fine*!" He tried to laugh, not quite succeeding.

"When was the last time you had a date?"

Ben didn't think the quick grope and blowjob with a random guy from Grindr in East Glacier Park Village counted as an actual date. He leveled Dee with an exaggeratedly accusing look. "And when was the last time *you* had a date?"

She barked out a laugh. "When you've been married thirty

years, it qualifies as a date when your husband takes you to the sports bar to watch the game, holds the door for you, and turns away to burp."

"And they say romance is dead."

The phone rang, and Dee retreated to answer it. The mention of the word "manhunt" piqued Ben's interest, and he came to lean a hip against her desk. He raised his eyebrows when she hung up. "Well?"

"There's a killer on the loose from Whitefish. Chance he might be heading into the park. Also a chance he already escaped south, but I guess we'd better be safe than sorry."

"What's the story?"

"Scumbag blew away his ex-girlfriend and her new guy in a convenience store last night. Did the cashier too for good measure."

"Oh yeah, I heard about that. Do we have a description?"

Dee nodded to the corner. "Fax should be coming any minute."

She went back to her paperwork, and Ben lingered by the fax machine. The mug shot was two years old according to the accompanying note. The beady eyes of a man in his thirties with unkempt hair cut into a mullet style stared back at Ben. The man had a thick, muscular neck, but his chin was small and weak, his nose crooked, as if it had been broken a few times.

"Looks like a real charmer," he noted.

Dee glanced up from her desk, and Ben turned the page toward her. She snorted. "Yep. If you're bored, want to make some copies for me?"

"Sure." The photocopier had been built sometime in the Stone Age, but it got the job done. According to the description on the police alert, this Harlan Brown was not only armed and dangerous, but was a paranoid survivalist who had extensive knowledge of the area and had been known to drop off the grid for weeks at a time.

Great. He might be hiding right under their noses. "I'll put these up. Can you make sure the other stations have them too?"

Dee didn't look up. "Will do. I'm sure there's nothing to worry about, but I wouldn't want to run into this creep out there."

Ben picked up the pile of copies and looked at the mug shot again. "Definitely not."

THE STARS TWINKLED into sight as Ben parked his truck near the entrance to the Bear Creek campground. He was a full hour early to begin his inspection rounds, but he wanted to find out exactly where Jason and Maggie were camping before they went to bed. Maybe he'd be invited back later if his instincts about Jason Kellerman were right.

Ben ambled down the dirt road that twisted through the campsites. He was hungry for the feel of another man beneath him. Seeing Brad had served to remind him how unsatisfying their sex life had become years before Tyson Lockwood had even entered the picture.

When Ben and Brad met in college, they'd been young and fumbling. Brad had never liked the idea of bottoming, refusing even to try it. Ben never pushed—Brad had every right to his preferences. But as the years passed and Ben had wanted to explore and expand their boundaries, Brad was never enthusiastic. He'd always hated the mess of sex, wanting everything tidy and contained.

Kicking a rock into the undergrowth with a violent rustle of leaves, Ben wondered if Brad was like that with Tyson. *Maybe he just didn't want* my *dick inside him. Probably bends over for Tyson Lockwood daily. Gives him everything I wanted. Adopts a baby with* him. *Why were we ever even together?*

It was all tainted now. Half his life, and he couldn't help but look back on it as a waste.

After the breakup, it had taken Ben months to even think about screwing other guys, and aside from the odd trip to Butte's pathetic excuse for a gay bar or a couple quick online hookups, there hadn't been anyone. Certainly not anyone who mattered.

The guy in East Glacier had been wearing a wedding band, and Ben had tried to ignore it, telling himself as the man sucked him that it was none of his business. But he'd felt dirty in a way that had nothing to do with the sex.

That had been months ago when winter was thawing, and now it was July, the heat of summer lingering as night fell, slick on his skin. He wanted more than nameless sex with a stranger.

Ben snorted to himself, mumbling, "So you know Jason's name. Yes, that'll make it *so* much more meaningful." Hell, he didn't even know if Jason was interested. He might think Ben was a creep. *And I just might be.*

Maybe he yearned for a bit of company too. His dad's old cabin had been a magical place when he was a kid, but now that it was home, it felt empty. He and Brad had had a group of friends in Kalispell, but it was awkward after the breakup, and Ben rarely saw them after moving out of town.

Dad was gone now, and Mom had passed when he was still a teenager. He probably had cousins somewhere, but he didn't know them. He'd always imagined having kids by forty. He told himself he was fine on his own, but sometimes he wished…

"Christ," he muttered. There was his sentimental streak, rearing its ugly, useless head. His family was gone, and Brad had made a new family without him. He needed to man up and deal with it.

The moon was almost full, so he didn't need to turn on his flashlight as he navigated the campground. Many campers were gathered around their fires, and he scanned the faces far too eagerly.

After half an hour, Ben still hadn't spotted Jason. He was just about to give up and get to work when he heard a man and child singing off-key. As he neared the campsite, he spotted Maggie's bright hair, the echo of firelight catching in the golden strands.

When he realized what they were singing, he smiled in the darkness. John Denver and his country roads had been a favorite of Ben's parents, and he joined in without thinking.

Jason shot up from his perch on a log beside the fire, squinting toward the dark road. "Hello? Who's there?"

Ben stepped into the campsite with a wave, pushing up the brim of his hat. "Sorry to startle you. I was just passing by."

Jason visibly relaxed. "Oh, hey." He rubbed his palms on his jeans, seemingly anxious all over again. "We were just…hanging out." He cleared his throat.

"You sounded great, and don't let anyone tell you any differently."

Ben could swear Jason was blushing. "Yeah, well. Maggie loves campfire songs even though I'm not good at them."

"You're awesome, Dad. Hi, Ben! Do you want a marshmallow?" She thrust a stick toward him, a gooey mess stuck to the end of it.

"Thanks, Maggie." He pulled off the warm marshmallow and savored the sticky sweetness.

"Can I get you something?" Jason asked. "Um, I don't really drink." He opened a nearby cooler and fished around. "There's soda, juice, water and, uh, milk. Or I could make some coffee?"

Ben smiled. "Soda's great." He took a seat on the log next to Maggie, resting his hat on his knee. Jason passed him a cold can of cola and sat on her other side.

"So. Um, nice night, huh?" Jason asked.

He was clearly nervous. Maybe a good sign? Ben didn't know why he was even entertaining this idea of starting something with

Jason. He should probably just leave the guy in peace, but there was something about him and his crooked smile that intrigued Ben in a way he hadn't experienced in a long, long time. He took a swig of cola. "Beautiful. I guess you don't see stars like this in Philadelphia."

"Nope. It's amazing out here."

Maggie speared another marshmallow with her stick and held it over the fire. "Ben, will you sing a song with us?"

"Well, I'm not much of a singer. You might regret asking me."

"It's okay, my dad can't sing either."

"Hey!" Jason faked offense. "You just said I was good. I'll have you know I was in the choir all through school. Sure, it was mandatory, but that's not the point."

Maggie giggled and turned her stick, browning the marshmallow. "Come *oooon*. Let's sing."

"Maggie, don't whine," Jason said. "It's okay, Ben. You don't have to."

"How about you sing one for us, Maggie?" Ben suggested.

"Okay. I learned this in Girl Scouts." She cleared her throat dramatically before launching into a slightly off-key version of "Puff the Magic Dragon." When she was finished, both Jason and Ben clapped. Ben asked, "You ever think about going pro?"

She grinned. "Maybe in a few years. I have to at least finish sixth grade first, and I'm only going into fourth."

Jason added, "Oh, you'll be finishing a lot more than sixth grade, young lady."

"You know, that song used to bum me out when I was a kid." Ben took a swig of cola. "Man, I haven't heard it in years."

"I guess it is kind of depressing, with Puff losing his friend and going to wallow in his cave," Jason said.

"Yeah, but I thought the kid died. You know, dragons live forever, but not little boys."

Jason laughed. "Okay, I can see how that would be a serious

downer."

Maggie frowned. "So Puff never finds another friend?"

"No, of course he did," Ben assured her. "He found lots of other friends. Dragons are never alone for long. They're way too awesome."

She seemed to ponder it before yawning widely. "Yeah, you're right."

"I think it's time for bed, Mags," Jason said. "It's been a long day."

She suddenly sat up straighter. "I'm not tired at all! Let's sing another song."

"No, it's time for bed." Jason nodded to the tent.

"*Dad,*" Maggie pleaded.

"Maggie, I said no whining. Bed."

"But—"

"No buts. Go get your toothbrush." He pulled the car key from his pocket and pressed a button. With a chirp and dull thud, the trunk opened. "*And* toothpaste."

"Fine." She huffed loudly and stomped toward the car.

"And no pouting, either!" Jason called after her. He turned back to Ben. "Sorry about that."

"Kids, right? Don't worry about it. I'd better get to work anyway." He got to his feet. "Thanks for the drink."

"Sure, of course. Um, thanks for stopping by. It was cool." Jason stood as well and offered his hand.

Ben took it, holding on for a moment longer than necessary. He had to fight the urge to draw him closer and skim his fingers over the hair on Jason's forearms. He wondered if he had hair on his chest, or below his belly button...

He blinked and dropped Jason's hand. He usually went for beefy guys his own age, but there was something about this young man. So responsible, but with that baby face and lean body. Shit, he was beautiful.

Shoving his hands in his pockets, Jason licked his full lips. "Um, I should…" He motioned toward the car, where Maggie rummaged in the trunk.

"I can stop by later." Ben's heart thudded. "If you'll still be up." *Say yes.*

Jason's brow furrowed slightly. "Later? I'll be sleeping. All this fresh air, and Maggie gets up at the crack of dawn."

Damn. Playing hard to get. Or maybe he was reading Jason entirely wrong? He smiled and tried not to feel too disappointed, failing miserably as he put his hat back on. "Right. Well, I'll see you tomorrow morning. For the hike." Could he have been imagining the undercurrent running between them? "If you're still interested. No pressure. I'm sure there are a hundred things Maggie wants to do and—" *And stop babbling like a goddamned idiot.*

"We'll definitely see you for the hike, and if you come by tomorrow night, Maggie can sing you another soul-crushing song."

Strange relief flowed, and Ben smiled. "Sounds like a plan. How long are you here for, by the way?" *What are my odds of getting you alone?*

"Ten days, so we've got eight left."

"Great." Ben glanced around the campsite. "You'll be sealing up that cooler, I'm sure?"

"Safe and sound in the trunk. And I'm glad you're checking to make sure everyone else around here has too." Jason grinned, his face lighting up as he brushed a stray lock of hair off his forehead, his red lips dark in the firelight. "Thanks again."

As Ben strolled off with a casual wave, he whistled to himself, imagining all the things they could do in eight days.

THE NEXT MORNING, Ben had a spring in his step when he saw Maggie and Jason waiting near the ranger's station. His stomach fluttered, and images of the dream that woke him up hard and aching flickered through his mind. He'd stroked himself roughly in the dawn light and imagined Jason on his knees, mouth hot and wet, those red lips stretched wide—

As his dick stirred again, Ben closed his eyes and gave his head a mental shake. Last thing he needed was to walk up with a bulge in his pants. He took a deep, steadying breath. If he played his cards right, that dream could become reality at some point during the week. Hell, he should probably go to town and fire up Grindr, but Jason sent a thrill through him that he hadn't felt in too long.

Rain drizzled from the steel sky, the air thick. Ben hadn't expected a big group for the hike, and so far no one else had arrived. "Morning," he called out as he approached.

Maggie waved excitedly. "Hi, Ben! What's today's hike going to be about?"

He grinned at her excitement. "What do you want it to be about? Doesn't look like too many other people are interested in this lousy weather."

"I want to know more about the birds around here. And people need to learn about raincoats." Maggie indicated her bright red poncho, the hood drawn around her face, making her hazel eyes look even bigger.

Ben laughed. "Apparently they do." He wore a dark green rain slicker similar to the navy blue jacket Jason wore. He tugged on the wide brim of his hat. "Need to learn about hats too." He turned to Jason, who wore a Phillies cap. "Have a good sleep?"

"Aside from the fact that it gets way too cold here at night for July. The tent didn't leak, so that's something."

"Cold? There wasn't even any frost this morning!" Ben teased.

"Did I mention it's *July*?"

"City slicker."

"Damn right." Jason grinned.

Ben waited a few minutes to see if any other campers would brave the sodden weather, but soon led the way onto the trail. Maggie and Jason listened attentively as Ben told them about the birds in the area, giving background info on the various species.

After he'd run through his bird lessons, he asked Maggie, "Do you remember what to do if you spot a bear?"

Jason snorted. "Pray? Kiss your butt goodbye?"

Maggie sighed. "*Dad.* Be serious, please."

He raised his hands. "Sorry."

She rattled off the information Ben had told them the previous day about bear attacks, and Ben nodded. "You know your stuff. Good job, Maggie."

"Oh, and we should sing while we walk so they can hear us coming. What do you want to sing?"

"Know anything by the Beatles?" Ben asked teasingly.

Her face lit up. "Of course! 'Yellow Submarine' is awesome." She loudly launched into the first verse.

Jason hummed along, peering into the dense woods, clearly ill at ease now that he'd been reminded of the potential for danger. "Whose idea was it to come out here again?"

Maggie broke off from singing. "Don't worry, Dad. Remember, Grizzly attacks are very rare."

"If you say so, honey."

"*I* say so. Sorry, didn't mean to worry you." Ben clapped Jason on the shoulder and led them farther down the path toward a lookout.

Beyond a wooden railing, a vista of trees unfolded below, with mountain peaks disappearing into the clouds in the distance. Even in the gray drizzle, the view was remarkable, but Ben wished he could have shown it to them in the brilliant sunshine.

"Wow," Maggie breathed. "This is so cool."

Jason pressed a kiss to her head. "It really, really is."

Ben felt strangely proud and pleased by their awe. Not that he had anything to do with the gorgeous view, but it was gratifying to see his home appreciated.

"Am I allowed to look for rocks?"

It took a second for Ben to realize Maggie was talking to him. "Sure, just be careful. Make noise in the bush, and don't go too far from the trail. Stay in sight."

"Okay!" Maggie darted off.

Jason frowned. "Are you sure that's okay? I don't want her to damage anything."

"Don't worry. The ecosystem isn't quite that fragile."

"She's a budding geologist too, as you can tell," Jason added.

"I can indeed."

They watched Maggie's progress with an easy silence between them. Ben was dying to ask Jason some questions, but he figured it was best to play it cool and start slowly. "So, Maggie's eight?"

"Yep. Well, eight and a quarter, as she will insist loudly if you ask her."

"Funny how when we get a little older, we're not so eager to add on to our age."

"True. Although I'm twenty-five, and I wouldn't mind looking a little older."

Whoa. Jason didn't just *look* young. Ben blinked at him, doing the math. "So you were…"

"Seventeen when Maggie was born. I know, I was young. Believe me, I know."

"Sorry. I don't mean to pry."

"Sure you do." Jason smiled easily, a little dimple appearing in one cheek. "Most people are curious. It's okay as long as they're not dicks about it."

"Well, I try not to be a dick. How am I doing so far?"

The dimple deepened. "Not bad."

In a rush of *want*, Ben leaned closer, taking a step despite himself. Jason was a grown man, but there was an innocence about him that affected Ben in a way he couldn't explain. Jason hummed with a sweet warmth he wanted to touch. *Needed* to touch.

Jason's brows drew together, and he licked his lips. "Ben?"

Maggie called out from the trees, "Dad! How many rocks can I bring home?"

Heart thumping, Ben reached down and plucked a wet rock from the sodden leaves and dirt. "Speaking of which, this is a…" His mind whirled. *Rock.* "Um, I'm blanking on the name, but maybe Maggie would like it." It was only an ordinary gray stone, but it was a little shiny in the rain, at least.

Jason answered Maggie. "As many as you can fit in the pockets of your jeans. The ones you're wearing, I mean." To Ben he said, "Cool, thanks." He took the rock, their fingers touching, and Ben could swear a spark shot all the way to his balls.

"Sure. No problem." He managed not to squeak like a teen-aged boy.

Jason shook his head as Maggie bent over again, her red poncho flashing through the leaves. "You should see her room. Rocks everywhere."

Breathing deeply, Ben regained control. "No Barbie dolls for her, huh?" He was being officially nosy now, but he needed to concentrate on something other than how hot Jason Kellerman was.

"Oh, she likes her dolls too. Maggie isn't…easily categorized."

"She's a great kid. You're lucky."

"I am." Jason looked distant for a moment before he shook his head and smiled.

"I'm sorry about her mother. It must be hard." He had so many questions that would likely fall into the "dick" category, so he bit his tongue.

Jason's voice was steady. "I lost Amy a long time ago. It's a challenge raising Maggie on my own, but you do what you have to do. I'd give up anything for her. Everything."

"You don't have any family helping you?"

"No." Jason's jaw tightened, his spine stiffening. "We're just fine on our own."

Hmm. Definitely a story there, but Ben didn't think it was wise to press it. "Most guys wouldn't be able to handle it—taking care of a little kid all alone. Sure as hell not as a teenager."

Jason shrugged and fiddled with a damp curl behind his ear, tugging down the brim of his baseball cap. "Guess I'm not most guys."

Definitely not. Ben watched Jason wipe a raindrop from his cheek. He cleared his throat. "How do you manage it?"

Jason was about to say something else when he stood up straighter. "Where is she?"

Ben realized Maggie had wandered completely out of sight while they'd been talking. "Don't worry, I'm sure she's right over there." He pushed up the brim of his hat, peering into the gloom.

"Maggie!" Jason called.

A lark's song whistled through the trees, and the raindrops seemed to echo in the stillness.

Before Ben could say another word, Jason bolted into the forest. "Maggie!"

Ben followed. "It's okay, don't panic."

"Dad, come look at this!"

Ben could practically feel Jason relax, his breath whooshing out in a long sigh as Maggie reappeared and pointed excitedly at something in her hand. Jason listened patiently, running a hand over Maggie's damp hair and pulling up her hood, retightening it under her chin.

Ben found himself smiling as he watched them. How had this young man handled raising a child? And raising one so well? Not that Ben was an expert, but he flashed back to muddy hikes with his parents and their endless patience as they taught him about the land. How happy and safe he'd felt exploring the wilderness with them.

Jason pulled his phone from his pocket, and Ben said, "No cell service anywhere out here. Sorry. You'd have to go down to Apgar Village."

"Yeah, it's been weird not going online. But a good weird, you know? I was just looking at the time. Shouldn't we be getting back? It's almost been an hour."

"Nah, it's okay. I don't have another tour until after lunch. There's a pretty cool cave nearby if you want to see it."

Maggie gasped and clapped, and Jason laughed, a throaty chuckle that tightened Ben's groin. "That's Maggie for 'yes.'"

As Ben led the way, he hoped he'd hear Jason Kellerman say *yes* again soon in an entirely different context.

CHAPTER THREE

"I DON'T KNOW about this."

Maggie rolled her eyes. "Dad, why do you always have to worry so much?"

"Because it's my job."

"No, it's not."

"Yes, it is."

"Is not."

"Is…" Jason stopped himself before he sounded even more like an eight-year-old. "Maggie, I just think it might be too dangerous."

Her sigh was decidedly longsuffering. "You're such a control freak."

"What? I am not. You don't even know what a control freak is."

"Sure I do. I saw it on TV. This is why you won't let me go to sleepovers. You want to be in charge of everything."

So maybe he was a little overprotective. He could admit it. But after almost losing custody of Maggie, he kept her close. "No, I want you to be safe. That's all."

"Look, those kids over there are younger than me. Besides, we have to wear life jackets."

"Right, because there's a good chance of *falling out.*"

"Dad, would you chill?"

Jason laughed despite himself. They were in line at a small wooden kiosk to sign up for a morning of white-water rafting. The day had dawned sunny and perfectly warm. Down a gentle slope, the Flathead River was calm and placid. However, Jason knew that less than a mile away, the river became a frothy, frenzied beast, crashing violently over massive rocks.

"The rapids are only twos and threes. That's nothing." Maggie had done her homework, as usual.

"Why don't we go canoeing on the lake back near the campsite? That'll be even more fun." He tried to sound enthusiastic.

Maggie's tone indicated that she thought her father was being completely lame. "You can still drown in a canoe, you know."

Terrific. "Is that supposed to make me feel better?"

Maggie lowered her voice and leaned closer. "Is it too much money?"

"No! Of course not. Don't worry about that." He smiled in what he hoped was a completely reassuring way.

Truthfully, at just over a hundred dollars for the half-day trip, it was pricier than Jason would like, but he hated that Maggie was even aware of money beyond her allowance. At her age, he hadn't had to think about what anything cost. Yes, his parents were rich, but still—kids shouldn't have to worry about money. A hot slither of guilt snaked down his spine.

They were almost at the head of the line, and the woman in front asked the ticket seller if she'd get wet. She wore pressed capris and a crisp white blouse, and her hands sparkled with jewels. Maggie and Jason glanced at each other and tried to hide their giggles.

Maggie whispered too loudly, "It's like she thinks this is Hersheypark."

"You will get wet on this ride," Jason intoned in a deep announcer's voice.

"Excuse me?" The woman turned and regarded him with one eyebrow arched over the rim of her gleaming sunglasses. With her blond hair she could have been his mother, right down to the French manicure.

Jason stammered. "I—I was just talking to my daughter."

"*Daughter?* You barely look old enough to shave. How sordid."

"You're sordid!" Maggie crossed her arms and glared up at the woman.

Jason pulled Maggie against him, arm around her tense shoulders. "I think it's our turn." He motioned to the teenage cashier, who watched the unfolding drama with wide eyes, twirling her ponytail around one finger. "If you'll please step aside."

The woman flounced off without another word, and Jason pulled out his wallet to buy their tickets. Maggie watched the woman leave. "Why would someone like that go on vacation in Montana?"

Before Jason could answer, a low voice behind them replied, "It's the 'in' thing these days. The rich and famous are getting back to nature in droves."

"Ben!" Maggie squealed, her anger dissolving. "What are you doing here?"

Wearing a tank top and shorts, with a life jacket hanging over his bare, hair-dusted arm, and a paddle on his wide shoulder, Jason was willing to bet Ben was going rafting. He tried to ignore the strange, spikey flush that spread from head to toe.

Ben had come by the night before for marshmallows, and had surprised Maggie with chocolate and graham crackers for s'mores. He'd also taught her an old campfire song about barges. While Ben insisted he wasn't much of a singer, his baritone was gentle and steady, and Jason wanted to hear it again.

Maybe Ben could take time off work and spend a whole evening with them. Jason would cook a fancier dinner than pasta and jarred sauce, and they could sit by the fire and talk after Maggie went to bed. With Ben there, he wouldn't worry about bears. Wouldn't worry about anything much at all.

Jason couldn't remember the last time he'd actually made a new friend. His coworkers at the cookie factory were nice and all, but he never saw them outside the assembly line. He was far too busy with Maggie.

He cleared his throat. "Hey. You're going on this trip too?" It was dumb to think of Ben as a *friend*. He was older and probably just being nice. Just doing his job as a ranger.

"I'm filling in this morning. I've been a guide here since I was a teenager. Still do it on my days off once in a blue moon."

"Cool! Can we be in your boat?" Maggie grinned ear to ear, and Jason found he was doing the same.

Ben winked at Maggie. "I think I might be able to pull a few strings."

Giddiness bubbled through Jason, his worries about safety evaporating. Ben wouldn't let anything happen to them on the river. To be polite he said, "Don't go to any trouble or anything."

"Nah, it's no trouble." Ben smiled, his cheeks creasing. "I'll see you down by the first raft there." He indicated with his chin.

Jason paid the cashier, who directed him to the equipment shed. Inside, a teenage boy wearing a Metallica T-shirt and what appeared to be a perpetual frown sized them up and provided life jackets and helmets.

Through the open shed doors, Jason watched Ben by the river's edge, bent over examining the rigging on the raft, his white tank top stretched across tan skin and firm muscles. Jason fidgeted, excitement ping-ponging through him.

The last time he'd felt this way about spending time with a friend was with Edward Martin at equestrian camp the summer before sophomore year of high school. Amy had teased him mercilessly about his "bromance," and he'd brushed it off.

"Dad, are you okay?" Maggie asked, hands on her hips. "You don't have to be afraid, I promise."

"I know, baby. Thank you." He dropped a kiss on her forehead and stood still while the teenager plonked a helmet on his head and tightened the strap.

Ben waited by the large inflatable raft as people trickled down from the shed. He crouched and tugged Maggie's life jacket. "You always have to make sure your jacket's on securely. See these buckles?" Maggie nodded, listening carefully. She was like a sponge, always eager to learn, and Jason watched with pride as Ben went on. "You have to pull them like this to double check that everything's nice and tight. Here, you try."

Maggie did as she was told. "Is that good?"

"Looks great to me, kiddo." Ben stood. "What about Dad?"

"Huh? Oh, I'm fine." Jason's fingers were suddenly shaky and useless as he tried to fit one side of the zipper of his life jacket into the other.

"Here, let me help." Ben gently pushed Jason's hands aside and zipped the jacket in one smooth motion. Standing so close, Jason stared at the curl of Ben's long, dark eyelashes. Up close without the ranger hat, he could see the warm hint of auburn in Ben's short, thick hair.

Ben slowly tightened the straps on the jacket. Jason's throat went dry, and he swallowed hard. Sweat trickled down the back of his neck, his heart skipping as Ben did up one buckle and tugged. One of his hands rested lightly on Jason's hip, and Jason swore his skin tingled even through the cotton of his shorts and T-shirt.

He held his breath as Ben tested the other buckle. A moment later, Ben stepped away with an easy smile. "There you go." He turned to Maggie. "Is your helmet comfortable?"

Jason loosened the strap of his own helmet to wipe a band of sweat from his forehead. He took a deep breath. Maybe a dip in the glacial water would do him good.

"Okay, everyone! Let's take our positions." Ben told the gathered group where to sit, placing Maggie and Jason near him in the back. There were nine people in the raft, including Ben. Everyone had his or her own paddle but Maggie, much to her chagrin.

"But that's not fair! I want to paddle too!"

"Baby, you're not big enough to reach. I'm sorry." Wincing internally, Jason could see a hissy fit coming on and kept his voice low and calm.

"It's not fair!" Tears welled in her wide, hazel eyes. She was a remarkably mature child most of the time, but her occasional tantrums could come on without warning.

"Maggie, stop it. Now. Or we're getting out and we're not rafting." Jason's skin itched with the judgy gazes of the other passengers in the raft. He hated it when Maggie acted out in public. He could practically hear the whispers saying he wasn't fit to be a parent. Not old enough, not responsible enough—look at how his child was behaving! Why couldn't he control her? Terrible father...

"But it's not fair!" Her lip quivered and she banged her fists on her thighs.

"Ben, I'm sorry. We're going to have to go." They hadn't left the shore yet, and Jason stood to step out of the raft, his arms out for balance.

"No, no!" Maggie wailed. "Daddy, I want to stay. I'm sorry. Please, please!"

"Okay, but no more of this attitude today. Or we're getting off." Maggie nodded vigorously, and Jason sat again and nodded to Ben, who seemed to be waiting for a sign that it was okay to shove off.

"You're the lucky one, kiddo. We have to do all the work, and you get to sit back and enjoy it!" Ben patted her back. "Pretty good deal if you ask me."

This got a tiny smile out of Maggie, which wasn't easy after one of her tantrums. Ben must have had children himself considering the patience and coaxing touch he had with her, and Jason was grateful for it. He realized he didn't actually know if Ben was married or a father. He didn't wear a ring, but that didn't mean anything.

Face down, Maggie wiped her red cheeks sheepishly, and Jason gave her a squeeze. She was always incredibly embarrassed after an outburst, and it made his heart ache.

They headed into the center of the river with Ben giving them basic paddling instructions. Then he told them to put their paddles across their laps, and the raft drifted lazily.

"Okay, so here's what you need to know if you fall out. You won't, but just in case, it's important to know what to do. First off, the water's darn cold, and it'll knock the air right out of you. So make sure you force yourself to breathe. Float down the river on your back with your feet pointing in the direction you're going. Don't ever try to put a foot down. It's very easy to get stuck between rocks, or any of the other detritus that might be down there—old tree branches and that kind of stuff. If you get stuck, you can be pulled under and trapped by the current."

Jason shuddered. "But we won't fall out, right?"

"Not if everyone paddles when I tell them to." Ben grinned. "Don't worry, I've got everything under control." He clapped Jason on the shoulder.

He swallowed hard as the warmth from Ben's hand seemed to shoot right down to his dick. He practically squeaked, "Right. Good to know."

As Jason struggled to process his body's reaction, Ben went on. "So, feet pointed downriver and don't try to touch down. The other thing to remember is not to fight the current. You will not win. To get to shore, swim sideways, and eventually you'll make your way over. Of course, if you happen to fall out of the boat today, we'll pick you right back up, or one of the other rafts will."

Ben's knee grazed Jason's lower back, just below his life jacket. Under the wide blue sky, blinking into the sun as the river ebbed and flowed, Jason gripped his paddle.

Holy shit.

Then he admitted the truth.

I'm attracted to Ben.

He rolled the words around in his head, new and confusing—but undeniable.

"Has anyone ever fallen out?" Maggie's voice had returned to normal, and her tears were dry.

"Oh, a few times," Ben answered. "But only when they weren't paying attention. I know I won't have that problem today with this crew. Okay, it's time to start paddling. Remember, do as I say, and know which side of the boat you're on—left or right."

"Isn't it port or starboard?" Maggie asked. "Like in the song about barges?"

Ben chuckled. "Jason, you've got quite the budding sailor here. Yes, port is left, and starboard is right. But we find it easier not to confuse people with nautical terms, especially on a raft. Okay, we're coming up on our first rapid. Can you hear the water?"

The group nodded, and Jason's pulse raced. The rapid came into sight, and Ben barked out an order for them to all paddle. Then the raft was flying through the air and splashing down in the roiling water, sweeping around rocks.

"Right side, paddle hard! *Hard!*" Ben shouted.

Jason was on the right, and he paddled as forcefully as he could, Maggie screaming with delight at his side. Almost like magic, the raft neatly avoided slamming into an outcropping of rocks.

They glided out of the rapid as the river calmed once again. The current remained strong, and pulled them along at a steady pace.

"That was awesome!" Maggie clapped her hands. "I want to do it again!"

Ben laughed. "Don't worry, there are plenty more where that came from."

"How do you know when to paddle and how to avoid the rocks?" Jason turned to ask, wiping the water that had sprayed up over his face.

"Experience. After you've been down this river hundreds and hundreds of times, you know it like the back of your hand. Every eddy, every rock, every tree stump."

"Nice to know we're in good hands."

"That you are." Ben smiled, and...*winked?*

Whipping back around, Jason clutched at the rope lining the raft. Ben didn't...there was no way he was...he couldn't be... He couldn't he *hitting on* Jason? Could he? Jason's new truth echoed through his head, joined by a question.

I'm attracted to Ben. Is he attracted to me?

"Paddles up!" Ben's low, commanding voice sent a shiver down Jason's spine. "We've got another rapid coming."

They were off again, water spraying up, cries of exhilaration all around as the raft successfully navigated the twists and turns of the river. After two rapids in close succession, the current calmed once more, and the raft drifted almost to a stop.

"Okay, here's the part where we all jump in and get the blood pumping." Ben gave Jason a playful nudge. "Come on, get the ball rolling."

Dipping his hand into the water, Jason couldn't hold in a yelp. "Oh my God, that's freezing!"

"Duh, it's from the glacier, Dad."

"Hey, watch it or you'll be the first one in!" Jason tickled Maggie under her arms, and she giggled and squirmed.

"It's hot out here. I'm ready for a dip." With that, Ben stood, dropped his helmet and life jacket at his feet, and somersaulted off the back of the raft. His splash soaked Jason and Maggie, who both gasped and sputtered.

"Come on, Dad!"

"Okay, okay." Jason took off his helmet and helped Maggie with hers. Keeping their jackets on, they paused at the side of the raft as another member of their group jumped. Was this really a good idea? What if Maggie caught a cold?

But she grinned up at him, face alight, her little hand clutching his, and Jason couldn't deny her. He called, "One, two, three!" and propelled them off the raft. The frigid water was a slap in the face, and his whole body seized.

Maggie shrieked and flapped around joyfully, screaming about how cold it was. Another raft had made its way down the river, and some of those people jumped in as well. Ben swam up and splashed water in Jason's face.

"Hey, I'm already soaked!" Jason laughed and splashed back, his heart like a drum.

Their legs tangled under the water, bodies pressed close, only separated by the bulk of Jason's life jacket. They both wore long shorts, and their calves rubbed together as they treaded water, skin slick, friction from their leg hair sending shivers through Jason.

He realized he didn't really need to try to keep himself afloat with the life jacket on, and with a nervous laugh that sounded like a weird honk, he propelled himself backwards and away as Ben watched him with a little smile. Jason's mind whirled.

Is Ben gay? Am I making something out of nothing? Is this something? *What's going on with me?*

Then it was time to heave themselves back into the raft. With helmets on and paddles ready, they prepared for the final set of churning rapids, which Ben navigated expertly. After the last bit of jostling white water, the river smoothed out again and they landed on the shore, where flatbed trucks for the rafts and minivans for the rafters waited to return them to the starting point.

Taking a towel from one of the staff, Jason watched as Ben helped hoist a raft, his wet skin glistening in the sunlight, the dark hair on his chest showing through the soaked white cotton of his tank top.

What would it feel like to rub against him?

"Helloo? Earth to Dad."

Jason forced his attention back to Maggie, helping her with the stubborn lid on a water bottle.

It was crazy, but he felt a strange pang of disappointment when Ben rode back in a different van.

Everyone clambered out in the parking lot, and he looked around for Ben. He caught his eye and waved. "Thanks for a great trip!" His pulse sped.

"Anytime," Ben replied as he approached, rubbing a towel over his hair. The fuzz on his chest was a shadow under his drying tank top, and Jason forced his gaze up as Ben asked, "What are you guys up to the rest of the day?"

Maggie glared at Jason. "I want to drive all the way up Going-to-the-Sun Road, but Dad's chicken."

"I'm not *chicken*. I'm cautious. The weather could turn again, and I don't want to be stuck on a two-lane road up a mountain."

"Oh, but you have to do the Road to the Sun." Ben smiled softly, a faraway glint in his eyes. "That's what my dad called it." He peered up at the sky. "I think it's a good bet to do it now." His gaze met Jason's, sending a bolt down Jason's spine. "If you want, I'll drive you in my truck. I've done it a hundred times." He motioned. "Besides, the road's right there. We're already on it."

"Awesome!" Maggie clapped and practically twirled. "Can we, can we? I'm sure Ben is a very safe driver."

"I like to think so." Ben laughed.

Jason had to smile. "How can I say no?"

And as they followed Ben to his truck, he realized the only word echoing faintly in his mind was *yes, yes, yes.*

CHAPTER FOUR

"Wow." Jason stared at the swath of green valley. A sharp blue river cut through it, rocky hilltops reaching up to the huge expanse of sky, a few fluffy white clouds making the blue even richer.

It had been slow going over the continental divide, the twisty road clogged with other tourists. They'd lucked into a prime location at one of the lookouts, and Ben had turned off the truck so they could stretch their legs and take in the view.

As Ben pointed to a rock formation and talked to Maggie about tectonic plates, Jason couldn't resist grabbing his sketchbook and pencils from his backpack. Leaning on the hood of the truck, he opened a fresh page, pencil flying.

"It's amazing!" Maggie exclaimed, and Jason glanced up to find her out of reach.

He called, "Don't go any closer to the edge, Mags."

She rolled her eyes over her shoulder. "*Dad*. It's, like, way over there."

"I know, but… Be careful."

Ben gave Jason a smile. "Don't worry, I'll keep her safe and sound." He nodded to the sketchbook. "I didn't know you were an artist."

Jason scoffed. "I'm not. It's just a stupid hobby."

"He's *so good*, but he doesn't believe me," Maggie said. "He should be drawing pictures instead of working at the cookie factory. Even though I like the free cookies."

Heat in his cheeks, Jason shook his head. "Unfortunately we need to eat and pay the rent." Ben hadn't asked what he did for a living, and Jason had been grateful. He knew there was nothing to be ashamed of since the factory was an honest job, but when he'd attended Waltham Prep, expectations were far different. Even if he hadn't wanted to go into business, he'd never envisioned a punch card in his future.

Either way, his art was never going to pay the bills. Most of the time he was too tired and busy to draw much anyway. He looked down at the scratchings on his pad, his cheeks burning hotter. "It's a waste of time."

"I disagree." Ben had come closer and was watching him with those intense eyes under thick brows. "Art or anything that inspires passion in us is never a waste." He swept his arm around. "Believe me, if I had an iota of artistic talent, I'd draw the hell out of the Road to the Sun. I mean, look at it. Look at all of this. To me, nature *is* art, and I think it's incredibly valuable. It needs to be protected. Cherished!" His words spilled out, and he took a breath, chuckling. "I guess you hit a nerve. I'm so lucky to be able to work here, and I wish everyone could discover their passion. Explore it and cultivate it. If you want to draw, do it!"

Jason's heart raced, goosebumps waving over his bare arms despite the heat of the afternoon sun. He returned Ben's smile, and the insane urge to hug him tolled through Jason like a bell. Ben *got it*. "You're right. I…" He looked down at his pad, gripping the pencil so tight he might snap it.

"Draw, draw!" Ben grinned. "Maggie and I will be over here talking about rocks and trees."

Maggie tugged Ben's hand, walking farther down the lookout, mercifully not any closer to the edge. Jason was completely confident she was safe with Ben, and he turned his attention to the paper, his pencil flying over the pages as he drew the view from different angles, capturing what he saw in each direction.

Then he focused on Maggie and Ben. Ben crouched, pointing into the distance as he spoke, Maggie nodding and listening avidly. Jason wished he had brought the colored pencils he'd left in the tent to capture the hint of dark red in Ben's thick hair, or the blue of his eyes...

I'm attracted to Ben.

The words were becoming familiar now, but no less frightening. Or maybe that was the wrong word.

Exhilarating.

Yes, Jason's belly fluttered with butterflies, nervous energy sending his pencil careening almost off the page. He turned to a fresh white sheet.

Although he didn't pay attention to women the same way, he'd always written off his long looks at other men as mere admiration. Envy of their fit muscles, appreciation of hard work at the gym. Nothing more. It had been easy to do because his recognition of other men's attractiveness had always been...theoretical. Safe.

He'd been able to tell himself it was like appreciating a sculpture in a museum because he'd had the same distance from them. But now here was Ben. Ben, who had smoothly slipped under the barricade in a blink.

For years, Jason's life had been Maggie and work. Work and Maggie, with as much sleep as he could steal in between. Now, far from the normalcy of home and routine, a protective layer had somehow been stripped away. He was feeling things the tunnel vision of his responsibilities had apparently blocked out. He watched Ben with a longing unlike anything he'd ever experienced, and it was more than physical attraction.

Breathing deeply, he calmed his shaking hands and drew one more image.

As they drove to the next lookout, Ben flicked on the radio, flipping through a couple of stations playing commercials. Then he hit one with music, and before Jason could stop himself, he said, "I love this song."

Ben turned up the radio with a quizzical smile. "Is this…Will Smith?"

As "Wild, Wild West" filled the truck, Jason's cheeks burned. "I loved this movie when I was a kid. Steampunk. It was cool."

Ben's eyes twinkled. "You know all the words, don't you?"

Screw it. "As a matter of fact, I do. No shame." He started rapping along as Maggie giggled. Ben drummed his fingers on the wheel to the beat, and joined in at the chorus. They sang terribly except for Ben, but it didn't matter. In that moment with the sun and sky and mountains all around, peace and happiness sang through Jason along with cheesy Will Smith.

When the song was over, Ben and Maggie applauded, and Jason gave a little bow. The traffic was slow as everyone admired the views. Maggie leaned forward as far as she could without taking off her seatbelt in the middle seat of the pickup bench. Jason and Ben shared a smile at her excitement, and Jason realized how rarely he had that gift. He'd been so determined to raise Maggie on his own.

He tried to keep his voice casual as he asked Ben, "Do you have kids?"

Ben kept his gaze on the road, his soft smile undeniably sad. "No. My ex and I talked about adopting, but it didn't happen for us. He has a baby with his new husband." The smile grew brittle, his hands tightening on the steering wheel. "It's great for them."

"Oh." Jason's head spun. Ben *was* gay or bi or whatever. When he'd winked at Jason when they were rafting… *Had* Ben been hitting on him? Breath caught in his throat as they rounded a corner, a glacial lake sparkling far below, Jason definitely wanted the answer to be yes. What did that mean?

"Is that a problem? That I'm gay?" Ben's voice had gone as sharp-edged as his brittle smile.

"What? No, no. Of course not." Jason shook his head.

"There's nothing wrong with gay people," Maggie said. "Mrs. Wexler's gay. She was my teacher last year. She's awesome. She let me bring in a little piece of dolomite I dug up in the woods for show and tell."

"It's not a problem at all," Jason added. "I was just... I—" He broke off, swallowing hard as Ben gazed at him over Maggie's head, the traffic at a standstill as they approached the next lookout.

Those blue eyes bore into him. "You...?"

"Um... Uh, I..."

I want to know if you've been hitting on me and if anything might actually happen. Do I want something to actually happen?

Fire scorched his veins at the thought of it—kissing and touching Ben for real. No theoreticals, no idle interest he could brush off and explain away. His heart tripped. What was he thinking? This vacation was for Maggie, and she was *sitting between them,* and he was wondering how Ben's lips would feel. He'd been celibate for years and had honestly never given it a lot of thought. There had been too much else to worry about.

But now his imagination worked overtime. He cleared his throat, pressing his sweaty palms to his thighs. "Just that I'm sorry to hear about your ex. You're so great with Maggie that I figured you must have kids."

Ben turned his attention back to the road as they crawled along. "Thanks. But I couldn't compete with Tyson Lockwood, so." He grimaced. "That's not really fair—Brad and I broke up for more reasons than Tyson."

"Your ex is the guy who married Tyson Lockwood?" Jason asked. "Huh. I saw something about it on Buzzfeed."

Maggie huffed. "Tyson Lockwood's a terrible actor. Dad,

remember how bad that movie about the volcano was? Not to mention completely scientifically inaccurate."

"God, that really was awful," he agreed. *Just act normal. Stop thinking about Ben's lips. Or his arms. Or his hairy chest. Just stop thinking completely.*

Ben chuckled. "Thanks, guys."

Jason blurted, "Are you going to adopt with anyone else?" He laughed nervously. "I mean, you probably have a new boyfriend, so maybe you guys could?"

Ben met Jason's gaze steadily. "Nope, no boyfriend. But I'm open to new possibilities."

"Great! That's good." Jason's heart thumped, his voice too high. "Wow, look at that view! You can see for so many miles. Maggie, look!"

"Obviously I'm looking, Dad. What's up with you?"

"Nothing! I'm just excited by the view. That's why we came up here, right? Amazing view." *Oh my God, stop talking.*

"Indeed it is." Ben edged into the back of the lookout parking area. "Maggie, I've got a great story about that lake. Want to hear it?"

Jason followed them out of the truck, grateful for the change of subject. But he could still feel the imprint of Ben's steady gaze, the low rumble of his voice echoing.

New possibilities.

Jason was walking through quicksand, and it was closing in, pulling him deeper and deeper. He breathed shallowly, not sure if he was afraid or all too eager.

"DO YOU THINK THEY found that fisherman?" Maggie asked from the back seat.

"I don't know, sweetie. I hope so." Jason flicked on the windshield wipers as he turned onto another dirt road that allegedly led to a remote trail Ben had recommended. They'd already been driving more than an hour from the campground, heading deeper and deeper into the middle of nowhere. They hadn't even passed another vehicle in ages.

"Do you think Ben will be able to come with us?" She toyed with the fraying lining of her red poncho, tearing off a strip.

"Honey, don't do that. That coat has to last you until winter."

He certainly hoped Ben could meet them. Being alone this far into the woods put him on edge. Ben had assured him the view was worth it and there was no danger as long as they took the usual precautions. Jason had told the campers in the next site where they were going, just in case they got lost. Still, he'd feel a million times safer if Ben came with them.

"I really want Ben to come," Maggie whined.

You and me both. "He said he would meet us this afternoon if he could. We're lucky he spent almost his whole day off with us yesterday." Jason had been working up the nerve to invite Ben to the campsite for dinner when Ben had been called away to join a search party for a fisherman who was hours overdue.

"But he said he had to do a trail inspection anyway, so he should come with us."

Jason drove into the middle of the narrow road to avoid a pothole. "I'm sure he will if he can."

"You like Ben, don't you?"

His laugh sounded slightly hysterical. "Of course. Why wouldn't I?"

"I dunno." Maggie flipped the back seat heating vent open and closed, open and closed. "You were acting funny."

"No I wasn't. Stop that." He reached back and nudged her hand away from the vent.

"Anyone who doesn't like Ben is a dummy. Like his old boyfriend."

ENDS OF THE EARTH

"Maggie, we don't call people names." The rain blurred the windshield, and he twisted the wipers up to the highest level.

"Come on, Dad. That guy is stupid. Ben would be the best boyfriend."

The brisk, rhythmic thumping of the wipers echoed his heartbeat. "I still don't want you calling people names. And I said stop doing that."

Maggie left the vent alone, crossing her arms over her chest. "Can I sit up front? I hate it back here."

"No. You know you're not allowed to sit in the front until you're twelve. The airbag could really hurt you if we got into an accident."

"You're careful. We won't."

He bit back a huff. Was it going to be one of those days when she argued with everything? "Someone else could cause an accident as you are well aware. Enough."

She sulkily asked, "Did you try to call him? He gave you his number, didn't he?"

"Yes, but there's no service in this area. You know that. We'll just have to wait and see if he meets us." *Please meet us.*

Being alone in the wilderness was definitely outside Jason's comfort zone. He thought of home—the lumpy futon and toilet handle that had to be jiggled, the small kitchen with neat shelves and labeled containers. Home, where everything was familiar and safe.

Where he didn't have all these new and confusing feelings for a man he'd just met.

After a stretch of silence, Maggie sighed wistfully, her mood apparently morphing, thank God. "Daddy? Can we live in the mountains one day?"

"Maybe one day, Mags." He glanced back and smiled before adjusting the wiper blades to a slower rhythm now that the rain was easing. They thumped from side to side with a gentle squeak across the glass.

If Ben had stayed for dinner, what would have happened last night?

Jason gripped the wheel as half-formed images cartwheeled through his mind. *Ben's eyes up close, big hands on Jason, arms wrapping around him, bodies rubbing and lips meeting...*

He gave his head a mental shake. Talk about being outside his comfort zone. He needed to focus on Maggie. This was *her* trip. It wasn't about him and his...crush, or whatever it was.

He followed the signs to a small, empty lot at the trailhead. Putting the car in park, he peered around uneasily. "Maggie, it's pretty deserted up here. I think we should go hiking on one of the more popular trails."

"But Ben said this one has an amazing lookout. Besides, he'll be with us."

"He *might* be with us. If he can't make it—"

"Less people means more nature!"

"More nature? We're in Montana. It's pretty much all nature."

"Dad, you promised." She stared at him with big, sad eyes.

It's true, he had promised that morning they would do the hike, rain or shine, but he hadn't realized just how isolated it would be. At least the rain was only a drizzle for the moment. It was mid-afternoon, but the sun didn't set until after nine p.m., and hopefully the skies would clear soon.

The hum of an engine approached, and Jason's belly flip-flopped as a familiar pickup truck drove into the small lot.

"He's here! See, I told you!" Maggie clapped.

With a rush of giddiness, Jason tried not to grin like a fool. He shouldn't indulge himself in pointless fantasies, but there was no harm in enjoying Ben's company. He cleared his throat. "Okay, honey. Let's do this thing." He held up his palm.

She high fived him before hopping out of the car, Jason shouldering his backpack with water, snacks, bear spray, and his sketchbook. Peering around at the dense forest, he shoved the spray canister into his jacket pocket.

"Ben!" Maggie raced toward him, skidding to a stop by his feet.

"Hey there, kiddo." Ben smiled widely. "Fancy meeting you here." He pushed up the brim of his hat. Beneath his open dark green jacket, the top few buttons of his uniform shirt were unbuttoned, exposing a vee of tanned skin with scattered dark hair.

Pulse galloping, Jason tried to greet him, but couldn't get a word in over Maggie's breathless questions.

"Did you find the fisherman?"

"We did. His boat had been damaged on rocks and sank, but he made it to shore. Cold and shaken, but he'll be just fine."

"How far did he swim? Was he hungry?"

"About a mile, and he sure was."

Jason cut in before Maggie could ask another question. "Glad you could make it. You're sure we're not taking you away from work?"

Ben smiled at him, and a shiver tripped down Jason's spine. "This is work. Trail maintenance is ongoing. Making sure the path isn't overgrown, no trees down, that kind of thing."

"You're so lucky you get to hike for money!" Maggie said.

"I sure am." Ben hoisted a small pack onto his back. His green pants were tucked into his leather boots. The cuffs of Jason's cargo pants were soaked already after stepping into a puddle getting out of the car, and he wished his hiking shoes were taller.

He said, "Maggie, roll up your khakis so they don't get too wet."

She bent and rolled her pants over her ankles, then popped back up and exclaimed, "Can we go to the lookout now?"

"You bet. It's about an hour away." Ben motioned Maggie ahead of them, and she skipped off excitedly, warbling the campfire song about barges, which was apparently her new favorite.

She darted back every few minutes with questions for Ben, and the time passed quickly. Before Jason knew it, they'd reached the lookout, and he had to admit it was another stunning view, even with mist hanging over the trees. Snow-capped peaks met the clouds, and it was like they were the only people left in the world.

Maggie clasped her hands joyfully, staring in awe. "It's so quiet. I love it."

Jason pressed a kiss to her damp hair. "Me too, baby." It had been worth every penny he'd saved to give her this gift.

"Can we go farther? Is there another lookout?"

Ben said, "There is. Another hour or so."

Before Jason could open his mouth, Maggie jumped in. "Yes. I'll totally be able to walk back, and no, it won't be too late for dinner. We have lots of snacks."

Ben chuckled with a flash of white teeth. "She's got your number, huh?"

Jason had to laugh. "She sure does. Okay, we'll go to the next lookout, but then we're turning back." He'd probably have to piggyback her later, but he couldn't say no.

Maggie bounced. "Thank you, thank you, thank you!" She darted off, full of energy as always.

"Not too fast," Jason called after her. "Stay in sight!"

As they walked on, it was peaceful under the shelter of the trees, the sodden, earthy-smelling leaves on the ground muffling their footsteps. Drizzle pattered on the glossy leaves and dripped onto Jason's head, but he didn't mind that he'd forgotten his cap in the car. He kept his hood down, watching Ben from the corner of his eye.

Ben moved through the woods with smooth grace, clearly at home among the oaks and pines, his steps even and sure, long legs striding confidently. Beneath the brim of his hat, faint stubble shadowed his strong jaw, and—

Jason's breath caught, body seizing as he tripped over a root, barely getting his palms out in time to break his fall as he thudded onto the wet earth.

Oh my God, I am such a loser!

He popped back up as Ben took hold of his arm, helping him to his feet, face creased in concern. "You okay?"

Laughing awkwardly, cheeks on fire, he brushed leaves and twigs and dirt from his jacket and pants. "I'm fine!" The sympathy in Ben's expression made the sticky flood of embarrassment worse, and Jason turned away. Maggie had rounded the corner and he could only see flashes of her red poncho through the trees, her latest song fading on the breeze. He called, "Maggie, wait up!"

Ben was still holding Jason's upper arm with a steady grip that sent Jason's pulse skittering. "Are you sure you're okay? You didn't twist an ankle?"

He circled the right and then his left ankle. "I think I'm fine. Just incredibly clumsy." He met Ben's warm gaze again. "Lame city slicker."

With a low laugh, Ben said, "I'll tell you a little secret."

"Uh-huh?" Jason swayed closer, sparks igniting on his damp skin, throat gone dry.

"One time I took a header right in front—"

A ragged scream tore through the air. *Maggie.*

Adrenaline ricocheting, Jason raced around the bend, expecting to see a grizzly, his worst nightmare come true. His heart pounded, sick fear strangling his spine as he blinked at the scene in front of him.

No bear. A man.

About twenty feet away down the trail, Maggie stood frozen, a big, scraggly man behind clutching her shoulder. He held a pistol in his other hand, pressed against Maggie's temple.

"Get away from my daughter." Jason barely recognized his

own hoarse voice.

The man smiled. *Smiled.* "Now, now. Let's all relax. I was just minding my own business, and your little gal here came across my path."

Jason's ears buzzed with rushing blood. "Then let go of her, and we'll get out of your way."

The man smiled crookedly as if he didn't have a care in the world. As if he wasn't *holding a gun* to Jason's little girl. Why did he have a gun? "Now I want to make sure you and Ranger Bob coming up behind won't do anything stupid."

"Let her go," Ben commanded, appearing in Jason's peripheral vision to the left.

Jason pleaded. "We won't tell anyone, I swear. Just let her go." Cold sweat sprang out on his skin, prickling the back of his neck.

"*Daddy.*" Maggie whimpered. The barrel of the pistol dug into her pale skin.

Jason held out his hands. "Please. Please don't hurt her."

"Brown, let her go." Ben's voice was steely. "You know she'll only slow you down."

This Brown person Ben somehow seemed to know cocked his weapon. The click of the metal was much louder than it sounded on TV. "Thing is, I heard her coming—what a sweet little voice she has. And I realized she's just the guardian angel I need."

"What?" Jason sputtered, his lungs struggling. *Wake up! This can't be real!*

"Well, those so-called lawmen after me aren't too interested in taking me into custody. I heard it with my own ears—shoot to kill. Had to hole up in a cave while those fuckers looked for me over to the east." He cackled. "Assholes went right by me, but it cost me a lot of time. I think it's best I take the girl with me now that the good Lord's put her in my path. Could use some insurance, and I'm not one to look a gift horse in the mouth."

A scream tore at Jason's throat, and his voice cracked when he managed to choke it down and speak. "Just let her go, please. I'm begging you." He was ready to drop to his trembling knees if that's what it took. Maggie cried, and he ached to have her in his arms again.

But Brown yanked Maggie closer to him. "I do have to be going now, and I'm afraid the little lady's taking a trip. The police ain't gonna shoot in her vicinity."

"No!" Bile rose in Jason's throat, terror clawing him open from the inside, stripping him bare and useless. *Can't be happening. Not real. Please let me wake up.*

Ben gritted out, "Leave her alone, you fucking bastard."

The man's nostrils flared, the tendons in his thick neck standing out. "I'm trying to be reasonable here. I could kill you both right now, so stop with the name-calling."

"No, please!" Maggie whimpered. "Don't."

"As long as no one does anything stupid, they'll be just fine, and so will you, honeypie." He backed up. "I don't have no quarrel with a little girl."

Jason's heart was going to explode through his chest. "We won't tell anyone, I swear!"

"I wish I could believe that. But my momma didn't raise no fool."

"Take me instead," Jason begged. "I won't give you any trouble. Take me. *Please.*"

"Daddy!" Maggie struggled in the man's grip, and he put his forearm across her throat, pressing hard.

"Now, now. *Daddy*, you tell her to mind me. Or you ain't never gonna see her again. I hate to make this unpleasant."

"What are you going to do with her? Where are you taking her?" Jason choked down another scream. He was flying apart, knives in his gut and fishhooks tearing his skin. "Don't you touch her. If you hurt her, I swear to God…"

Brown's spine went rigid, his chin lifting. "What kind of man do you think I am? I don't interfere with little girls." He spat on the ground. "I helped give that pervert over in Lupfer a good beatdown before the fucking useless cops came. That sick son of a bitch was lucky. That shit ain't right, messing with kids. I'll forgive the ugly accusation since I know you're a little out of sorts right now. But watch your mouth, boy. In fact, I think you owe me an apology."

The syllables were glass shards on his tongue, but Jason gritted out, "Sorry."

"Okay now. Let's be civilized about this. Everyone do as I say, and I'll treat her real good and let her go when I don't need her any more. I'm being fair as can be. Don't make me kill you."

"Harlan, let's talk about this." Ben held out his hands.

The man's beady gaze narrowed. "Shut your trap, Ranger Bob. We ain't friends." He spat again, refocusing on Jason. "Boy, take off your bag and throw it this way real gentle-like."

Heart roaring, Jason slipped off the pack, gripping the straps with his left hand. As he pulled his arm back and tossed, he dug in his right pocket, slick fingers tightening on the metal canister. Getting his shaking finger on the nozzle, he made sure it pointed the right way.

He couldn't let Maggie go. If this man took her now, Jason would never see her again. A reporter's voice from a *Dateline* episode echoed through his mind.

Never go to a second location. Odds of survival drop drastically.

"Pick that up and put it on." Brown kept the gun pointed directly at Maggie's head, stepping forward with her as she bent and slung the pack over her trembling, narrow shoulders. "Tighten the straps," he ordered.

She lowered her head, doing as she was told, and Jason leapt forward, spraying the bear repellent with a hoarse shout.

Brown roared and gunshots blasted, thunder cracking through the air. Jason instinctively dropped to the muddy ground, and as he reached out and grabbed Maggie's ankle, she was torn away, hauled under the monster's meaty arm with a scream that reverberated through Jason's bones.

In a heartbeat, Maggie and Harlan Brown vanished around the next bend in the path. Jason scrambled up, slipping in the mud and crashing down again, blinking against the residual bear spray in the air, his eyes watering as he clawed at the ground and shoved to his feet.

Barreling forward, Jason chased after his baby.

CHAPTER FIVE

F UCK!
Pepper burning his eyes as the wind changed, Ben scuttled backward around the curve in the winding trail, his heart about to hurtle from his chest. He'd tossed his pack into the trees when he'd heard a stranger's voice and instinct told him it was Harlan Brown. Now he still had the radio, at least.

He crawled into the bush, gasping and rummaging through wet leaves, pain searing every pore. He was allergic to peppers, and he tried to hold his breath, squinting into the gloom. If he didn't wash his eyes out immediately, they could swell shut and he'd be helpless to help Maggie and Jason. *Useless.*

Have to find them!

Finally his grasping fingers found fabric, and he dragged the pack over desperately. Breathing too harshly with the pepper in his lungs, he managed to unscrew his water bottle, shaking as he tossed aside his hat and rinsed his eyes, water pouring over his face as he struggled to keep them open.

Every blink torture, he dug out his radio and jammed his thumb on the speak button. "Mayday, mayday, mayday. This is Park Ranger Ben Hettler. Wanted criminal Harlan Brown has abducted a child. Maggie Kellerman, eight years old." He rattled off Maggie's description and what she was wearing, then gave their coordinates, cracking his burning eyes open enough to find the antihistamines in his pack.

Dee's voice crackled over the radio. "Copy that, Hettler. We're calling the local cops and the FBI, but it'll take some time getting out there. You and the father sit tight."

Ben pushed three pills through the blister pack and choked them down before rasping, "Can't. Jason's gone after her. Have to find them. Jason Kellerman: twenty-five, six foot, shaggy blond hair, slim build. Blue raincoat."

"Ben, this is way beyond your pay grade. Park your butt."

"I can't leave them alone." An iron band squeezed his chest, and it wasn't just the pepper spray. He had to find Jason and Maggie. Had to protect them. They wouldn't have even been out this far if not for him.

He jumped as a gunshot echoed in the distance, hollow through the mist and rain. Another followed, and he was on his feet. "I'll report back soon. Over and out." Switching off the radio so it wouldn't receive transmissions and make noise, he strapped on the pack and stormed back to the trail, ignoring the burning in his eyes and on his skin.

Jason. Maggie. Oh God, please.

Icy terror rattled his spine. What if they were shot? What if that was Harlan killing them both? He shoved branches out of his way. Or they could be hurt, helpless on the ground, bleeding into the earth. Dying.

Faster!

He flew along the narrow path, panting roughly, boots pounding the sodden dirt. He'd left his hat in the scrub, and the wind whistled in his ears.

He ran and ran—then, rounding a bend, he skidded to a halt, struggling to make sense of what he was seeing.

Swallowing hard, a chubby, older man swiped at his round glasses, blocking the trail. He had a rifle jammed into his shoulder, pointing it at Jason, who'd stopped about ten feet away from Ben.

Jason practically vibrated as he shouted, "Listen to me! He's getting away! He has my baby! Move! Let me go!"

The man's nervous gaze flicked to Ben. "What the hell is going on?"

"Yes." Ben had to cough, his lungs rattling. "There's a man with a gun. A criminal. He has a little girl."

Jason jerked his head over his shoulder at Ben, his eyes red from the pepper spray. "Tell him! Tell him he has Maggie!"

Breathing hard, the hiker looked back and forth between them rapidly. "I saw her. Son of a bitch shot at me before I even knew what was happening. I shot back, and then this guy showed up. How do I know he's not packing too?"

Ben took charge and spoke as calmly as he could, every breath burning. "He's not. Listen, we need your help. This man's daughter was just abducted. The police are on the way. Can you meet them at the western trailhead? Can you do that for me?" The last thing they needed now was a shocked and scared gun owner with a jumpy trigger finger.

"He's getting away, you asshole!" Jason screamed. "Fine. Shoot me." He tore off into the bush in a wide circle around the hiker blocking the path before hitting the trail again and disappearing around a bend.

Fuck!

The hiker didn't shoot, thank God. He spun, shaking and sputtering before wheeling back to Ben. Ben barked, "Get that out of my face!" and the man instantly complied, pointing the barrel at the ground.

"I'm sorry. Oh my God, what's happening?"

"I need your weapon," Ben commanded, not giving the skittish man a chance to argue as he snatched it from his hands. "Get to the trailhead and meet the police."

"I... What? Is this some joke? What the hell is going on? Your face is all weird."

"Bear spray." He gripped the rifle. "Extra ammo?" He hated

that people insisted on carrying guns in the park just because they could, or because they were poaching, or because they thought they could be a hero and stop a bear when they'd only ever fired on a range. But right now, he was grateful as hell to have the heft of the rifle in his hands.

The man handed over a box, and Ben stowed it in his pack. "Thank you. Go meet the police."

Running down the winding trail again, he gripped the rifle, ready to fire. His father had taught him, and he'd hunted for years. He was ready. He'd get them back. He had to get them back. His pulse raced, the drum of his heart thundering in his ears as fresh panic ripped through him.

Fuck, fuck, fuck!

There was a flash of movement ahead through the trees, and Ben jolted to a stop, squinting. The drizzle had increased, and he wiped at his sore, puffy eyes. He wanted to scream for Jason, but how far ahead was Brown? Hard to say at this point.

Tentatively, he jogged on, calling, "Jason!" Stopping to listen and scan the trees, he raised the rifle, sucking in lungfuls of air.

"Ben?"

Relief rushing through him, Ben sprinted along the path to find Jason standing there, chest rising and falling, rain streaming down his face like tears. For a heartbeat they stared at each other before Ben slung the rifle over his shoulder and grasped Jason's arms. "It's okay," he lied.

"Oh God. Please help me." Jason's breath gusted over Ben's cheek as he swayed. "I have to find her. They went that way. He's fast, even carrying Maggie, even after I sprayed him. I think I missed and just pissed him off. They could be anywhere. Anywhere!" Words spilled out, Jason vibrating and tugging Ben forward.

"Shh, it's okay. I've got you. We're going to find her." He ran his hands over Jason's back and arms. "Are you hurt?"

"Huh? No, come on. Hurry!"

"Listen, the police are on their way. The FBI too."

"Have to find her. We can't stop. No!" His fingers dug into Ben's arms. "I'm not waiting. I'm not leaving her out there alone with that psycho. We have to go now!"

Ben wanted to argue, but with each minute, the odds of finding Maggie alive diminished. Brown could decide it wasn't worth the potential advantage of having a hostage. Could leave her for dead. Could do anything.

Jason let go of Ben and backed away. "I'm going to get Maggie. You can wait."

The cold truth plummeted through Ben, settling in his gut like concrete as he stared into Jason's wild eyes. They were hours from civilization. The FBI would have to fly into Kalispell. It would be at least an hour until the local cops even made it to the trailhead, miles away. Meanwhile, Maggie would be farther and farther into the wild.

If she died and he didn't even *try*, Ben would never forgive himself.

He reached back for the radio in the side pocket of his pack. "This is Hettler. I've located the father. We're continuing the search, heading north." He gave coordinates and finished with, "Over."

Dee's voice crackled through the speaker. "Hold on. They want you to wait for the cops. Brown is dangerous."

"That's exactly why I'm not waiting." Ben chased as Jason took off up the trail. "I know these woods better than they do, and the only way I'm going to stop Jason from going after his daughter is knocking him unconscious. Over and out." He flipped off the radio, and they ran.

They'd gone about half a mile when he had to stop, doubled over, hacking. Feeling his face, he could tell the antihistamines were kicking in and reducing the swelling, and his eyes only stung now as opposed to scorched. His lungs struggled to clear the remnants of pepper spray he'd ingested. The rain had slowed once more to a fine mist.

Jason hovered at his side, panting. "Shit, I'm sorry. You must have really gotten a face full of the bear spray. What if it hit Maggie? Do you think she's okay? It barely seemed to slow that bastard down. He's huge. The way he just hauled her off…"

Ben straightened up and gulped water from his backup bottle. "I'm allergic to pepper spray. I'm sure she's fine. The effects don't usually last this long. She'll be okay." He passed Jason the bottle.

After Jason swallowed, they stared at each other, chests heaving. "Who the hell is that? You knew his name."

"Harlan Brown. I saw his mug shot at the station a few days ago. The police are after him."

Jason stared at Ben, breath coming more shallowly, his hands twitching. "What did he do? Tell me."

"He's wanted for murder."

"Oh my God. Maggie. How could I let this happen?"

"You didn't. It's not your fault. It was bad luck."

"No, I wasn't paying attention. I was too busy—" He motioned toward Ben. "I should have made sure she didn't get out of sight for a second!"

Guilt prickling, Ben remembered helping Jason off the ground, standing closer to him than he should have, leaning in to flirt. He repeated, "It wasn't your fault."

"You said he's a killer. What if he's a pervert?" Jason shuddered, reddened eyes stark in his pale face. "I know he said he wouldn't, but do you think he'll touch her? God, if he lays a finger on her…" He pressed his lips together, pacing back and forth.

"There was nothing in his criminal history about sexual violence that I saw. He did seem genuinely offended at the thought, so let's pray it wasn't an act. I don't think it was." To imagine otherwise was unbearable. "Let's keep moving." It was the only thing they could do.

After another hour without any sign, they reached a ridge overlooking the wide expanse of a lake. Gray, choppy water flowed to distant shores. Trees carpeted the hilly ground as far as the eye could see until mountains rose to meet the clouds. Ben carefully sipped water, aware that they'd run out soon. He passed the bottle to Jason and peered around.

"This is the farthest point the trail goes. At the end of this ridge over there, it loops back toward the parking lot." Coughing again, his throat raw, he examined the terrain to their left. The mountain was far too steep to scale without equipment. Brown was a survivalist, but did he have ropes and crampons? It was possible, but highly implausible to attempt it with Maggie. Peering up, Ben couldn't see anyone, although fog obscured the higher peaks.

Maybe he tossed her over the side.

A fist around his heart, he edged to the railing and squinted down for any sign of her red poncho. In the mist he couldn't see all the way to the ground hundreds of feet below. He pulled out his binoculars, but there was still nothing but green and brown through the patches of fog, the forest standing sentinel as always.

Ben cleared his throat, taking another sip of water. "I don't think he'd head left. Too steep, and Whitefish is to the east. He wants away from there. South will take us back toward the trailhead and roads. To go north, he'd have to get down off this mountain first. West is the only way that makes sense. It's the way I'd go if I were him. Off the trails."

Nodding, Jason followed Ben along the ridge. They stopped where the trail looped back to their right. Ben had hoped desperately to have heard helicopters overhead by now, but there was only the rustle of leaves and the distant tapping of a woodpecker.

The land sloped, but leveled off again after fifty feet. Ben wasn't much of a tracker, but he eyed the bush for signs that someone had recently passed through. With Jason on his heels, he led the way, careful on the muddy ground. Wet branches and leaves slapped their faces, and Ben squinted for footprints.

There!

Adrenaline zipping through him, he skidded down, boots squelching in the mud. At the bottom of the slope, he bent low. It was a heel print. No doubt.

Jason clutched Ben's shoulder, his voice sharp. "Look!" Ben straightened and stared carefully into the bush ahead of them where Jason pointed. When he saw it, his heart leapt and they ran over.

Red.

Jason plucked the torn strip of red fabric from the mud with trembling fingers. "It's from the lining of her coat. I'm sure of it."

Maggie was a bright kid, and there was no doubt she knew the story of Hansel and Gretel. Ben nodded. "Breadcrumbs."

Without another word, they rushed on, deeper into the heart of the endless forest.

CHAPTER SIX

J ASON SHIVERED AS HE squinted through the fading gray light, scanning the undergrowth for a sign of red. They'd found two more scraps of material as the hours had ticked by relentlessly.

His adrenaline high had crashed, and they'd slowed to a walk, too exhausted to run and afraid they'd miss Maggie's trail. One word echoed through him with every ragged beat of his heart.

Maggie, Maggie, Maggie, Maggie.

He prayed they'd find them and then…

Then what?

Harlan Brown was still armed. They'd be stuck in the same situation they'd been before, but Jason had to go after her and hope they could get the upper hand. Hope he could tackle Brown and get Maggie away from him. It was all he could do.

Hope.

A fresh burst of primal panic clawed his gut. Maggie was scared and she needed him. He had to find her. Couldn't just sit back and wait. He'd go crazy.

"You okay?" Ben's low voice beside him soothed some of the jagged edges of Jason's terror like water over a rock. At least Jason wasn't alone. He nodded, but Ben added, "Sorry. Stupid question."

As Ben rubbed his red eyes, Jason asked quietly, "Does it still hurt?"

"Getting better. How does it look? Swelling feels like it's going down."

Jason nodded. "You're not coughing much now either."

"Yeah. Took more antihistamines and some ibuprofen. We need to find water."

Jason nodded and they continued on. They'd half-filled Ben's two bottles with rainwater during a short downpour, but it wouldn't last long. Had to stay hydrated and alert. Had to be the best he could be.

What kind of father am I?

In his life, Jason thought he'd known fear and pain. Grief. Amy's round face filled his mind, her joyful bark of a laugh ringing in his ears. But he'd lost his best friend years ago, and it paled in comparison to the horror that gripped him now. He took a shuddering breath, fighting back a sob.

My baby.

He had to try. Had to protect her. It was his job, and he'd failed.

One foot in front of the other, he plowed on, following Ben, whose surefootedness and broad shoulders comforted. Rangers weren't cops, but at least he knew the land.

As night fell, Ben wordlessly offered a granola bar, and they rested for a minute. Jason took a swig of water. "You think Brown will keep moving?"

Ben held up his palms. "Hard to say. He'd want to get far away as soon as possible, but without light, it'll be nearly impossible." He tipped back his head. "Doesn't look like there'll be any moon or stars visible tonight."

"Are they going to send out a search party? Like for that fisherman?"

"Not in the dark. That's why I had to rush off yesterday and help. We were fighting the clock. And the lake he was on was much closer to the campgrounds and main area of the park. Getting out here isn't as easy, and with Brown armed with a hostage, it's not a typical search and rescue. Rangers aren't equipped for this."

"Right." Jason peered around at the shadowy forest. "Maggie doesn't do very well without sleep. He'll have to stop, or—" Bile rising, he squeezed his eyes shut. He'd tried not to think about it. Didn't want to make his fears real by voicing them.

But he knew what happened to kidnapped little girls.

Then the oats and raisins of the granola bar were coming back up. He dropped to his knees, heaving up the bit of food and water he'd consumed, the wet earth soaking his pants.

"It's okay." Ben crouched beside him, rubbing a hand slowly up Jason's back, his fingers warm on the nape of Jason's neck.

For a few heartbeats, Jason didn't move. He knelt there, head hanging low, letting Ben rub the strip of exposed skin. He fought the urge to bury himself in Ben's arms. He had to be strong. He was Maggie's father. He had to be a man.

Coughing, he swiped at his eyes. He took the bottle of water Ben offered and sipped. "Thanks," he croaked. "I'm fine. Let's go. We can keep looking until we can't see." Ben had a flashlight, but it would be too dangerous to use. They needed the element of surprise. It was their only advantage. Jason would tackle Brown. Trade his life for Maggie's, and Ben could get her to safety.

Ben watched him for a long moment. "Okay."

But Jason didn't move, his knees cold in the wet leaves, a pinecone digging into his flesh. Terror paralyzed him, and even though Ben didn't have the answer, he had to ask again, "Do you think he'll hurt her? Do you really think he meant what he said about not molesting kids?"

"His offense did seem genuine. Like he has some weird code of honor. I saw his rap sheet and it was robbery and assault. Like I said before, nothing sexual."

Jason exhaled. It was no guarantee, but at least it was something. He had to put the horrible possibilities out of his mind or he'd be hobbled. Just had to concentrate on finding her and getting her safe. If Brown felt like he needed her as a bargaining chip, he'd keep her alive. Jason had to believe that.

Ben quietly checked in on the radio, and the woman on the other end told them there'd be helicopters out in the morning, and that the local police were on their trail, but had to turn back and regroup, get organized and supplied up for first light. The FBI was taking over, and had ordered Ben be told to stop searching and "contain" Jason.

His gaze on Jason, Ben simply said, "Copy that. Over and out." Then he kept walking, and Jason followed gratefully. He couldn't stop. Maggie was leaving a trail. Maggie was waiting for him to find her.

They went another quarter mile and reached a babbling stream. It hadn't been a warm day to start with, but now the temperature dropped like a stone as the hidden sun sank. With numb fingers, Jason filled their two bottles with fresh water. He closed his eyes briefly.

Maggie was gone.

Grief lashed through him for the hundredth time since she'd disappeared, screaming as that psycho carried her off. Jason fought the tears and rinsed his face, slapping his cheeks with glacial water. Sitting around crying wasn't going to get her back.

He muttered, "I can't believe I let this happen."

Ben stood against a nearby tree, rubbing his face. "It's not your fault."

Jason shoved to his feet with a burst of impotent fury. He wanted to throw his head back and scream, but had to stay quiet. Before he knew what he was doing, he was in Ben's face, gripping his jacket, gritting out, "Stop saying that. Stop it!"

Ben raised his hands. "Okay."

"Of course it's my fault! And why did you tell us to go on that isolated trail? We drove out to the middle of nowhere and now she's gone."

Face creasing, Ben whispered, "I'm so sorry. I'll get her back. I promise. God, I'm sorry."

In the face of Ben's guilt, Jason's rage dissipated, whooshing out of him like air from a balloon. "No. It's not your fault. I'm sorry." He shut his eyes, trembling as he clung to Ben's coat, leaning into him. "She's alone. Maggie's alone with that killer. What if she fights him and he hurts her? I always taught her to fight. To kick and bite and scream if someone tried to grab her. But he had a gun and…"

"She's a smart girl." Ben's warm breath ghosted over Jason's skin. "She's leaving us a trail. She'll get through this."

"I never should have brought her to Montana. If we'd stayed home, she'd be safe." He opened his eyes, staring into Ben's. "I was supposed to keep her safe."

Ben gently pushed Jason's damp hair off his forehead, and Jason leaned into his palm. "You couldn't have known this would happen. You're not to blame. Do you hear me?"

"Everyone said I wouldn't be able to do it. That I was too young." He gasped, his lungs tightening unbearably. "They said I should give her up. My parents tried to take her. They said it would be better, and I could go to college and be normal and Maggie would be my sister instead. I wouldn't. She's mine, *my* child. But they were right. I can't do it. I've lost her."

Ben enunciated carefully. "*Bullshit.* Listen to me. You're a wonderful father." He held the back of Jason's neck. "You brought her to Montana because it was her dream. You didn't do a damn thing wrong."

Jason was still gripping Ben's slick jacket, and his icy fingers relaxed. His legs shook, and Ben eased him to the ground, both of them on their knees.

From the corner of his eye, Jason caught a flash of red on Ben's wrist in the weak light. He reached for it, sucking in a breath at the angry hives.

"From the bear spray? I did this. I'm so sorry." He held Ben's hand in his, aching to make it better.

"It's fading. I'm fine. I'll put on some Polysporin."

"I'll help. It's in your bag?" At least this he could do. Pulling out a Ziploc bag full of bandages and gauze, he dug in the bottom for the tube of gel. Jason had used it a hundred times on Maggie's scraped knees and elbows, and he quivered with a pang of longing.

"Here," he said, twisting off the cap and storing it safely in his pocket. He carefully spread the gel over the hives on one hand and then the other, pushing up Ben's sleeves to see if there were more. Fortunately there weren't. Ben breathed softly, warmth whispering across Jason's cheeks.

Holding Jason's fingers, he squeezed lightly. "None of this is your fault."

"But—"

"None of it." Ben tugged gently, wrapping Jason in his arms.

Shutting his eyes, Jason leaned into the solid warmth, too tired to argue as darkness closed in around them. Ben ran his fingers gently through Jason's hair. God, it felt so *good* to be held, and Jason couldn't find the words to tell Ben to stop, or keep himself from inching closer, pressing his face to the bare skin at Ben's throat.

It had been so long since he'd been close to anyone but Maggie, since he'd even hugged another adult. So long since he'd let someone else take care of *him*. But Ben was steady and strong. Secure.

In that moment, all Jason could do was let go and sob.

THE NIGHT WAS never going to end.

Huddled next to Ben under an emergency blanket that allegedly would reflect their body heat, Jason fidgeted. After a dinner of beef jerky and protein bars, Ben had spread a blanket underneath them as a groundsheet and pulled another on top. Jason curled on his side, and Ben's bulk behind him was a comfort.

If only he could sleep.

But how the hell was he supposed to sleep? Keeping it under the lightweight, orange blanket, Jason checked his phone, blinking at the stark light. He knew there was no cell service in the backcountry, but he needed to know the time. His heart sank. Not even midnight.

Ben's voice was a low rumble. "Do I want to know?"

"Nope." He shifted restlessly, a stone that felt like a boulder jammed into his hip. He knew he had to try to sleep, but it was impossible. The darkness surrounding them was complete—he could barely even see the shadow of Ben behind him if he craned his neck.

At least it had stopped raining, although drops still fell from leaves rustling in the wind. An owl hooted, and insects chirped. Otherwise it was silent, the forest peaceful.

Too peaceful.

Jason couldn't take the eerie quiet. He whispered, "I'm sorry. For…" Remembering Ben's arms around him, holding tight and comforting, he tried to find the right words. "For losing my shit and stuff. You were really nice. I hope that wasn't weird or anything."

Ben's exhalation tickled the back of Jason's neck. "It wasn't weird."

His heart skipped, and he shifted again, fiddling with the blanket. "Good thing you brought this stuff."

"Once a Boy Scout, et cetera."

"I never was."

"No?"

"My parents wouldn't let me join. Boy Scouts were

too…grungy. Let's just say they don't camp."

"So what did you like to do as a kid?" Ben asked.

"I was a great swimmer. Used to spend all the time I could at the pool in our country club. I was pretty good in prep school. But drawing was my favorite thing. I wanted to go to art school so much."

He wasn't sure why he was rambling. Curled up in the wilderness in the pitch black with Ben inches away was like the strangest dream. He shivered on the hard ground, yet felt outside himself at the same time.

He choked down the swell of panic and grief. He'd get Maggie back. He had to.

Ben asked, "Why didn't you go? Oh, of course. Maggie."

"She changed my life." Jason had to swallow hard, his throat burning. "And people felt sorry for me, like I was losing everything, but they didn't get it. They don't understand how much she gave me. She's…" He took a shuddering breath. "She's everything."

"We're going to find her, Jason. She's going to be okay."

"This is a nightmare and I don't think it's ever going to end." He blinked against a rush of tears. "I can't live without her. I can't." His guts were torn out, flapping in the cold slice of wind, his heart exposed and bloody.

Ben pressed closer, rubbing a comforting hand over Jason's shoulder and arm.

Jason fought for air, blood rushing in his ears. "I can't. I need her back."

"Shh. It's okay."

Jason's pulse thundered, desperate need burning. He couldn't think—he was all raw nerves, trembling and grasping. He needed warmth to cling to like a life raft, and he turned over, burrowing close to Ben.

"I've got you. I'm here." Ben held him so tightly, murmuring into his hair.

It wasn't enough. Jason needed more, needed something to fill the gaping hole inside him. He panted harshly against the rough stubble of Ben's throat, searching.

Then he was kissing Ben, jamming their mouths together, still drowning and grasping for the surface, clutching Ben close. He opened his mouth on a gasp, and their tongues met, wet and thrusting. Ben groaned, and Jason's head spun.

What the hell am I doing?

Shoving backwards, he scrambled to his hands and knees, pushing away the blanket. "I'm sorry."

"It's all right," Ben soothed. In the pitch black, his searching hand made contact, and Jason jerked out of his grasp.

Jason babbled, "I don't know why I did that. I... What's wrong with me?"

"Nothing. You're under an enormous amount of strain. You want comfort. It's normal to reach out."

"But I've never... I don't..." Jason scrubbed a hand over his face, the darkness pressing in. He wanted to wake up. He had to wake up from this hell.

"You're in shock. Let's get some rest."

Shame slithered through Jason with a low hiss. His daughter was out there with a psycho, helpless and alone, and he was *kissing* someone. Kissing Ben.

But thinking of Maggie was gut-wrenching agony, and he desperately wanted to retreat into Ben's arms so he could forget, only for a minute. Waiting in the dark, he was utterly powerless, and he wanted to shut off his mind and connect with Ben—warm, breathing, soothing. He yearned to feel anything but soul-shattering terror.

So weak!

He struggled to be strong. "No. This isn't... I can't." He pushed to his feet.

Ben's hand gripped Jason's calf. "It's fifty degrees, if that. It's windy and cold, and hypothermia is a real threat. Get back here, and don't make me chase you. This will not help Maggie."

He was right, and Jason dropped back to the ground. "I'm sorry."

"Don't be. We're just going to sleep, okay? Come on. That's it." Ben gently pulled Jason onto his side, spooning up behind him and tucking the blanket over Jason carefully before slipping his arm inside, solid around Jason's chest. "Sleep," Ben whispered.

Quicksand sucked Jason in all the way to his armpits. Echoes of sensations wheeled through his ragged mind: Ben's strong hands, the salty taste of his lips and warm puff of breath, his low groan, barely out loud. The smell of sweat and dirt and *Ben* that filled his nose now.

God, Jason ached to lose himself in Ben's arms, press against him from head to toe so he didn't know where he stopped and Ben started. The only person he'd ever kissed had been Amy, awkward and fumbling, punctuated by giggles.

He wanted to laugh now at how ridiculous he'd been. All those times he'd leafed through *Details* or men's fitness magazines, telling himself it was because he admired their physiques, because he wanted a body like that. No, he'd wanted *them*. He'd wanted to touch those hairy muscles and feel bristle against his face when a hard mouth took his.

The thought of their bodies together—of pulling Ben on top of him, being covered by his weight, tasting his mouth again, hearing him moan—coiled a hot spiral of desire through his belly.

Shame joined desire, fire and ice all at once, churning his stomach. He shouldn't have been thinking of anything but finding Maggie, but he was completely out of control—all sensation and emotion, hunger and need and desperation.

Their breathing sounded overly loud in the blackness. Images ran riot through Jason's mind: Joy blooming over Maggie's sweet face as she found a pretty rock. Harlan Brown's gun pressed against her head. Ben's wide, easy smile. Jason squeezed his eyes shut and curled into a ball, wishing desperately he could switch off his mind.

The night was never going to end.

I WANT TO GO home. I want Daddy.

On the stone floor of the tiny cave, Maggie hugged her knees to her chest as she curled on her side. It was wet, dark, and freezing, and her dad felt a million miles away. The bad man snored loudly next to her, his head pillowed on his small back-pack, her dad's pack tucked under his arm.

He blocked the entrance, the stone ceiling only a few inches above them. There was no way she could crawl over him without waking him up. She was stuck.

She could still hear the echo of her dad's voice screaming for her as the bad man had carried her off. Daddy's shouts had gotten fainter and fainter, and she'd sobbed, the bear spray burning in her eyes. It barely seemed to bother the man, and he was so big and strong and ran so fast.

Then they'd walked forever—hours and hours. He'd piggy-backed her sometimes, and she hated hanging onto him, having his scraggly, greasy hair in her face. The day had gotten colder and colder. Finally, he'd stopped when it got dark.

Her fingers had been numb, so he'd unwrapped a gross energy bar for her and given her gloves. She didn't understand why he was nice sometimes. Why didn't he just let her go? He'd given her his water too. She hated putting her lips to the same bottle he used, but she was so thirsty.

He'd given her a sweatshirt to put on under her poncho. It was damp and smelled gross, but she'd been afraid to say no, and had pulled the stinky cotton over her head.

The man had fallen asleep almost right away somehow, but Maggie shivered and jumped at every noise. It was so dark outside that she couldn't see a thing. Tears filled her eyes, and she cried as quietly as she could.

At least with the bad man, she wasn't alone.

CHAPTER SEVEN

"D ID YOU EVER want to leave Montana?" Jason's voice was barely a whisper, but it still made Ben jump in the darkness.

"What?"

"You grew up here, you said. Sorry, I'm just..." Jason blew out a shuddery breath. "I can't sleep. I'm going nuts waiting. Will you talk to me? Please?"

Ben kept his tone hushed as well. "Of course." His arm was still around Jason's chest, but he'd left an inch between their bodies, even though he wanted to press close, especially as Jason shivered in the piercing wind. There were still two hours before dawn, and neither of them had slept.

Jason asked, "Do you have lots of family around?"

"No. My mom died when I was in high school, and my dad several years ago. But this is the only home I've ever known."

The seconds ticked by before Jason murmured, "Did...did he know? Your father. About you. Being..."

"That I'm gay? Yes. He was never that keen on Brad, but he had no problem with it. Well, after an adjustment period. My mom never knew. Or at least she never said anything. I was still a kid when she died. Tenth grade." Ben wriggled the arm curled beneath him, trying to ward off pins and needles. "I wonder sometimes if she ever really knew me. I wish I'd told her before the accident. She hit a tree skiing." That he hadn't been honest with her was a hollow in him that would never quite be filled. "I was too afraid back then. Too much of a coward."

Jason was silent, and Ben wished he could see his face. Wished he could kiss him again, gently this time, soothing and sweet. Then Jason said, "I'm sorry about your mom. And you're not a coward."

Ben grunted. "Sure feel like one sometimes."

"You're out here with me in the middle of the woods in the pitch dark chasing a killer."

"It's not... Not that kind of coward. More about my life. My choices. I could transfer to another park and have far more opportunities. Opportunities I deserve after all these years and training."

"Why don't you?"

"That's the million-dollar question, isn't it? Instead I live up in my dad's old cabin alone. I stay at a job where my ex is my boss and he and his movie star husband parade their new baby in front of me. And why? What do I think is going to change? I wouldn't even want Brad back. But I'm still here because I'm afraid to leave. Montana is all I've ever known. I've barely even been out of the state except for driving up into Alberta over the Road to the Sun."

"It's beautiful here."

"It is. But I'm not happy. I haven't been for a long time." As the words came out, Ben realized they were absolutely true. "I need to shift out of neutral. What am I afraid of?"

"I wish I could tell you. I'm afraid of everything." Jason shifted with a little sucked-in breath.

"You okay?"

"Leg's cramping. Need to turn over."

Ben pulled back his arm as Jason squirmed around under the blanket, his breath gusting over Ben's face as he settled facing him. Ben wanted to reach out again and touch, but he tucked his hands under his cheek. There didn't seem to be any danger of Jason running off half-cocked and irrational, so there was no excuse to hold him close now.

He wished he could see his face, but the darkness was complete. "Jason, you're one of the bravest men I've ever met. Hell, you've got to be brave to even think about raising a kid alone. At any age, let alone as a teenager."

"I wasn't brave. I was terrified." He was silent for a long few moments, breathing softly. "Sometimes I can't really remember what she looked like. Amy, I mean. Maggie's mother. Like, I have pictures and stuff, but in my head, she's all…faded."

"I'm sorry." Ben was dying to know more, but bit his tongue.

"We were best friends since middle school. She got a scholarship to my prep school, and she was on the swim team too. We did everything together."

After a few moments of silence, Ben prompted him. "Including…"

Jason exhaled noisily. "I should have said no. But I was curious. Amy wanted to lose her virginity with someone she trusted, and she decided there was no one more qualified than me in the trust department. Even though I'd never had a girlfriend aside from Regina Potter in the second grade. Anyway. We used a condom, but I'm not sure I put it on right, or maybe it broke. I don't know what went wrong. It was all so weird and awkward and over almost before it started. Of course she got pregnant."

"That must have been a shock. What did your folks say?"

"To say I disappointed them would be an epic understatement. First, they wanted Amy to go away to have the baby and give it up so no one would find out. Offered to pay her as much as she wanted."

"Wow."

"Amy's parents wouldn't dream of it. Not that they were happy about the situation, but they accepted it, at least. They let me come over and be a part of everything. My parents barely even saw Maggie after she was born. They were so ashamed of me. They wanted to pretend it hadn't happened."

"I'm so sorry." He itched to slide his arm over Jason's shoulders, but kept his hands pinned under his cheek. He shouldn't ask, but had to know. "What happened to Amy?"

"It was an accident. I went over to their house to be with Maggie for a few hours so Amy and her parents could go out for dinner. Her dad's birthday. They got hit by a train at a level crossing. The police weren't sure if the signal was faulty, or if Mr. Summers just didn't see it somehow. Didn't matter. Either way, they were dead. Amy lived for a few days, but she never woke up again."

"God. That's awful." Saying he was sorry again seemed woefully inadequate.

"Maggie was only six months old."

"I can't even imagine what that was like. Before, you said your parents tried to take Maggie away from you?"

Jason's voice was scraped raw. "First they did everything they could to convince me to give her up. Finally they decided it would be best if *they* raised her. They wanted to pretend Maggie was theirs, even though all their country club friends would know the truth. I'd just be her brother off at college. A stranger."

"Must have been tempting though?" He added, "Because you were so young. I don't mean…"

"I know. Yeah. For a minute, I guess. It would be a do-over. I'd get to be a kid again. But there was no way. Maggie was my daughter and I couldn't pretend she wasn't. I was all she had. I couldn't leave her. To only see her at Christmas and in the summers, and give all the control to my parents? They said they wanted to raise her properly since I couldn't. I was too young. I have a younger brother, and they said it would be perfect for him to have a sister."

"And what about for *you?*"

"I was the failure. I didn't seem to matter anymore. I refused, and thank God I turned eighteen so there was nothing they could do. I left and took Maggie. They hired a lawyer and tried to get custody. Said I wasn't fit to be a father."

"Jesus."

"Ah, but it was for my own good, and Maggie's." Jason huffed, a puff of warmth on Ben's skin.

"Did Amy have any other family to help?"

"She had an aunt and cousins who helped out a little at first, but you know how it is… People have their own lives. They meant well, but they were busy. They send Christmas cards and we're friends on Facebook, but that's about it. In the end, it's always been just me and Maggie."

"What did you do for money?"

"Got the job at the cookie factory. It's not exciting, but it pays well enough and there's a union. A daycare down the block at the YMCA. I basically worked just to pay the fees. We lived in a tiny studio apartment the first few years, but it was worth it."

"How did you know what to do? To take care of a baby, I mean."

"Googled a lot. Read parenting books from the library. Winged it and prayed I wouldn't break her."

Ben smiled in the darkness. "I imagine that's what most people do. Did it go to court with your parents?"

"Briefly. Judge sided with me, and that was it. I haven't seen them since."

Ben wanted to say good riddance, but instead said, "Most people would have given in. I admire you so much."

Jason snorted. "Me? I'm nothing special."

"You realize how hard it is to raise kids? Or so I'm told. I always thought I'd have some, but I guess it's not in the cards."

Jason's fingers wrapped around Ben's forearm, squeezing and

sparking a shiver in him even through his jacket. "You'd be an amazing father. You're so good with Maggie. She really likes you." He inhaled sharply, grip tightening. "God, I can't…"

"We'll find her. I promise." Ben knew it wasn't a vow he should make, but he wanted to believe it was true with all his heart.

FAINT LIGHT FOUGHT through the thick foliage as Ben stirred. He'd dozed maybe an hour, and Jason had finally settled, exhaustion winning. Carefully pushing himself up to sitting, he could just make out Jason's face, slack and even younger-looking in sleep, his lips parted and sandy waves sticking up every which way.

Before he could even think, Ben reached out to smooth down Jason's hair, snatching back his hand just in time. He didn't have the right.

He crept away to piss against a tree and wash his face in the stream, bracing against the splash of freezing water. At least his face felt normal now, and the hives had faded. He popped a few more antihistamines to be on the safe side and splashed his face again. Despite shuddering in the early cold, a flush heated Ben's skin as memories barged through his mind.

He should never have returned Jason's frantic kiss. The man was at the end of his rope, utterly desperate. But along with desire—and he couldn't deny that it still stirred in him now, his groin tightening as he imagined kissing Jason again—the urge to protect and comfort tugged sharply.

With Brad, naturally they'd had moments of comforting each other over the years, but Ben had never felt such a powerful urge to shelter and care for someone. Of course he and Brad had never experienced such a trauma. Maybe Jason's age played a role as well. He was a grown man, but he carried an innocence that went beyond his baby face.

The night before, Ben had been desperate to take Jason in his arms, if only to hold him close. But kissing him back had nearly sent Jason running into the darkness.

Not that Ben blamed him, especially after the stuttering revelation that Jason had never kissed another man before. At least that's what Ben had gathered from the halting admission. Jason had been forced to grow up so quickly to be a father, and Ben wondered just how much he'd missed out on.

The emergency blankets rustled, and Ben braced himself to face Jason in the murky dawn half-light, fog hanging low over the trees and thick moisture in the air. Jason rubbed his face blearily before focusing. Their eyes locked for a moment before Jason hurried to the bushes, head down. Ben folded the blankets and packed up the rest of their gear, shouldering the rifle.

When Jason returned, Ben held out a protein bar. "Eat this."

He shook his head with a grimace. "Not hungry."

"You need to eat."

"Can we just go?"

Ben still held the bar out. "We can, but you need to eat this first."

"Fine." Jason snatched it, unwrapping it and gnawing off a piece.

After examining their surroundings through the binoculars, Ben called in on the radio for news. The FBI were setting up a command post at the southern ranger station, and helicopters would go up as soon as the fog cleared.

The bad news was that the forecast called for cool temperatures and more rain, and the fog might not lift, making a search from above useless. Tracking dogs were en route, but everything took time in rural Montana. There was nothing else to do but keep going, and they scanned the ground and bushes carefully for footprints and clues from Maggie, heading steadily west.

Going downhill was hard on the knees, and as they neared the valley floor in a steady rainfall midday, Ben's muscles protested from the marathon hike the day before and cold night on the ground. He could only imagine how Jason felt. Jason had probably never hiked more than several miles at a time in his life.

Stopping to gulp water, Ben assessed Jason's condition. He was pale, dark circles under his eyes, hair plastered to his forehead. He clutched the last piece of red fabric they'd found a mile back in his fist like a talisman.

Then Ben peered into the distance. His heart skipped. *Red. Red!*

"Ben?"

He wore the binoculars around his neck and yanked them up. "Come on, come on…"

"Do you see something?" Jason stood beside him, vibrating with sudden energy.

"I think I saw her."

"*What?*" Jason clutched Ben's arm.

"It was just for a second. I might have imagined it." He held his breath as he scanned the endless green of the forest, fog obscuring the treetops. There! Red poncho and a flash of golden hair. "I see her. It has to be her."

He was about to pass the binoculars over, but Jason was already off and running. Heart in his throat, Ben raced after him, the rifle ready in his hands.

I WANT TO GO home.

It was the only thing Maggie could think about as she plodded along behind the man, her dad's backpack digging into her shoulders. The man made her carry it when they moved, then snatched it away as soon as they stopped. It had barely been light out when he'd made her eat and drink and ordered her to walk. He was angrier with her as time went on, yelling at her to go faster.

Her lungs rattled when she coughed, and all she wanted more than anything was to be home and warm again. Making sure the man wasn't looking, she ripped off another strip from beneath her poncho, hooking it onto a bush and praying her dad would find it.

Tears streaked down her face as she thought of him, and she cried out when she stumbled over a fallen branch.

"Get up. You're slowing me down on purpose—don't think I don't know your little game," the man snarled.

"I'm trying. My legs hurt. I have a big blister. Please, I just want to go home."

He yanked her up by the arm, her shoulder screaming. "You can go home after I'm a long ways away. You're my little insurance policy. No telling when the cops might find us, and I need to get—"

"Where?"

"Never you mind. Move!"

Teeth chattering, Maggie concentrated on putting one foot in front of the other, and when the man piggybacked her again, she didn't mind as much. Her stomach growled, and she was so cold.

Then she heard a strange humming noise in the distance. The man began to whistle, jogging now. Maggie hoped that wherever they were going, they were almost there. She couldn't go much farther.

Daddy, where are you?

The humming grew louder, and she realized it was one of the white-water rivers that ran off the glacier. As it came into sight beyond the trees, the man whooped with joy. "There she is!"

At first Maggie couldn't see anything but green and the swirling water beyond. Then she realized that hidden in the foliage was an old wooden lean-to like the ones the Native Americans built.

"Old man Gilderoy uses this place for hunting. No one even knows it's here."

"But you're not allowed to hunt in the park."

The man laughed, his yellow teeth bared. "What they don't know don't hurt 'em."

He disappeared around the other side of the lean-to and returned dragging a small inflatable raft. "My buddy Dwayne comes out here to ride the rapids sometimes, and sure enough we're in luck." His ugly face creased. "Poor ol' Dwayne won't be needing this boat no more."

Maggie couldn't stop herself from asking, "Why not?"

He spat on the ground. "Because he won't. Because he made me do something I really didn't want to do, but a man has to protect his honor. Now stop asking fucking questions. And give me that." He flicked his fingers, demanding the backpack.

She was more than happy to slide it off her sore shoulders, flinching when he snatched it away. Rummaging through it, he swore loudly.

"Why didn't your dumb daddy pack more food?"

Maggie bit back a smart aleck answer and meekly replied, "We were only hiking for the day. You already have a lot, don't you?" She was surprised to see how much he'd squeezed into his pack.

"Never too much food," he muttered as he turned the knapsack upside-down. The only things left were a whistle, first aid kit, and her dad's pencils and sketchbook, which the man pawed at with a sneer, opening it and tearing at pages.

"Carries this crap around but not more food." He spat on the ground. "Namby-pamby waste of time."

"It's not crap! You're stupid! My dad's a great artist." Maggie sucked in a breath as the man jerked his head up.

"What'd you say to me?"

Inching away, she shook her head, lowering her gaze as she mumbled, "Nothing."

"Great artist," he muttered, tearing at the pages and scattering them over the dirt.

Maggie blinked rapidly, eyes burning as she tried so hard not to cry. She wanted to pick up all the pages and fold them safely into her pockets, but didn't move a muscle.

Now the man muttered to himself as if she wasn't there. "Won't be watching the river. Won't know I've got a boat."

Her throat hurt, but she had to ask, "Then you'll let me go soon, right?" She knew it might make him mad, but needed to hear him say it.

The man gazed at her steadily and smiled with his crooked teeth. "Course I will. Don't you worry about a thing."

Liar.

The fear that had been her constant companion since he'd torn her away from her daddy made it hard for Maggie to breathe. Her heart pounded over the rush of water. He was lying. He was never going to let her go.

She needed to get away. But she couldn't run faster than him. She might be able to hide, but what if he found her?

It would be really bad.

The man opened the lid of a wooden crate sitting under the lean-to. He pulled out a weird rubber thing with a hose and started pumping air into the raft with his foot. As he worked, Maggie noticed the bright orange strap now hanging out of the box.

A life jacket.

Slowly, she walked over to the box and looked inside. There it was—an old, dirty life jacket that probably hadn't been worn in years. It was too big for her, but it was better than nothing.

Maggie tried to think. Okay, running wouldn't work—the bad man would catch her. If she rafted down the river with him, he was probably going to kill her when he decided he didn't need her anymore. Or maybe he'd just kill her now if she made him too mad.

Reaching into the bin, Maggie pulled out the life jacket, her heart beating so hard she was sure he could hear it. She put it on over her poncho and tightened the buckle as far as it would go with trembling hands. She was pretty sure it would stay on.

"What're you up to?"

She turned to face the man, who was still pumping away with his foot. "I'm afraid of the water."

He only grunted. She slowly walked sideways toward the water's edge, only moving a bit at a time so he didn't notice. The bank was about ten feet above the whirling river, and it looked so far. The water was going so fast, and she knew it would be freezing cold.

She took one last look over her shoulder. A knife hung on the bad man's belt, and as he pumped, he fiddled with it. Maggie thought of how the metal of the gun had felt pressing into her head.

Turning back to the water, she closed her eyes and thought of Declan Michaelson's birthday party the summer before. She'd been too afraid to jump off the diving tower at the pool, so her dad had climbed up with her.

"You can do it, Mags. We'll do it together. One, two, three!"

He'd held her hand, and they'd flown through the air before hitting the water with a big splash. It was so fun, and she'd wanted to do it again and again. Daddy had jumped with her every time.

Standing on the very edge of the riverbank, Maggie counted in her head and imagined he was with her, his big hand tight around hers, keeping her safe like always.

One, two, three!

CHAPTER EIGHT

THE RUMBLE OF white water thrummed through the forest, a powerful heartbeat.

Ben couldn't imagine why Brown would have ventured that way, but perhaps he hadn't known the fast-flowing water was there. He'd have to go south as the river cut off his route to the west, but he could still stay hidden for days. Weeks. Months.

As they neared the throbbing river, a growl vibrated through the air. Ben stopped in his tracks, grabbing Jason's arm. Jason stared at him, waiting.

Not a grizzly. A voice.

"...God damn." Over the white water's drone, a man swore faintly. "*Motherfuck.*"

Ben had to wrap his arms around Jason from behind, holding him back from barreling onward. Jason's chest heaved, and Ben whispered in his ear.

"Be smart. Breathe." Ben's heart pounded, and he imagined he could hear the drum of Jason's as well in a terrible, terrified unison. They were pressed close, and Ben calmed his own breathing until Jason followed suit, quivering in his arms.

Jason mumbled, "Okay. Slowly."

"Slowly," Ben agreed. "Follow my lead." Not that he knew what the fuck he was doing, but Jason was all raw emotion and the deep, instinctual desperation imprinted into a parent's DNA when their child was in danger.

They veered to the right to approach at a distance. Ben slipped off his pack and crept through the trees. Tension radiated off Jason in waves, but there was nothing Ben could say to calm him at this point. Ben just prayed that Maggie was there. That she wasn't hurt.

He couldn't believe they'd actually found Brown. Blood thundered in his ears as loud as the white water, and his heart was going to shatter his ribcage. He forced an inhalation and exhalation.

A dilapidated lean-to lay ahead, and Brown suddenly walked into view on one side of it. Jason stared with wide eyes, vibrating but not charging forward, looking to Ben instead.

What am I supposed to do?

Jason and Maggie needed him. They needed him to be strong. To take charge. He could do this. He could do this for them.

He and Jason crept forward, and Ben's breath lodged in his throat, cold sweat on his neck as he readied the rifle, Brown out of sight again. No sign of Maggie, but one thing at a time.

Another curse rang out, louder this time. *Go, go, go!* Ben lunged into the clearing, the rifle jammed into his shoulder, barrel up, twigs snapping under his feet. Brown rounded the lean-to with his handgun raised.

"We just want the girl," Ben gritted out. Jason was in his peripheral vision, ready to explode.

A smile broke over Brown's scruffy face. "Aw, Daddy to the rescue. Too bad you're too late."

The bottom of Ben's stomach plummeted, and he tasted bile. *Please, no. Please!*

"Where is she?" Jason croaked.

"Went for a swim, I'm afraid. After I cut her little throat open a few miles back so I wouldn't have to listen to her fucking questions no more."

Grief shot through Ben like a snakebite, poison in his veins, and Jason staggered beside him.

"No!" Jason cried out. "*No*. You're lying!"

"Why kill her now? You took her so you'd have a hostage when the police closed in." Ben glanced around as if there'd be glaring evidence that Brown was lying. He had to be lying. *Had to be.* His throat burned with emotion, and he could only imagine Jason's horror.

Harlan shrugged, spitting carelessly on the ground. "More trouble than she was worth after a while. Slowing me down. And shit, the mouth on her." He sucked his teeth, eyeing Jason with a sneer. "Should have taught that little bitch some manners."

Rage burned through Ben, and he pulled the trigger before he could think twice, clipping Harlan in the shoulder as the man dove behind the lean-to. Ben hauled Jason behind him and crouched.

Now the only thing that separated them from Brown was splintered wood and bark. Ben dared a look around the side by the river. There was no sign of Brown, but he did see a deflating raft.

"Looks like your boat sprung a leak, Harlan."

Aside from the river rushing by, Ben couldn't hear a thing. He waited, then dared another look, this time around the other side of the dilapidated structure. Fifty yards away, Brown disappeared into the forest. Ben sucked in a breath, but kept the rifle at his shoulder, eyes scanning the trees. As much as he wanted the bastard dead, Brown was far too dangerous to take on, and Ben was happy to leave him to the authorities.

The minutes ticked by with no movement. Birds chirped faintly over the rush of the river. A chipmunk scurried through the underbrush, Ben training his rifle in that direction until he saw the flash of white-striped tail. The forest went quiet again in the gray murk.

Beside him, Jason stared blankly, his eyes unfocused. Ben scanned the area again before slowly lowering his rifle. Brown would surely have gotten as far away as possible. It was just Ben and Jason now.

"Jason…" Ben's voice sounded hoarse and distant to his own ears. "I'm so sorry."

"She can't be gone. It can't be true. I…" Jason blinked, opening and closing his mouth. A wail escaped him. "I *can't.*"

Then he collapsed in on himself, hunching forward as sobs racked his slim body. Ben watched helplessly, fighting his own tears. There were no words to make it better. Ben had failed, and all he could do was wrap Jason in his arms and pray for a miracle.

IT WAS LIKE BEING in a gigantic washing machine.

Maggie's lungs burned as she fought her way back up. The water spun her all around, and she gasped for air. Even with the life jacket, the force of the rapids sucked her under every chance it got.

The river whirled and thundered, twisting and turning as it swept her along. Ben's voice echoed in her mind, and she tried to keep her feet pointed downriver. The water was freezing, and her fingers were numb. She wasn't sure how long it had been since she'd jumped. It seemed like forever and ever, but was probably only minutes.

Another rapid approached, and she just missed a rock before she corkscrewed down under the water. When she came up again, she gulped for air, coughing and spitting. The river seemed to be slowing. She could barely move her arms and legs, but tried to get closer to the shore.

Then she saw it.

At the water's edge, where the riverbank wasn't so high, a grizzly leaned over, pawing at something under the surface.

Maggie held her breath as the river swept her closer and closer.

The bear was so big it didn't look like it could actually be real. Its brown hair was wet, and she prayed it didn't want to go swimming again.

I'm a piece of wood. Don't look up. I'm nothing you want to eat.

As she drew nearer, Maggie squeezed her eyes shut, her heart beating so hard it sounded really loud even over the noise of the river.

When she opened her eyes again, she was past. Glancing back, she could see the bear still on the shore, splashing its huge paw into the water.

She could breathe again, but she was still stuck in the river and it was too cold. Her muscles were so tight she thought she might break apart.

Rocks jutted out into the river in the distance on the right. As the current brought her closer, she reached out. Her fingers skimmed over the slick surface of the rock, but she couldn't grab hold.

Ahead, a low rumble meant there were more rapids. She kicked harder, swimming sideways toward the shore. Downriver, a fallen tree jutted out into the water. With every ounce of strength she had, Maggie reached out and closed her fist around the slick wood.

It slipped from her hand as the force of the water carried her away. Just as she cried out, she jolted to a stop. The river rushed by, but she wasn't moving. After a few seconds, Maggie realized her life jacket was caught on one of the branches.

She struggled to take hold of the branch that stuck out of the water. After a few tries, she managed to get a solid grip, and swung her left arm over the branch as well. Now she needed to get the life jacket unstuck without being carried off by the current.

"Daddy!"

She cried, wishing with all her might that he was there to help her the way he always did. But he wasn't, and she had to do something even though she was so tired.

Maggie couldn't just hang there from the tree, so she reached down with her foot. She knew she shouldn't, but couldn't think of another way to get unhooked. Her foot touched another branch under the water that seemed pretty thick. Still holding on tightly with her arms, she tried standing.

Immediately, her feet slipped off in her heavy hiking boots, and she screamed as she lost her grip. She bobbed under the freezing water, but the life jacket tied her to the tree. Sputtering, she wiped the water from her face and reached out for the branch again. After a few tries, she had the branch in her hand again, her fingers barely able to curl.

Maggie tried standing again, and this time she managed to keep her balance. The shore was ten feet away, and if she could reach behind and unhook her life jacket from the tree, she could climb on the trunk and crawl to the riverbank.

She twisted her right arm behind her and felt around for the strap snagged on one of the branches. Her fingers wouldn't work right, but finally she grabbed hold. She considered taking the life jacket off, but if she lost her balance again, she didn't want to be in the river without it.

Trying to stay as still as possible, she worked the strap loose. When she was free, she clung to the tree, afraid to move. Tears fell down her cheeks, and she whimpered, teeth chattering painfully. But she knew her only choice was to keep going, so she slowly worked her way down the length of the tree, hooking her arms through branches and holding on so hard even though she couldn't feel her fingers.

When she reached out and touched solid ground, she sobbed harder. Pulling herself up onto the bank of the river, the dirt and grass beneath her were so wonderful to feel. She was almost there, almost free of the tree. As her left knee rested on the earth, she pushed off with her right leg.

Her foot slipped wildly as the tree suddenly shifted. She cried out as her ankle was caught between the ground and the trunk. Gingerly, she tried to pull her foot free, but it was wedged in tight. She sat up and pushed at the solid weight with all her might.

It didn't budge.

Maggie shivered helplessly. She couldn't stop more tears as she realized there was nothing she could do to move the tree. It was too big. At least it didn't really hurt. She was cold all over, almost like she didn't feel anything at all anymore. For the millionth time, she wished her dad was there to fix it. He always fixed everything.

Sinking back to the ground, she pressed her cheek to the grass and shut her eyes, wishing and wishing her dad would find her.

BLINKING, JASON LIFTED his head and peeled a woodchip off his cheek. He was on the ground, Ben huddled close behind him, and—

Maggie.

Squeezing his eyes shut, he braced as the grief scoured him all over again, leaving him an open, bleeding wound. He had nothing. He *was* nothing. This was it. The world had become a black tunnel, and he'd never get out.

He'd failed. It was his job to keep his baby girl safe.

Jason prayed he'd wake up and this terrible nightmare would be over. That Maggie would be there in the door of the tent, tickling his foot and telling him he was a lazybones.

That he would never see her again was impossible. He was still breathing. The planet still spun on its axis—it must since the sun blinked out from behind moving clouds, the weather finally clearing as the afternoon brightened.

How?

How was the world still turning? How was he not dead too? He should be. Maggie was everything. How could he still breathe, heart still beat? He should be dead.

Again and again in his mind he saw it—Harlan Brown's grin as he mimed slashing Maggie's throat. Did she know what was happening? How much did it hurt? How long before…

No. No, no, no.

His arm was asleep under him, and Jason inched away from Ben's grasp. Ben had spooned up behind him, and now breathed deeply, his face slack. Jason had cried himself to sleep, and Ben had clearly given in to exhaustion too.

Pushing to his feet, Jason stumbled and rolled over his ankle, but it didn't hurt. He was numb now, gazing around at the sun-lit trees, blue sky revealing itself patch by patch. He shivered as the cool breeze whispered, part of him wanting to drop back to the earth and huddle close to Ben—wanting Ben's strong arms around him again, his deep murmur gentle, his skin smelling of pine.

Maybe that was just the trees all around, but Jason would always associate it with Ben now.

He wrapped his arms around his stomach, looking left and right as if there would somehow be an answer. As if Maggie would somehow appear, whole and real and alive.

Something rustled near his feet, and he blinked at the stark white…pages? Reaching down, Jason's trembling fingers grazed the paper. Standing tall, he mechanically flattened a page against his thigh.

He stared at his own drawing, the breath whooshing from his lungs as if he'd been punched in the gut. There were Maggie and Ben on the Road to the Sun, Ben kneeling and pointing to something in the distance of the valley, Maggie beside him in her too-short capri pants, tipping her head to follow the trajectory of Ben's finger. Jason had drawn them mostly from the back, with just a hint of their faces, eyes alight.

Through the unbearable ache of grief, fury flowed like the river at his back, crashing over rocks and slicing through solid ground, flooding him.

Fists clenching, crumpling the paper again, Jason wanted to howl at the moon and tear Harlan Brown apart with his hands and teeth. He wanted to rip into him until he saw bone, until the bastard's guts stained the earth.

Eyes darting everywhere, Jason was untethered, his knees about to buckle under the agony.

Then he saw it.

It was on the ground beside Ben, resting innocently. Jason's eyes darted to Ben's still, handsome face as he took one step, then another.

Bending, he wrapped his hand around the rifle. It was heavier than he'd imagined, but the weight was reassuring somehow. In the shadow of the lean-to, Ben still slept, and Jason didn't blame him. He'd done more than Jason could have hoped.

Now Ben could rest. He was safe, and he'd earned it. Jason's lips burned to bend and kiss him again, just once.

If he ever saw Ben again, he'd tell him how grateful he was. For now, he smoothed out the drawing once more and left it tucked in the shelter of the lean-to by Ben's head. Jason hoped he'd see gratitude in the strokes of charcoal.

He tread softly in the direction Brown had fled, gripping the rifle with both hands. Once he was far enough away, there was only one thing he could do, vengeance drumming his heart.

He ran.

CHAPTER NINE

GROANING, BEN STRETCHED. Where—

With a jolt, he opened his eyes, pushing up to sitting, stiff and cramped, remembering. He choked back a sob. *Oh, Maggie. I'm so sorry.*

The ground beside him by the lean-to was empty. "Jason?"

His only answer was the sway of leaves overhead. All was peaceful and still. Too still. Where was Jason? In sunlight blinking through the trees, he scrambled to his feet. Maybe Jason went to piss. Straining, Ben listened for any sounds of life in the nearby bushes. He could only hear the thump of his own heart.

"Jason?"

Ben circled the lean-to and searched the surrounding area, calling out. There was nothing. It was as though Jason had simply vanished. Where could he have gone? They'd both been utterly drained, but Ben hadn't intended to fall asleep. He'd just wanted Jason to rest, but now here they were.

Well, here *Ben* was.

"Shit, fuck, fuck!" he muttered, searching farther from the lean-to and calling Jason's name again. *Should never have fallen asleep!* But the urge to escape the terrible reality and give in to his exhaustion had overwhelmed him.

Guilt pricked his skin, and he rubbed his face as he neared the river. Then his knees almost buckled as a terrible thought occurred. He raced to the river's edge, the roiling, silver-tipped water a good ten-foot drop from the bank.

Of course there was nothing there, because if Jason had jumped, he would be long swept away now. Long dead.

Ben's empty stomach clenched, bile in his throat. In his despair, would Jason have tried to end his life? He gazed about frantically, screaming, "Jason!"

The thought of both Maggie and Jason dead eviscerated him, his guts spilling out as tears sprang to his eyes. He'd only met them less than a week ago, but now they felt as vital as oxygen.

"Jason!" He ran back to the lean-to, circling it again as if Jason would magically appear.

Then he staggered to a halt, staring at the ground. The rifle was gone.

Relief flooded, sweet and pure. It was possible Brown or someone else had taken the weapon and kidnapped Jason without waking Ben, but unlikely. Much more likely was that Jason had slipped away and taken the rifle, chasing after Brown for revenge. Or maybe he planned to shoot himself and end his misery.

Have to find him!

Ben jerked on his pack, cursing himself for his failure.

From the corner of his eye, he spotted a piece of paper in the shadow of the lean-to, skittering a few inches this way and that in the late-afternoon breeze. It had been crumpled and then straightened out, and his breath caught as he took in the drawing of him and Maggie on the Road to the Sun.

Yes, Jason had left this. He had to have. Now that Ben was looking more closely at the ground and not for a person, he noticed a backpack by the deflated raft. It was Jason's, the sketchbook torn and abandoned nearby.

Carefully, Ben tucked the drawing of him and Maggie inside the sketchbook and stowed it in his own pack, praying Jason didn't have too much of a head start. His skin prickled at the thought of Jason out there alone, grief-stricken. If only he could fly over the trees and scoop Jason up to bring him somewhere safe. Somewhere Maggie was still alive.

His radio battery would run out soon, so he kept his report brief and was told helicopters were in the air, but there wasn't much daylight left. The river rushed by on his left, obscuring any sounds Jason might have been making in the forest. Would Brown have stuck close to the river's path? Would Jason? Ben could only guess. He hedged his bets by staying near the river while still exploring the endless forest.

He kept a careful watch, conscious of the fact Jason might shoot blindly if he realized anyone was close by. As he tried to formulate a plan to get the gun away from Jason and bring him back to safety, thoughts of Maggie tugged incessantly.

He'd only known the girl for days, yet bottomless grief spiraled. He supposed it was only normal to feel such sadness for a dead child, but the thought of never seeing that sweet smile again, never hearing a clever question or excited answer, stabbed at him with every step. It wasn't *fair*.

A twig snapped nearby, loud and sharp. Ben froze, his breath in his throat. His eyes darted left and right, but he saw nothing. A moment later, some kind of small animal—he didn't see which—scurried by in the underbrush.

His breath whooshed out in a rush, and he turned in a circle just in case. No, he was still alone.

Reaching into his pack, Ben took out his water bottle and swallowed a big mouthful. It was almost empty, so he headed over to the river while he had the chance. Here, the bank was almost level with the rushing water, so it was easy to crouch and fill his bottle.

As he stood, screwing the cap back on, he glanced farther downstream. A large tree had been felled—by lightning, probably—and it stuck out into the river, its branches grasping the flowing current like fingers, and—

Red.

He took a few tentative steps, narrowing his eyes as he peered at the tree.

A few steps more and he could see the red clearly, as well as the orange band of a life jacket. His mouth went dry. *Oh God.* Her body must have been snagged by the tree or washed up on shore.

He forced his lead feet to move, stopping by the tree's exposed, torn roots. Maggie was just on the other side of the trunk, tucked in close, her face obscured.

Motionless.

Harlan Brown's evil words replayed in Ben's head as if shouted on a megaphone. *Cut her little throat open.* Ben knew what he would see, but he had to look. Had to bring her home to Jason.

His hand trembled as he reached down to roll her over. His fingers closed over her shoulder, and Maggie twitched.

Ben gasped and staggered back, crashing onto his ass. Scrambling forward, he rolled Maggie toward him gently, bracing himself. No, he hadn't imagined it—her chest moved up and down, and the skin on her neck was smooth and white and *whole.*

Relief and joy mingled, and he barked out a laugh that echoed through the trees. She was alive! He said a silent prayer to whatever deity might be listening. "Maggie!"

She might have moaned softly in response, but Ben wasn't sure. Her body was twisted awkwardly, and he realized her foot was pinned beneath the fallen tree. He tentatively poked and prodded her limbs, checking for broken bones. Not finding any, he stood and heaved the trunk a few inches, adrenaline sparking through him. Maggie moaned as he carefully pulled out her foot.

Cradling her in his lap, Ben pressed a finger to the pulse point on the side of her throat, just to double check. Sure enough, he felt a steady beat. "Maggie, wake up. Maggie!" He rubbed her sternum.

Her eyes flickered open briefly, and she made a low noise. Her skin was ice, and she'd obviously been in the river, her clothes still damp. Dirt smeared her, stark against her pale face. Even though the sun had come out, Maggie was obviously hypothermic, and he had to get her back to civilization, which had never seemed so far away as another night fast approached.

The quickest route to find help would be down to the most remote campground the park offered. Ben called in on his radio, telling them to send an ambulance.

He tossed the life jacket aside and hoisted Maggie into his arms. He wanted to yell for Jason, but couldn't risk it now. Brown was still armed, and Ben wasn't. Risking himself was one thing, and he would have done it in a heartbeat for Jason. But Maggie's life was literally in his hands, and he had to get her to safety.

Heading south as night fell, Ben moved steadily in the fading light. His arms burned before long, and he stopped to drink more water and rouse Maggie. He managed to get her to swallow a few sips, but she couldn't seem to really wake up.

He wanted to move as swiftly as possible, but paused to get her out of her wet clothes. The poncho had dried, but her pants and sweatshirt were cold and soggy.

With efficient movements, he peeled off her wet things and dried her with his T-shirt. The turtleneck he kept folded in his pack came down almost to Maggie's ankles, and he pulled his spare socks onto her little feet, tugging them up over her knees. It was the best he could do under the circumstances, and he wrapped her up in the red poncho.

Maggie remained unconscious throughout, making only the odd noise. He had to move faster. Instead of holding her in his arms, this time he slung her gently over his shoulder in a fireman's carry, the moon and stars illuminating the way.

Now they just had to make it back to civilization in time.

An hour later, Maggie squirmed on Ben's shoulder, making

muffled sounds of protest. Ben shifted her into his arms, kneeling on the ground. "Maggie. It's Ben. You're okay."

Her eyes opened with some struggle, and she blinked a few times before focusing on him. "Ben?" Her voice was little more than a croak.

"It's me. You're safe now, sweetheart."

"Daddy?"

The lie came easily. "He's still looking for you, but he'll be back really soon. Don't worry."

"Jumped in. Kept my feet up like you told me."

Ben's heart clenched. "You're so brave. I'm so proud of you. Your dad will be too." He could only imagine the courage it had taken to leap into the freezing white water. "We followed your trail. You were very smart."

"Cold." Her teeth chattered.

"I know, sweetheart. We'll be somewhere warm soon, I promise." He really hoped he wasn't lying this time. "I'm going to carry you, okay? This is the easiest way." He didn't wait for an answer before hoisting her up on his aching shoulder. He'd get her to safety. He wouldn't let her or Jason down again.

He exhaled in relief when he spotted tents through the trees, pale blue nylon. This campground could only be accessed by boat taken across a lake, so the journey wasn't over yet.

As he approached a tent, Ben called out, "Hello!"

Moments later, there was the sound of a zipper opening, and an older man's head appeared, suspicion evident in his creased face. "Who's there?"

"I'm Ben Hettler. I'm a park ranger. I've got an injured little girl here and I need help."

A woman's voice murmured from inside the tent, and the man crawled out and got to his feet. He took in Maggie draped over Ben's shoulder. "My God, what happened? Where did you come from?"

"The backcountry. Look, she's hypothermic and needs medical attention immediately. An ambulance is on the way to the other side of the lake. Where's your canoe?"

The man motioned to his right, and Ben could just make out a dark green canoe at the base of a tree. A woman in her fifties clambered out of the tent, pulling a sweater over her head. She peered anxiously at Maggie. "Is she all right?"

"She needs to get to the hospital," he repeated impatiently. "I'll be sure your canoe is brought back to you, but I need to take it."

Another camper appeared beyond the blue tent. He was short and stocky, in his forties with a thick head of red hair. "Everything okay over here?" He eyed Ben warily.

"This man says he's a ranger," the woman answered. "The girl is sick."

"Where are her parents?" The redhead asked.

Jesus Christ, Ben didn't have time for this. "Her father's lost in the forest."

"How do we know you're telling the truth?" the woman asked.

"He's wearing a ranger uniform," her husband noted.

"There's no time to debate. I'm a ranger, and this child was missing in the forest and is going to die unless she gets medical attention *now*."

His authoritative tone must have done the trick, because soon the two men had the canoe over their heads and they moved down toward the water's edge some fifty feet away. The redhead volunteered to help the older man take Ben and Maggie across the lake. He introduced himself as Eric.

"It'll be faster with two of us paddling." Eric was no-nonsense and Ben didn't argue.

The woman fetched her sleeping bag and helped Ben wrap Maggie in it snugly. He gently deposited Maggie in the middle of the canoe and knelt behind her. She didn't wake, and Ben checked her pulse, exhaling when he felt it, still steady.

Soon Eric and the older man were hard at work, the canoe slicing through the mercifully calm water. Ben felt useless huddled with Maggie and not helping, but he kept her warm in the chill of the night, rocking her in his arms and murmuring that she was safe now.

When the front of the canoe jammed finally into the wet sand on the other side, Eric jumped out, splashing in the shallow water and hauling up the boat. "Let's hope the ambulance is almost here." He started up toward the tree line before stopping. "Do you want me to carry her?"

Ben realized he hadn't moved, cradling her to his chest and watching her breathe. Eric was looking back at him with eyebrows raised. "No, I'm fine. I've got her," Ben insisted. He mentally shook himself and climbed out.

The older man whose name Ben still didn't know squinted into the trees. "I think I see some red lights coming."

Ben could have cried with relief when an ambulance, police, FBI agents and his fellow rangers streamed along the dirt service road, vehicles crowding a small clearing, lights and shouts shattering the peace.

In the back of the ambulance, he held Maggie's small, limp hand and stroked her hair. She blinked drowsily and managed to mutter, "Where's my dad?" before falling under again.

Ben allowed himself to close his eyes just for a moment as the vehicle bumped along, wishing desperately he knew the answer.

CHAPTER TEN

H E COULDN'T SEE.
Leaves and tree trunks surrounded him in dappled moonlight, and Jason knew it was the forest—endless miles of green stretching out. But nothing looked right, his vision tunneling and warped like a funhouse mirror. He couldn't hear anything, the chirp of night birds and rustle of leaves faint as if he wore earplugs, the sound of his own harsh breath blasting in his ears.

He'd run haphazardly, charging through the wilderness, branches slapping his face, no longer looking for fluttering pieces of red fabric—now red a thick haze over everything, rage fueling his stumbling steps.

Halting, Jason realized he wasn't sure when it had gotten dark. He lifted his hands and found he still carried the rifle. He stared at it, his numb fingers clenched around wood and metal.

Maggie.

Bright, beautiful Maggie. That he would somehow never see her again had seared through him, leaving a hollow, charred husk behind. His baby.

He'd once seen a piece of cheap art at TJ Maxx, one of those inspirational quotes mass-produced in China in pastel watercolors with a rainbow. It had said something about being a parent was like choosing to have your heart living outside your body. The truth in it had made him smile, because Maggie was absolutely his heart. His everything.

Now he recognized the horror of it. The unending agony of his little girl gone.

Faintly, Jason realized he was screaming, collapsed on his knees in the dirt and leaves, hunched over the rifle. He prayed he'd wake in Philly, alarm blaring, announcing the start of another monotonous day at the factory. He'd do anything, give *anything* to be back at his dead-end job, with Maggie waiting to be picked up at day camp.

She'd stand on the sidewalk outside the YMCA, a newly created piece of art in her hand—an orange juice can covered in spray-painted macaroni, or a fluttering drawing of mountains and lakes.

Gulping, Jason choked on a sob. His heart was gone, and he wasn't going to survive.

"NO WAY."

Ben took a deep breath, trying to remain calm. "I'm going to find him. So get out of my way." They were in an exam room off the ER since Dee had insisted Ben be checked over. "I got the all clear from the doc. Nothing wrong with me."

Dee gave him the glare that Ben knew made most men quake in their boots. "Except exhaustion, which can lead to fatal mistakes. The search party will find Jason Kellerman. And that cowardly piece of shit Harlan Brown."

"I'm going with them."

"No, you're sure not. You look like hell."

Dee had been waiting at the hospital, where Maggie was now safe and sound and in good hands. Ben had to find Jason. "I'm going."

"They're already out there. Sun's coming up any minute. Just hang tight." She reached for his shoulder, but he dodged.

"I promised Maggie I'd bring her father home. I'm going to keep my word."

Dee sighed. "Ben, you've done more than enough. Kellerman isn't your responsibility."

"Of course he is! I should never have fallen asleep. I should have kept watch over him. Now he's out there alone."

She stood her ground in the doorway, hands on hips. "You can second guess yourself 'til you're blue in the face, and it won't change a damn thing. Fact is, you saved Maggie Kellerman's life. You've already done more for these people than anyone would expect, so just get some rest. They'll find him."

"What if they don't?" The thought of never seeing Jason again was a shard of ice wedged between his ribs. "What if they don't find him?"

"There's nothing more you can do right now. Come on, get some rest." She gently tried to nudge him back to the exam table, but he jerked away, jamming his lower back against a counter corner.

"I can't just go to sleep knowing he's out there! Knowing I might be able to find him. I have to find him. He needs me! I need him!" His eyes burned with the threat of tears, and Ben clenched his jaw, trying to breathe. With a fervor he didn't quite understand, he needed to have Jason in his arms again, safe and whole.

Realization dawned on Dee's face, and she nodded slowly. "Ah. I see."

"I know we just met, but I…" It sounded crazy, but the words whirled through him.

I could love him.

He cleared his throat. "Jason's out there alone, thinking his daughter's dead. I can't just sit here. I'm going."

She nodded. "I'll drive you back out. There are five armed search teams going at sunrise, along with the choppers again now that that damn fog and rain have finally cleared. Let's get moving."

Jason, hang on. Maggie needs you. I think I need you too.

THERE WAS DIRT in his mouth.

It was gritty on his tongue as Jason coughed and spat, collapsed on the ground, still clutching the rifle beneath him. He wasn't sure how long he'd been laying there. Pins and needles pricked his hands and arms trapped beneath him.

Shivering, Jason pushed himself to his knees. A woodpecker drilled into a tree faintly, or was that his teeth chattering?

He squeezed his eyes for a second, remembering the warmth of Ben's strong arms.

No, he had to keep going. Had to…what? Jason blinked in the watery dawn light, thick tree trunks rising around him. It didn't matter if he found Harlan Brown. Didn't matter if he killed him. It wouldn't bring Maggie back. She was gone, swept away into the raging water that cut through hundreds of miles of wilderness.

Will they even find her?

He bent in two, his face in the dirt again, the metal of the rifle barrel freezing against his cheek.

Just shift it back a few inches and pull the trigger. It'll all be over.

Jason was on the edge of a canyon, swaying in the wind. He wouldn't have to feel this anymore. He wouldn't have to live without her.

You have to find her first.

A sob tearing from his raw throat, he sat up. He had to find his baby. Give her a proper funeral. He was her only family. He had to take care of her to the end. It was his job.

What if she's still alive? You haven't seen her yet. He might have been lying.

A flare of hope ignited in the ruins of his chest, deep in the ragged hole where his heart used to be, and he grasped for it desperately.

"Please, God." On his knees, tilting his face to the heavens, Jason promised to be a better father if Maggie could only be returned to him. He swore to never fail her again.

With a burst of manic energy, his breath coming harshly, he ran, not sure where he was going, but needing to move, muttering prayers and making bargain after bargain if this could not be happening.

He bulldozed through the trees, pushing onward desperately as the sun came up in a huge blue sky.

Ben, where are you?

Maybe he should turn back and find him. Ben would help. Everything would be okay if Ben was there.

Jason spun in a circle, trying to figure out which way he'd come. Where was the river? Which way was east? North? He stared up at the sun, heart beating too fast, throat dry. When had he last had water?

Where was he?

Where was Maggie? He had to find her! He spun again, staring up at the sky, trying to figure out the position of the sun. He staggered under a rush of dizziness, empty stomach heaving. *Ben! Where are you?*

Had he shouted it out loud? He wasn't sure. His chest tightened, and he looked up again, feeling more alone than he ever had in his life. He had to find Maggie! She couldn't be dead. He spun one way and then the other. No, no, no, no—

When the shot came, it echoed distantly, and he stared down at the rifle, expecting to see blood flowing over his hands. There was only dirt.

Another shot rang out, birds squawking in startled flight. Jason looked down again at the rifle. It wasn't him. Someone else was shooting. Was it Brown? Oh God, what if Ben was in trouble?

Images flickered through his mind—Ben sitting by the camp-fire licking gooey marshmallow off his fingers, singing along with them. Buckling Jason's life jacket, his blue eyes clear and close, cheeks creasing in a smile. Crouching by Maggie on the Road to the Sun, telling her all the things she wanted to know with endless patience.

Jason charged toward the sound. He hadn't protected his baby. He wouldn't fail Ben.

CHAPTER ELEVEN

H EART THUMPING, BEN stared down at the body, cataloguing its features: greasy mess of brown hair, weak chin, bulky muscles and broad chest with a gaping, bloody hole torn through it.

Not Jason. Not Jason. Not Jason.

They'd heard the shots coming from the next search quadrant and had raced over, Ben running until his lungs burned even after the report on the radio said it was Brown. He just had to make sure.

"You're trampling the scene. Move back," an FBI agent ordered him, her tone brooking no argument.

Other agents spoke on radios, clipped voices buzzing around him. In the distance, the thumping of helicopter rotors drowned out the usual sounds of the forest—birds and insects and the scurrying of animals through the underbrush.

"We have to find him," he said stupidly.

The woman nodded briskly, her short red hair falling over her forehead. "It'll be easier now. Straight forward search and rescue. Don't worry."

Don't worry.

His bark of laughter had her eyebrows shooting up. "Maybe you should head back. You've had a rough couple of days." She called to someone, "Jones! Let's see about—"

Through the trees, a flurry of voices exploded like a grenade.

"Put the gun down. Now!"

Ben shook off the agent and pushed through the foliage, leaves slapping his face. In the space between two ancient pines, Jason stood, the rifle in his shaking hands, pointing forward.

Pointing toward at least four agents, who'd pulled their weapons and barked commands, shouting over each other as Jason blinked at them, eyes wide in his dirt-streaked face.

"What?" Jason rasped.

Ben was in-between the agents and Jason in a heartbeat, reaching out as voices cursed and ordered him to move. He ignored them. "Jason, it's me. It's okay. They're FBI agents. No one's going to hurt you. Give me that."

"Ben? Are you okay?" Jason stared, lips trembling.

"Yes. I'm fine. Give me the rifle." The tip of the barrel brushed his chest.

"What?" Jason looked down, shaking his head and exhaling sharply as if surprised to see the weapon in his hands. "I thought you were in trouble. I didn't mean to…" He released the rifle, and Ben held it back behind him for an agent to take.

"It's okay." Ben cupped Jason's face in his hands. There were dried tear tracks through the dirt, and Ben ached. He never wanted Jason to hurt again. "Maggie's alive. Brown was lying, and he's dead. He'll never hurt anyone again. Maggie's safe, Jason. Do you hear me?"

Jason panted, his chest heaving. "Maggie?"

The short, redheaded woman Ben had been speaking to pushed in. "He's clearly in shock. Jason, I'm Agent Reardon. We're going to—"

Ben ignored her. "Maggie's alive, and she needs her father."

"Maggie's alive," Jason repeated. His voice strengthened, and he grasped Ben's shoulder. "She's alive?"

Ben's throat tightened, tears and a joyful smile battling. "She's alive. She's okay, Jason."

Jason shuddered, clinging to him. Relief at having Jason in his arms again sang through Ben's veins. "You're both safe."

"Thank you. Oh God. Maggie's okay." Jason repeated it a few times, as if it would make it more true. "How?"

"I found her by the river. She's at the hospital in Kalispell. They said she'll be just fine." He glanced at Reardon.

She nodded. "We just got a report that Maggie's doing great. Very anxious to see her dad, so let's get you moving. Chopper's coming to the closest landing spot, by the Silver Bark campground."

Ben kept his arm tightly around Jason's shoulders as they followed through the trees and to a ranger jeep. They bounced along a curving dirt road, Agent Reardon in the front and Jason and Ben in the back. Ben's co-worker Jim was behind the wheel, grinning from ear to ear.

Jason sagged into Ben's side. "You saved her. Thank you."

He shrugged. "She saved herself. That's one tough kid you raised. She jumped in the river to get away."

Choking on a sob, Jason exhaled. "My poor baby. Thank you for finding her. Thank you." He reached across Ben for his hand, threading their fingers together, squeezing so hard their nails went white. "Is this real?"

Ben squeezed back. "Yes, I promise. You and Maggie are safe." He drew Jason's head down onto his shoulder, Jason's uneven breath warm on his neck.

Maybe it was crazy, but Ben wanted to keep them safe forever.

"DADDY?"

Jason's heart exploded, joy and relief flowing through him like electricity as he leaned over her hospital bed and gathered her close, careful of the IV in her arm. "I'm here." He inhaled deeply, smelling medicinal soap and *Maggie,* the indefinable scent she'd had since she was a baby in his arms.

It was really her. She was really okay. She wore a blue Montana sweatshirt over a hospital gown, a plastic ID bracelet on her wrist.

"I missed you, Daddy. I'm so glad you're here." Her voice was hoarse, and when she coughed, her lungs rattled with congestion, but she was alive. His little girl was breathing and talking and *alive.*

"I missed you too, baby. I missed you so much. I love you, Maggie. I love you more than anything." He leaned back and perched on the plastic guest chair. "You know that, right?"

"Duh. Of course."

He laughed, and it felt so damn *good.* "Same old Maggie." He glanced at Ben, who stood inside the doorway, his wide smile creasing stubbly cheeks.

"I love you too, Dad. Are you okay?"

He'd let Ben take him into the bathroom and wash his face and hands so he didn't scare her by looking filthy and crazed. He'd closed his eyes and let Ben wipe his face with a warm cloth, Ben's big hands gentle. "I'm fine. Better than fine. I'm amazing now that I'm here with you."

"Me too."

Jason stroked her hair and examined her face. She was pale, dark circles under her eyes, but he didn't see any marks on her aside from a scratch on her cheek. He took a deep breath. "You told the doctors that man didn't hurt you. Are you sure? You don't have to be afraid. You can tell me anything, no matter what."

"I know. He just yelled at me when I was too slow. Sometimes he was nice. It was really weird. But he didn't do anything bad like what you're thinking."

Jason exhaled slowly, letting the relief fully sink in. "Okay, baby."

She smiled over his shoulder. "Hi, Ben."

"Hi, Maggie." He came to stand beside Jason, solid and reassuring.

"Did Ben tell you he saved me, Dad?"

Ben said, "You saved yourself. I was just lucky enough to stumble across you."

"When I woke up and you were there, I knew everything would be okay." She gave him another smile.

A warm whirl of emotions filled Jason—gratitude, comfort, affection. He wanted to take Ben's hand, but brushed back Maggie's hair instead, unable to get out any words.

"Where were you, Dad?"

Guilt slashed with razor claws. He should have been the one to find her. Instead he'd been wandering dazed and useless. "I…"

Ben said, "We split up to look for you. Could cover more ground."

Jason found enough control to add, "Ben told me how brave you were. You jumped into the river?"

She nodded solemnly. "I pretended you were there with me, like at Declan's party, remember?"

Jason swallowed hard, eyes burning. "Of course. We had so much fun jumping together. Didn't even seem high after the first time." He'd actually been nervous every time they'd climbed the stairs of the pool tower, but Maggie had been fearless after the first plunge, and he hadn't wanted to hold her back.

"I don't think I want to jump into the river again though. It was really, really cold and I had to stay in too long." She coughed, and Jason helped her sip water.

"You must have been really, really scared. I'm very proud of you." *Don't cry.* Jason exhaled slowly. "Do you want to tell us more about it?"

Her eyes filled. "I was super scared. But I don't want to talk about it anymore. You already know the important parts."

"Okay," Jason soothed. "We don't have to talk right now."

"Not *ever*. It doesn't matter anymore. I want to talk about good things." She pointed beyond them. "Like what's in that bag Ben brought?"

Jason realized there was a plastic bag on the chair in the corner as Ben fetched it. His mind swirled, acid in his belly. Okay, he wouldn't push Maggie to talk about it today. She'd been through more than enough without him forcing the issue. Surely she needed some time to process.

Ben said, "Just a little something I saw downstairs in the gift shop that made me think of you." He pulled out a thick book called *Birds of Montana and How to Spot Them.*

Eyes alight, Maggie clapped weakly. "Oh, thank you!" She thumbed through the pages. "And it's not for kids. It's a real grown-up book!"

"You already know way too much to go for the kiddie books. Right, Jason?"

Jason had to blink away tears rapidly as he nodded. Ben's thoughtful gift and Maggie's sheer delight even after everything she'd been through had his chest tightening with almost unbearable tenderness.

Sitting there watching his daughter read until her eyes grew heavy and she slept, Jason felt as though his nerves were exposed, his whole body, mind, and soul flayed open.

"Time for Dad to rest too." Smiling kindly, Dr. Sharma stood in the doorway. "Let me give you a quick exam to make sure everything's ship-shape, and then you can go get some sleep."

Ben, who'd pulled up the other guest chair, chimed in. "I spoke to the FBI agent in charge, and they have a room for you in the hotel right next door. You can be back here in five minutes. I know you're going to say you're not leaving her for a second, but you need some sleep."

Jason snapped his jaw shut, since that was precisely what he'd been about to say. "I'm fine. I need to be here in case she wakes up."

Dr. Sharma tucked a stray piece of dark hair behind her ear. "I understand, but trust me. She's going to be out for hours." She checked her watch. "Very likely all night at this point."

The light through the window waned, and Jason couldn't deny he was exhausted, but no. There was no way. "I can catch some sleep right here."

The doctor and Ben shared a glance. Dr. Sharma said, "How about you go take a shower and sleep for a couple hours. I promise we'll text you the moment she wakes up. Which I don't think will be until the morning, as I said." She grimaced. "To be frank, you stink. Both of you."

Jason found himself laughing, and God, it was surreal. Maggie was alive, and they were back in civilization. Ben was by his side, and Jason was *laughing*. He felt like he was outside his body, observing. He caressed Maggie's hair, only a whisper of a touch to prove she was really there, the golden strands silky between his fingertips.

"Jason, it's going to be a big day tomorrow." Dr. Sharma's face pinched in concern. "Maggie is going to have a lot to process. You're both in shock. You need your strength to support her. Get at least a few hours of quality sleep. I promise Maggie will be okay."

He scratched at his neck, digging in his nails. "I just... I don't want to let her out of my sight."

"Of course you don't," Ben said, squeezing Jason's shoulder, sending sparks of warmth down his arm. Jason leaned closer as Ben asked, "Can Jason have a cot here next to Maggie?"

She sighed. "Okay. Jason, I completely understand your re-fusal to leave Maggie, but please get some real rest. And I'm examining you—no arguments. I know you insist you're not hurt, so it won't take long at all." She nodded toward the adjoining bathroom. "Afterward, there's a shower you can use since this is a private room. It's better for Maggie to see you clean and looking the way you normally would. Normalcy is comforting after trauma like this."

Agent Reardon spoke from the doorway, saying, "Sorry to eavesdrop" in a tone that wasn't remotely apologetic. "Jason, I took the liberty of having your belongings from your campsite moved to the hotel next door. I'll have some clothes brought over immediately." She eyed Ben in his dirty, creased uniform. "What size are you? There's an adjoining room you can have and I'll make sure clean clothes are waiting. You live out of town, yes? It'll be easier if you stay put until our investigation is complete. Won't take long at all, don't worry."

Ben nodded. "Absolutely. I'm not going anywhere."

Jason smiled gratefully, trying to keep up with what Dr. Sharma and the FBI agent had said. His brain was wrapped in cotton, and he straightened up as the words penetrated. "Wait—a private room? Our insurance doesn't cover that. How much is it?" He'd have to get a loan, and with interest rates it would take years to pay off. He barely had enough for food and rent, and Maggie would need therapy and—

"*Jason*. Breathe," Agent Reardon ordered. "It's all handled. Don't worry about a thing. Maggie needs rest, and we require privacy to speak with her tomorrow and get more details of her abduction. We don't need sick kids sneezing and hacking and crying behind a curtain. We're covering the room upgrade."

He exhaled slowly. "Okay. Thank you."

"Of course. Also, we've posted agents by the elevators, at both ends of the hall, and outside the door here. Media are crawling all over downstairs and outside."

"Media?" Jason asked dumbly. "Why?"

Her lips quirked into a brief, sharp smile. "You're a big story,

Jason Kellerman. Single father, dramatic kidnapping, hunky, heroic park ranger thrown in for good measure. The villain was vanquished and the pretty little blond girl saved. This is like manna from heaven for the news outlets. The public are desperate for a feel-good story right now."

"Oh." How bizarre to think about people talking about them. Jason took Maggie's lax hand, her curled fingers warm and real.

"Don't talk to anyone about what happened. Not even nurses or orderlies. Only Dr. Sharma." The agent gave Ben another assessing look. "I'm going to assume you're trustworthy, but if you blab anything to the media, there will be hell to pay."

Jason sputtered. "He would never!"

Ben held up his hands. "It's okay. I understand you have a job to do. You can trust me."

Agent Reardon nodded briskly. "Good. One of my agents killed the suspect, and we need the complete picture before the media starts spinning its usual bullshit and half-truths. All they know so far is what we're telling them. Let's keep it that way." She turned on her heel. "Sleep well. And you both really do smell like shit."

In her wake, Jason, Ben, and Dr. Sharma looked at each other. Ben said, "She's a real people person, huh?"

Then Jason was laughing again—*laughing*—and he leaned over Maggie to breathe her in.

BEN JAMMED HIS baby toe on the wheel of the cot, and bit back a curse as he hopped on one foot. That's what he got for pacing in socks. His muddy boots were tucked under the chair in the corner, and he really didn't want to put them back on.

The plain T-shirt he'd been given was a little tight across his shoulders and boxers a little loose beneath okay jeans, but it would do. He'd left to give Jason privacy while Dr. Sharma examined him, and had practically run to the hotel next door, accompanied by agents who whisked him in and out through a side entrance, away from the buzz of reporters around front.

Part of Ben had wanted to stand under the stream of hot water for hours, but he'd hurried back, promising Jason he'd watch Maggie while Jason showered after being declared only bruised and exhausted by Dr. Sharma.

Ben peered at Maggie again in the low yellow light of a lamp in the corner. She was sound asleep, lips softly parted, the blue tint fading. Her chest rose and fell, lungs still rasping, and he carefully tucked the blanket up around her a little higher.

Then he paced again.

To the window, past the cot to the door, then back. He hadn't even glimpsed the sky in the alley between hotel and hospital, but now he could see the moon's pale glow through the glass.

All was silent beyond the closed bathroom door, and he stared at it on each pass of the small room. There'd been no running water. Maybe Jason was just on the toilet, and Ben shouldn't interrupt.

But what if he passed out and I didn't hear the thump? What if he's hurt after all? What if he needs help?

Stomach tight, he knocked on the bathroom door, just a brush of his knuckles. "Jason? Are you okay in there?"

"I'm…"

Twisting the handle after a few ragged heartbeats, Ben edged the door open. "Everything okay?"

Jason was still dressed in his filthy clothes, his back to the door. In the mirror, Ben could see that Jason was holding up his hands, staring at them. Ben rushed the couple of steps to his side. "Are you hurt?"

"No. Are you sure this is real?" Jason glanced up into the mirror and down again at his scraped palms. "It seems like it is, but…"

Through the open door, Ben glanced back at Maggie, who was still fast asleep. Standing behind Jason, he gently took hold of his shoulders. "We're here. Maggie's safe and sound."

Jason met his gaze in the mirror, his brown eyes shining. He whispered, "I keep thinking I'll wake up, and now I don't want to."

"Maggie will still be here." He squeezed with his fingers. "So will I."

Nodding, Jason swayed a little on his feet.

"Let's get you cleaned up." Ben flipped down the toilet lid and guided Jason to sit, then leaned over the tub and pushed in the plug. He was afraid Jason was too drained and unsteady for a shower. As warm water filled the tub, he unlaced Jason's hiking shoes and peeled off his socks.

Jason wrinkled his nose. "God, I really do stink."

They smiled at each other as Ben tossed the offending socks into the corner. Jason lifted his arms when asked, pliable as Ben undressed him. There was nothing sexual about it, the emotions filling Ben ones of tenderness and nurturing.

He swirled his hand through the water to make sure it wasn't too hot, then guided Jason into the tub. Jason moaned softly as he sank back.

"Oh God. That feels good." He closed his eyes.

Ben folded up a hand towel. "Here, try this." He lifted Jason's head and placed the padding on the rim of the tub against the white tile.

"Mmm. Thank you." A few moments later, Jason's eyes popped open. "Is Maggie still sleeping?"

Twisting to peer around the doorframe, Ben nodded. "Out like a light."

Jason visibly unclenched, his limbs flopping. "Okay."

After rolling up his sleeves, Ben unwrapped a bar of soap and grabbed a rough washcloth. "Just relax, okay?"

"Uh-huh."

With every stroke of the cloth over his skin, Jason relaxed until he was utterly boneless. Ben lifted his arms and legs, cleaning him efficiently, wiping Jason's soft cock and cleaning his groin. The water sloshed like placid ripples on a shore.

Jason's skin glistened, slightly reddened in the warm water and from the friction of the cloth. Ben wanted to run his hands all over Jason, just to feel him safe and solid. He longed to climb into the tub and hold him close, but instead pulled down the hand shower, running more warm water.

Ben murmured, "Keep your eyes shut and tip your face forward a bit," then perched on the side of the tub to wet Jason's hair. He switched off the water and let the hand nozzle hang low toward the tub. Uncapping a bottle of generic shampoo, Ben lathered Jason's hair, massaging his scalp.

"Mmm." Jason leaned into his touch, and after Ben rinsed out the shampoo, he wanted to rub his face all over Jason's head. Instead, he worked conditioner into the shaggy hair, Jason sighing, eyes shut.

Jason's legs were bent to fit in the tub, and he was beautiful through the soapy water, loose and unquestioning. His trust filled Ben with a sense of peace. Wholeness.

Once the conditioner was rinsed out, Ben rubbed a towel over Jason's head. "Let's get you out of there before you prune up."

After Jason climbed out, dripping onto the floor, Ben knelt at his feet and dried him, the cheap hospital towel rough but efficient. A change of clothes sat folded on the counter, and he helped Jason on with the briefs, track pants, and T-shirt. Resisting the urge to wind his arms around Jason's waist and keep him near, Ben led him to the cot beside a slumbering Maggie.

He pulled up the blanket around Jason's shoulders. "Sleep well. I'll be right here."

"Mmm." In the soft light, Jason could barely keep his eyes open. "You should sleep too."

"Nah. Grabbed a coffee and now I'm wired."

Blinking heavily, Jason groped for Ben's hand. "Thank you."

Even once Jason was sleeping, Ben kept hold, their fingers twined together.

CHAPTER TWELVE

THE CRY WAS plaintive and desperate, and Jason jerked up on the cot, blinking in the sunlight. On the other side of Maggie's bed, Ben was bolt upright in his chair, his hand hovering as if to wake her. He nodded to Jason, pulling back his hand.

Jason rolled to his knees on the cot, keeping his voice low and calm. "Mags? Wake up, you're having a nightmare." He shook her shoulder gently as she whimpered. "Maggie?"

Gasping, her eyes popped open. "Daddy?"

"It's me, baby." Jason pulled her into his arms, rocking her gently. "Everything's okay now. You're safe."

Maggie clung to him, tears streaming down her face as she gulped noisily for air, coughing, her lungs still rattling a little. The helplessness that had become so familiar returned with a roar, and Jason wished he could do more than rub her back and murmur words of comfort. At least Ben was there with him, silent and reassuring.

Eventually she cried herself to sleep again, and Jason leaned over her, brushing back her hair and watching for any signs of another nightmare.

After a little while, he sat crossed-legged on the thin cot, eyes still glued to Maggie. He murmured, "I can't believe I actually slept."

"You needed it."

Jason looked across the bed to Ben, who rolled his head from side to side, grimacing. "You must be exhausted."

Ben shrugged. "I'll take a nap later. Do you want anything? Coffee? Water?"

Jason bit back a moan at the very thought. "Coffee would be amazing. Sweet, sweet caffeine."

Ben's cheeks creased. "Ah, so the way to your heart is through a venti cappuccino."

"Definitely." His stomach somersaulted as he returned Ben's flirty smile. Because it was definitely flirty, right?

While Ben was gone, Jason rolled over the question in his mind. The night before, Ben had seen him completely naked—had given him a bath like he was a child. And maybe that's why Jason hadn't felt uncomfortable at all, because Ben hadn't been flirting with him whatsoever then.

Jason had been able to close his eyes and be taken care of for the first time in… He honestly couldn't remember. With Ben, he didn't feel as if he was being judged for needing help. He didn't feel weak or not-good-enough.

With Ben, he could breathe.

He'd been able to close his eyes and put himself completely in Ben's strong hands, let everything go and sink into trust and comfort. Memories bloomed: the lap of warm water and wet cloth against his skin, Ben's steady breathing matching Jason's heartbeat. He hadn't had to try to impress or be anything. He'd only had to *be*.

"Dad?"

Blinking, he snapped his attention to Maggie, who smiled up at him blearily. "Hey, sweetheart. How are you feeling?"

She stretched her arms over her head. Her eyes were puffy and voice hoarse, but he wasn't sure if it was from crying or the lung congestion. "Good. Is it breakfast time?"

"Yes, I'm sure it'll be here any minute." He kissed her forehead. "Do you want to tell me about your dream?"

Her gaze skittered away. "No. I don't remember it now."

"I know it's not easy, but I think you should tell me. You'll feel better."

"I told you—I don't remember it anyway. I'm fine."

Jason normally knew how much to push, but the rules had all changed. "It can be really hard to talk about scary things. I just want to make sure you're okay."

Her eye roll was reassuringly familiar. "Daaad, I'm fine." Her face lit up. "Hi, Ben!"

"Good morning, sleepyhead." Ben stood in the open doorway, a cardboard drink holder in one hand, a large paper bag in the other. To Jason, he said, "I can come back?"

"No, it's okay." If Maggie wanted to pretend nothing was wrong, he'd play along for the moment. He smiled. "Don't you dare take my coffee away."

Ben settled himself in the chair across the bed, passing over the coffee and an orange juice for Maggie. He sipped his own coffee and opened the paper bag. "I thought doughnut holes were in order."

Maggie gasped with joy before coughing. "Is there powdered jelly?"

"Absolutely." Ben folded down the bag and put it on the bed so they could peek in and pick. Jason popped a chocolate glazed into his mouth, savoring the soft sweetness and washing it down with a perfect coffee, strong and with just the right amount of milk.

While Maggie and Ben talked doughnuts and favorite baked goods, Jason thought of a list of questions for Dr. Sharma. He'd ask what Ben thought too about how much to push Maggie to talk. He didn't want to upset her, but choking down her feelings wouldn't work.

It was a relief to have a friend to consult for an opinion, and as he sipped his coffee and watched Ben and Maggie laugh, it really hit Jason just how isolated he'd been. He hadn't allowed himself to become more than passing acquaintances with anyone after Amy's death and the drama with his parents.

Now he had Ben, although he knew he shouldn't get used to it. He and Maggie would have to go home soon. On one hand, the thought of his own bed and their familiar little apartment was wonderful. On the other, he'd probably never see Ben again. His gut clenched. Maybe they could stay in touch on Facebook or through email and texts or whatever.

Maybe we could be more than friends.

"Dad, tell him to stop being silly." Maggie giggled.

Ben flattened his hand on his chest, faux wounded. "Silly? I am *never* silly."

"Woodpeckers and beavers aren't cousins! That's impossible."

"So it would seem," Ben said. "Let's examine the evidence. Jason, you can be the judge."

He realized he was grinning. "Okay."

Ben returned his smile, and a tingle ran down Jason's spine. Ben opened his mouth to make his case when a deep voice rumbled.

"Ben, there you are. I've been calling." The man loomed in the doorway, his ranger hat in his hands and dark green uniform hugging a fit body. "I'm Brad Cusack. You must be Jason and Maggie. We're all relieved to have you back safe."

Ben had pushed to his feet, and he wiped doughnut powder on his jeans. "Brad. Sorry, I turned my ringer off."

Brad strode into the room and opened his arms, pulling Ben into a hug. "We were so worried. You're sure you're okay?"

Ben hugged him back awkwardly, stiff and uncomfortable, and Jason realized this Brad person was Ben's cheating ex. The man who'd been stupid enough to let him go. Anger and a murky swirl of jealousy rolled through him.

Ben extricated himself from the hug and turned to Maggie and Jason. "This is my... Uh, Brad. My supervisor."

Maggie's eyes narrowed. "Are you married to Tyson Lockwood?"

Brad smiled widely, white, even teeth flashing. "I am indeed, darlin'. Do you want an autograph? I can get one lickety-split."

Maggie gave him a level stare. "No thanks."

Brad's smile faltered. "Okay then. Well, how are you feeling?"

"I wish people would stop asking that." She huffed. "I'm fine!"

Jason jumped in. "Maggie, Mr. Cusack was only being polite. Which you need to be." He stood and extended his hand. "Good to meet you."

Brad shook his hand firmly with a surprisingly damp palm. "I'm sorry to barge in. I wanted to make sure Ben was all right."

"Of course." Jason gritted out a smile, ridiculous jealousy spiraling as mental images of Ben and Brad together spun through his mind. He'd never hated someone on sight, but Brad Cusack was coming close.

The three of them stood awkwardly while Maggie glowered from the bed, the strange tension palpable.

Ben cleared his throat. "We were just... Did you need an official statement or something?"

"Yes, yes." Brad seemed relieved to discuss business. "You can imagine the follow-up to this incident will be intensive. I'll need to ask you some questions."

An orderly appeared with a breakfast tray, and Brad moved to stand beside Ben as Maggie grumbled about her eggs being scrambled and not over easy. Jason could sense a full-blown tantrum coming on, and he went the route of soothing her and promising they'd get perfect eggs as soon as she left the hospital.

"When? I'm better now."

"We'll see what Dr. Sharma says, but she thinks you should spend two nights just to make sure everything's okay." He braced for impact.

Sure enough, Maggie's face went red and she wailed, "I have to stay again tonight?" Then she had a coughing fit, congestion still clogging her lungs, and Jason helped her sip water.

"It's okay. Breathe. I promise we can go home soon."

Sniffing, she nodded, her rage disappearing as quickly as it'd appeared. She mumbled, "I'm sorry."

Ben poked through the paper bag and pulled out a powdered doughnut hole. "Here. Saved the last jelly for you."

She beamed and stuffed it in her mouth, getting powdered sugar all over. Jason and Ben shared a laugh, and Ben handed Jason a napkin, Maggie giggling and squirming as Jason wiped her face.

"Well. I should…"

Jason realized Brad was still there. "Oh, sorry. We're keeping you from your work."

Brad's smile was decidedly uncomfortable. "No apologies necessary. We'll leave you two in peace. Ben, I need to get a few details for the department report, like I said. I'll just make a recording on my phone and transcribe it later."

Ben nodded. "Of course." He tickled Maggie's feet through the blanket. "Don't get into any trouble while I'm gone."

With a little shriek, she agreed, and Ben gave Jason a soft smile. Brad watched them with a furrowed brow as Agent Reardon strode into the room, flanked by two male agents.

"All right, everyone who isn't Jason and Maggie Kellerman, there's the door. This is going to take some time, and then it's your turn, Mr. Hettler."

Jason sat up straighter in his chair and took Maggie's hand. After sharing a glance with her, he nodded.

"We're ready."

FOLLOWING BRAD INTO an alcove down the hall, Ben caught a familiar whiff of spicy cologne. Even after everything, it was strangely comforting, and he breathed a sigh of relief that he wouldn't have to deal with a stranger right now.

Brad turned, sporting a sly, crooked smile. "You fucking that kid?"

Relief evaporated into a bolt of fury. "Excuse me? No, I'm not."

He was still smiling. "But you want to."

Ben couldn't deny it, and he pressed his lips together, nostrils flaring.

"Hey, I'm not trying to be an asshole." Brad held up his hands defensively.

"It just comes naturally."

"Okay. I deserve that."

"Damn right you do!" Ben paced, two strides one way and then the other. "You don't get to comment on my life after you cheated and dumped me."

"You're right. I'm sorry."

"What? You're not going to try and make it my fault?"

"No." Brad's mouth turned down, and he shook his head. "None of it was your fault. And it wasn't mine either." He held up a hand and added, "Except the cheating. That was a hundred percent my fault."

"Yeah, it was. I never would have done that to you!" They hadn't discussed any of it since the initial explosion of a breakup when Brad had confessed the affair and Ben had moved out of the house the same night. "We pretend to be friends at work like everything is just fine. It's ridiculous! It's not fine. What you did is not fine and it never will be."

"I wish I could change it. I really do. But I'm not sorry we broke up."

The unearthed hurt piled up, resentment choking Ben, closing his throat. "Good to know. Thanks."

"Ben, it could never have—"

He exhaled sharply. "Let's just get this done. What do you need to know?"

Sighing, Brad pulled out his phone and tapped at it. He stared at the screen for a long few moments before looking up, his face drawn and tired. "We weren't happy together. We weren't happy for a long time. It doesn't excuse what I did. I know that. But shit, Ben. Don't you want to be happy?"

He stared at that familiar face, one he knew almost as well as his own. The long brows over wide-set green eyes. Laugh lines that had been etched beside Brad's mouth as long as Ben had known him. The little scar on his cheek from a piece of flying glass at a country bar in college when a fight broke out.

Brad swallowed thickly. "I don't think we ever really fit right. But we sure loved each other. So we stayed together years longer than we should have. And I'm so sorry for how it ended, but I'm glad it did. You are too. Maybe you don't want to admit it, but you are."

Ben's resolve started to crumble, the blaze of bitterness dampening.

Brad stepped closer, beseeching. "I want you to be happy. I want you to find what I have. God, being a father, it's everything you've imagined and—"

"Don't." He gritted out, "Don't throw that in my face."

"That's not what I'm trying to do," Brad pleaded.

"You didn't want kids with me. I wasn't good enough, but *he* is."

"No. That's not true. I didn't want kids with you because I knew it wouldn't fix us. It would have been a distraction for a while, but it wouldn't have changed the fact that we weren't right together. I didn't want a child caught in the middle of that."

Obviously Ben wouldn't want that either, and now he could

see the logic.

Brad motioned with his hands in the way he always had when he was passionate about something, swoops and cuts through the air. "I'm saying it's not too late. Damn it, you're not dead! We're not that old yet. Find joy, Ben. Be a father. Go after it! You're the master of your own destiny. Stop feeling sorry for yourself and grab your future by the horns. What are you waiting for?"

Ben opened and closed his mouth. He didn't have a good answer.

Hands falling to his sides, Brad said, "I don't want us to *pretend* to be friends. We shared our lives for twenty years. I don't want there to be nothing left of that. I realize that's easy for me to say at this point. But I'll always care about you and want you to be happy."

Jerking his head in a nod, Ben swallowed hard.

Brad's cheeks puffed as he blew out a long breath and tapped his phone again. "Okay, I just have to ask you some questions. Ready?"

Ben thought of Jason down the hall. His sweet smile with a dimple in one cheek, and the way his hair curled at the ends. His utter dedication to Maggie, the loyal, beautiful love filling Jason's heart.

"Ready."

BEN BOLTED UP, staring around at the hotel room, drenched in early evening sun. He'd only stretched out on the bed for a minute after showering, a towel around him. Had there been a knock, or was it in his dream?

No, there it was again, insistent. *Rap-rap-rap.* He flew out of bed and tossed the towel, stepping into the loose boxers before unlocking the door and flinging it open. Jason stood there with his fist raised to knock again.

"Oh, thank God. You weren't answering your phone. I just…" Jason shook his head. "Shit, I'm sorry to bug you. I'll let you sleep."

"No, no. I'm awake. Is Maggie okay?"

"Yes. She's fine. Playing games with another kid on the ward. I didn't want to leave her, but when you didn't answer… I don't even know why I was worried." Jason looked down at the phone clutched in his hand. "She insisted I go, and I don't want to smother her. She's safe there, right? They promised to call if anything happens, but I should get back."

"Come in for a minute." Ben stepped back and ushered Jason inside. "I'm sorry to worry you. I must have been passed out hard." He strode to the bedside table and grabbed his phone. "Or maybe it was because I plugged it into the charger and then didn't actually plug the charger into the outlet. Not my brightest move. I'm sorry."

But I'm happy you were concerned about me.

"No, don't be." Jason shook his head ruefully. "I'm not sure what I thought could have happened. Pretty sure you didn't run into a grizzly in the alley. I guess I'm just—" He waved his hands around. "Antsy. You know? I mean, you might have just gone home to your cabin. It's not like you have to hang around here anymore."

After hours spent with Brad and then the FBI, he'd come to the hotel for a shower, and he realized he hadn't even considered going home.

Not without Jason and Maggie.

It was another crazy thought, but it resonated deeply, the chimes of a bell he was helpless to unring. He tried to smile and keep his cool, but the words came out low and earnest. "I don't want to go anywhere if you and Maggie aren't with me."

Did I just say that out loud?

Jason stared with wide eyes, then licked his lips. Ben followed the movement, the urge to kiss and taste overwhelming. He itched to touch, to reassure himself that Jason really was okay and whole, that he was *safe*.

"I… Uh…" Jason stammered. "Did Agent Reardon find you after she was done with us?"

"Yes." He tried to joke. "She has excellent attention to detail. Asked a lot of questions. How did it go with Maggie?"

"Okay, I guess. Maggie answered the questions, but she really didn't want to. I mean, I get it, but I don't want her to bottle it all up. I'd rather she have one of her tantrums, you know? I talked to the hospital shrink, and he said to give her some time, especially right now when it's so fresh. She probably needs to process everything that happened herself first before she's ready to talk."

"That makes sense. How about you? I bet you could use some unbottling yourself."

Jason's small smile tugged at Ben's heart. "I'm okay, but thank you. You were there for most of it, and… Thank you for that too. I don't know what I would have done without you."

"You don't have to thank me. I wanted to help." Ben longed to breathe Jason in from head to toe. He wanted to show how much he cared, how much Jason could mean to him. How much he already did.

Ben wanted to love him.

Fidgeting, he shifted from foot to foot, his throat closing, fingers twitching. Emotion swelled and pushed through every pore.

This is insane. I hardly know him. We went through a traumatic experience together. I feel bonded to him, but it's not real. It can't be. Can it? I should get dressed and get my shit together.

Jason's brows drew together as he stepped closer. "Are you okay?"

Brad's voice echoed in Ben's mind.

What are you waiting for?

"I want to touch you," he blurted. "I want to kiss you and lick you and fuck you and hold you all night." He motioned to the window. "Or all day." He tried to laugh. "Whichever."

Jaw dropped, Jason stared with wide eyes.

Ben scrubbed his face. "Oh, wow. I'm sorry. I shouldn't—this isn't—you don't…" He exhaled sharply. "I'm being incredibly inappropriate."

"You… You really want that?" Jason asked. "*Me?*"

His body thrummed, hope buzzing through him. "I do. Yes."

I want to get you on your hands and knees and pound your ass. I want you to ride me and come on my chest. I want to fuck your pretty mouth until my cum drips down your chin.

Slow down. Don't scare the crap out of him.

Ben never engaged in cum play with hookups. It was too intimate in a way he didn't really understand. He'd tried with Brad, but Brad had hated it, so it had remained in the realm of fantasy. Maybe Jason would hate it too, but Ben couldn't deny that he was praying Jason wouldn't mind—would even enjoy it. That was if he even wanted to have sex.

"But…" Jason shook his head. "I…"

"What?"

"But I'm not allowed!" Jason exclaimed. He dropped his gaze, cheeks flushing even darker. Staring at the carpet, he mumbled, "I want to be with you, but I can't. I shouldn't."

Barely restraining himself from yelling, *"For the love of God, why not?"* and hauling Jason into his arms, Ben reached out and took his hand instead. "Okay. Because I'm a man?" Keeping his tone soft, he held on firmly, rubbing Jason's knuckles gently with his thumb.

"No. Not really." Jason opened his mouth and closed it again, clearly searching for words. He lifted his head. "I never really thought about it. Being…attracted to men. It was there, but I brushed it off. Told myself I liked looking at hot guys because I envied their bodies. It was all theoretical anyway. Because I'm not allowed to have…"

Ben softly asked, "What?"

"*This.* Any of it. I made my choice. I picked Maggie. I picked being a father. Everyone told me I wouldn't be able to do it. I was too young. Teenagers are selfish, and I'd want too much for myself. I would never be able to sacrifice college and parties and dating. All that stuff. But I chose my baby, and I swore I'd prove everyone wrong. I'd prove that I didn't need anything but her."

Smothering a swell of rage at the faceless people who had heaped so much pressure on Jason's young shoulders, Ben caressed his hair with his other hand, the waves curling over his fingers. "You're an amazing father. But that doesn't mean you're not allowed to have a life of your own. That you're not allowed to draw and be an artist. That you can't want things for yourself. A relationship. Sex."

Jason shook his head, knocking against Ben's hand. "Maggie has to come first."

"And she does. But what's second? Third, fourth? You get to have a life. You're allowed. I promise."

Tears glistened in Jason's brown eyes. "I'm such a mess. Why would you even want me?"

"You're intelligent and kind, and you sing terribly around campfires to make your daughter happy." As Jason laughed unsteadily, Ben took his face in his hands and thumbed the tears from his warm cheeks. "You're sexy and sweet and you unironically love nineties pop music. You're brave and strong, and you make me feel inspired for the first time in years. God, I want you."

Jason sniffed and licked his parted lips, his gaze flicking between Ben's eyes and mouth. "I… I'm…"

Marshaling all his self-control, Ben stepped back, dropping his hands, his fingers clenching into fists. "It's okay. We don't have to do anything. We can just talk and—"

His words were swallowed by Jason's kiss. Jason gripped Ben's head almost painfully, his lips bruising and pleading. All the blood in Ben's body rushed south, and he hauled Jason against him, fire zipping through his veins.

With a gasping breath, Jason broke the kiss, chest heaving. "I don't know what to do. I want...everything. I want it all."

Ben could only kiss him in response, pressing Jason back onto the bed, his heart singing with every little moan and whimper that escaped Jason's lips. Hungry, Ben wanted to rip off Jason's clothes, throw his legs up, and fuck him into next week.

But he concentrated on kissing him—licking into his mouth, sucking his tongue, reveling in every hitched breath and jerk of Jason's hips. Their stubble rasped roughly. Jason tasted vaguely of coffee and tangy orange sweetness. His hot breath puffed over Ben's face as Ben nipped and teased before diving back in, tongue stroking.

The denim-covered ridge of Jason's hard cock nudged Ben's hip, but Ben touched everywhere but there. He caressed his cotton-covered arms and shoulders as they kissed, one hand tangling in Jason's shaggy hair, the other snaking down to rub his thigh. He delighted in Jason's breathy shiver when his fingers stole under the hem of Jason's Henley, teasing his sensitive stomach and circling his belly button.

Flushed and beautiful, his thick lips red and wet, Jason pant-ed. "Please. I can't wait." He raked his fingers through Ben's chest hair. "Please."

Nodding, Ben scooted off the bed to kick free his boxers and fish a condom and packet of lube from of his wallet. When he turned back, Jason was peeling off his jeans and underwear in one go, his shirt already abandoned, sneakers tossed to the floor with dull thunks.

Jason's cock was a thing of beauty—uncut and flushed red, the glistening head poking out, thick shaft curving away from wiry hair. Jason had probably never had a mouth on his cock or tongue on his balls. That Ben could be the first sent a powerful, protective surge through him.

Ben couldn't wait to show him how incredible sex could be.

As Jason peeled off his socks, Ben have his own prick a hard tug, biting back a groan. Jason watched with wide eyes, waiting. He whispered, "Holy shit."

Kneeling on the mattress, Ben stopped. "Second thoughts?" *Please say no. Please say no. Please—*

"No. I want this. Want you. Want to know." Jason nodded, breathing deeply. "Please, will you show me?"

CHAPTER THIRTEEN

"**S**PREAD YOUR LEGS for me."

Mouth dry and body tingling, Jason did as Ben asked, stretching out on his back, his legs wide and bent, cock curving up. For a few thumping heartbeats, Ben just looked at him, rubbing Jason's calves, teasing the hair there lightly. Ben was naked—they were both *naked*—and Jason stared at Ben's hard, veiny dick, red and shiny with precum.

Holy shit that's big.

"You're beautiful," Ben murmured.

Heat flowed down Jason's chest, and Ben leaned forward with his hands on the mattress, bracketing him. He dipped his head to lick one nipple, sucking it into his mouth as Jason cried out and clutched at his arms.

Ben nuzzled his way to the other nipple, kissing lightly before sucking it into a peak. Jason thrashed, digging his blunt nails into Ben's skin. Ben chuckled, huffing warm air onto the sensitive nub. "And I haven't even touched your cock yet. You want that?"

His face surely lobster red, Jason could only nod.

Ben kissed him deeply and tantalizingly slowly, Jason chasing after him for more when Ben pulled back and murmured, "Tell me what you want."

"I… I don't know the right things to say." He turned his head away, squirming.

"Hey, it's okay." Ben took Jason's chin and eased his head

back until their gaze met. "There's no wrong answer. You don't have to say anything. Should I tell you what I want?"

Exhaling, Jason nodded gratefully.

Ben sat back on his heels, tracing Jason's chest with his fingertips. "Hmm. What *don't* I want? It's tough to narrow it down."

Jason laughed, a nervous little titter.

"I'm serious." He played with Jason's nipples, and Jason arched his back with a moan. "There's so much. This is what I'm going to do today." Ben leaned over him again, planting his hands on the mattress, his voice low, their bodies barely touching. He stared into Jason's eyes, the blue somehow darker. "First, I'm going to suck your cock. Swallow you into my throat so all you can feel is *hot-tight-wet*."

Shuddering, Jason pushed up helplessly with his hips, their dicks grazing. "Yes."

"I'm going to lick your balls while I put a finger in your ass. Have you ever had anything inside you?"

Breath coming in short bursts, Jason shook his head.

"You're going to be so close to coming, and if you do, that's okay. I'll get you hard again and put another finger inside. Stretch and get you ready for me." He pushed his hips lower, rubbing his dick against Jason's hip. "Do you want me inside you?"

"I don't think you'll fit," he blurted.

Smiling, Ben leaned down and kissed him lightly. "I will, I promise. But we don't have to do that. When you looked at other men at the gym or in magazines, did you ever think about having their hard cocks in your ass? Your mouth?"

Jason shook his head. "Never let myself."

"Not even when you jerked off?"

"No. Didn't think about much of anything. It was always quick. In the shower in the mornings. I had so much to do." *I wasn't allowed.*

Ben still braced himself on his arms, his cock only brushing against Jason. "You're sure you want this?"

"*Yes*," Jason moaned, the word bursting out. "Show me what you like."

"Cum play turns me on," Ben said, his arms trembling enough that he pressed harder on top of Jason. "I like it messy. I want to roll you over and fuck you, make it good for you, make you come. Then I want to jerk off on you and see my cum on your skin."

Jason's brain short circuited, and all he could do was stare up at Ben, who licked his lips nervously and added, "We don't have to do that. I'm weird, I know."

The thought of Ben coming on him was so dirty, but in a good way—a way Jason wanted to explore. "I guess I'm weird too." Trembling with need, he wrapped his legs around Ben's hips as they rocked with a shared groan. His dick leaking between them, Jason nodded. "Do it."

With a grin, Ben kissed him hard and muttered, "First things first."

When Ben swallowed his cock, lips stretched over Jason's throbbing shaft, pushing the foreskin back, Jason whined and moaned, noises slipping between his lips helplessly. Ben's mouth was hot and wonderfully wet, saliva dripping as he licked and sucked.

It was the first blowjob Jason had ever had, and he hadn't known anything could feel so *perfect*. He closed his eyes, fisting his hands in the sheets and trying not to come already.

Ben popped off with a slurp, lips red and shiny, and Jason wanted to beg him not to stop. But then Ben tore open the lube and slicked his fingers, and Jason could only watch, a thread of fear spiraling through him.

Big hands covering Jason's knees, Ben urged them higher and even wider. "Let me see you."

Knees almost to his shoulders, Jason fidgeted under Ben's hungry gaze, too exposed. *What does my ass look like? What if he doesn't like it?*

"That's it. So good. Hold your legs up for me."

Fingers slipping in the sweat under his knees, Jason did, desire and unease battling.

Ben asked, "Do you like that? Opening up for me?"

"I think so. Yes," Jason whispered. He did like it, despite the simultaneous urge to run away. His dick leaked, legs trembling.

"And you'll tell me if you don't like anything?"

"Uh-huh."

Ben inched in the tip of his finger, hard and slick, and licked Jason's balls, his tongue wet and textured and perfect. Jason suddenly came with a shout, back arching. He painted his belly and chest with semen, cock twitching. He actually saw starbursts behind his closed eyes, the orgasm scouring him, wringing out every drop of pleasure.

Panting, legs flopping down around Ben, Jason muttered, "Sorry."

"I told you this would happen, remember? Don't ever be sorry for coming." Ben ran his fingers over Jason's sticky, quivering stomach.

"Do you like that? You said…you like this?" Jason nodded his chin down at the mess on him.

"Your cum? Oh hell yes. I like that." Leaning over, Ben licked it up, rubbing his face into Jason's slick skin, swallowing every drop. Jason gasped softly, Ben's tongue and stubble rough, relentless. Ben murmured against his belly, "Now I'm going to get you hard again."

Jason almost told him to stop, the idea of coming again suddenly too much. But he only twitched and gasped as Ben licked and nuzzled his tender cock and balls. Then Ben sucked him fully into his mouth, and Jason's flesh throbbed although it was oversensitive.

When the stretch of one of Ben's fingers gave way to the burn of two, Jason clamped down, eyes shut and heart pounding at the idea of Ben's whole cock squeezing in there.

"Breathe. Are you okay? Jason, look at me."

Am I okay? He honestly wasn't sure, but when he opened his eyes to find Ben peering down at him with concern so palpable Jason swore he could *feel* it, his heart slowed. He trusted Ben.

Jason cleared his dry throat. "I'm okay."

His fingers still inside, Ben leaned down and kissed Jason softly, patiently. Jason panted against his mouth as Ben worked farther inside him, and then he seized up like he'd been electrocuted, the pleasure and pain too much.

He wriggled as Ben touched the spot inside him again. He'd heard men talk about their prostates and how good it felt. Jason was a live wire, nerves jangling, utterly exposed. He didn't know if he liked it or not, but he whimpered when Ben pulled his fingers free, the new emptiness overwhelming, his balls tight.

Ben pressed a kiss to Jason's soft inner thigh, then urged him over onto his stomach, slipping a pillow under his hips. Jason watched over his shoulder as Ben squirted more cold lube into Jason's ass and rolled on a condom, slicking it as well.

Then Ben eased up Jason's knee, parting his legs and fitting on top of him. He pushed the head of his cock against the rim of Jason's ass, running a soothing palm down his side.

"That's it. Let me in."

Jason shook and moaned, but pushed back, lifting his knee higher to the side and trying to open himself. He was afraid, but he knew Ben wouldn't hurt him. The need to complete this ritual beat in him like a drum, insistent and unrelenting, the pure desire overpowering.

The head of Ben's cock shoved inside as Ben said, "There. Yes, open up. Relax. I'm here."

"Too big," Jason gritted out, his ass burning. But when Ben eased the pressure, Jason reached back blindly, grasping. "Don't stop."

Wet kisses pressed to the top of his spine and over his shoulders, Ben's breath hot. "You're doing so well. It gets easier, I promise." He pushed again, filling Jason inch by inch with murmurs of support. "There, like that. Perfect."

Then Jason realized Ben was in all the way, so deep inside him he felt split open completely. He could only moan and gasp, words out of reach as Ben kissed his hair and said, "You're so beautiful. Fuck, Jason. Wanted to do this the first time I saw you."

He could feel it as Ben rocked—not only the thrusts of his cock filling him, but Ben's desire, the laser focus of that want trained on Jason, stripping him bare to his very core.

He reached back again wordlessly, needing an anchor as he came apart piece by piece, thrust by thrust, their skin slapping and breath harsh in the silence of the room. Ben threaded their fingers together, pressing Jason's hand into the mattress as he fucked him. *I'm being fucked.*

His straining cock was trapped against the mattress, and sweat dampened his brow. Ben grunted with each plunge into Jason, squeezing his free hand underneath to touch him. Ben's fist around his shaft was merciless, the pleasure almost too intense, and it only took a few rough strokes before Jason was coming again, shattering completely, mouth open in a silent shout.

Part of him wanted Ben to stay right there inside him forever, warring with the urge to run and hide until he could breathe and get back in control, until he could pick up all the pieces of himself and be Jason, not this quivering, defenseless jumble.

He watched over his shoulder as Ben eased out of him and tore off the condom, eyes bright and lips parted as he stroked himself and spurted, white splashes of his cum painting Jason's back and ass, pure ecstasy on his face.

Pride soothed a few of the raw edges in Jason, gratitude that he could give Ben this release. Ben smeared his semen over Jason's sweaty skin, and Jason's spent dick twitched with a few more drops, sparks shooting from his balls. It was like he was being marked—claimed—and deep satisfaction flowed through him, chasing away his fear for the moment.

Covering Jason's body, Ben kissed his shoulder, fingers tangled in Jason's hair. "Sorry," he whispered. "I know it's messy."

"Don't be sorry," Jason croaked.

Chuckling, Ben slid off him. "Think you've worked up a thirst. Hold on."

The loss of Ben's heat had Jason shivering, and he reached down for the sheet. The tap ran in the bathroom, and he took the glass of water Ben offered, not meeting his eyes as he gulped gratefully.

Ben climbed back into bed and wiped a washcloth over Jason's sticky skin before stretching out beside him on his side. He traced a fingertip down the ridge of Jason's nose. "How do you feel?"

Jason met his intense gaze—so blue and endless, like Ben was seeing right into the deepest, most fucked-up part of him. Jason was too raw, and he rolled Ben onto his back so he could lay his head on Ben's chest and close his eyes. He said, "Good. I don't know the right words."

Exhilarated. Terrified. Amazing. Exposed.

Ben's heart thumped steadily, and Jason breathed along with it, calming himself. Ben's voice rumbled in his chest. "You don't have to do or say everything 'right.' Not with me."

That generosity was frightening too, but Jason tried to slow the whirl of thoughts whipping through his mind. "I actually *had* sex." He laughed at the surrealness of it all. "I mean—you know what I mean? I had sex once before, but it was so quick and awkward and hardly anything at all." He pondered it, waiting for a rush of guilt about Amy. But no, Amy would want him to discover his true self. She'd want him to be happy.

Should I be happy? Am I really allowed to have this?

"And how was this time?" Ben asked, tracing his fingers up and down Jason's back.

"This was…" He rubbed his cheek against Ben's furry chest, trying to stay centered and in the moment. "This felt like the *real* first time. Is that dumb?"

"Not at all. You're incredible, you know that? I'm so lucky." He kissed Jason's head, caressing his hip. "Thank you for sharing this. For sharing yourself."

Is this me?

Another burst of panic sent Jason's heart racing, and Ben's hand froze. "Okay?"

He realized he'd gone rigid, and forced himself to relax. "Uh-huh."

Ben's fingers grazed Jason's swollen, tender hole. "Does it hurt?"

Jason's breath caught, and it was too much—he was too bare, all soft vulnerability like he'd been turned inside out. And Ben had already seen him helpless and pathetic, had *bathed* him for fuck's sake, but this was different somehow.

He'd actually been inside, stretching him so much he could still feel it, and even though Jason had let him in his body—more than *let,* had needed it like oxygen—now he'd careened too far out of control.

"Baby, are you okay?"

Baby. A kneejerk reaction struck, a defensive bolt of resentment. *I'm not a kid! I don't need you to be so nice and act like I'm going to break. I'm fine! I can take care of myself!*

Raw instinct kicked in—fight or flight—and there was only one thing he could do.

CHAPTER FOURTEEN

ROLLING AWAY, JASON pushed to his feet and gathered his strewn clothes. "I'm fine. Feels fine. Feels great!" He cringed at the forced cheerfulness as he dressed, looking everywhere but at Ben. "Just have to get back to Maggie." And God, he really did—he'd been gone too long. Guilt joined the chaotic confusion of emotions.

"Jason, wait. It's normal to be sore. Are you—"

"I'm good! But I need to get back. You understand." He bent to lace his shoes with shaky fingers, his ass twinging.

"Of course I understand. Can you just take a breath?"

Jason rocketed upright as his phone jingled on the side table, the chimes ringing out that indicated a text message. He lunged for the phone, only seeing the words: *"This is Karen at the hospital. You should come back"* before panic set in, acid flooding his belly. "Fuck! I have to go."

He stumbled over his still-untied lace, cursing as he bent, ignoring the flare of soreness in his ass. How could he have been so irresponsible? Shame burned, and he hated himself for his weakness. His selfishness. "Maggie's on her own, and she needs me. I should never have left."

When he jerked upright, his head spun. Ben stood naked in front of him, hands at his sides and forehead creased, now-familiar tenderness in his eyes. Jason averted his gaze, suddenly embarrassed by Ben's nudity and irrationally angry at the concern. He'd done everything on his own for years—he didn't need Ben now.

Couldn't need him.

Shaking his head, Jason skirted around Ben, a weak part still aching for him to reach out. "I'm sorry. I have to go." He didn't wait for an answer.

Clutching his phone, he ran into the hall and barreled down the stairs since he'd fly out of his skin waiting for an elevator. Reporters shouted questions as he rushed back into the hospital, security keeping them at bay as he took the stairs to Maggie's floor two at a time.

"Where's my dad? I want my dad!" Maggie's cries echoed off the linoleum, and Jason's heart clenched as he skidded into her room.

By Maggie's bed, Karen the nurse sighed in relief and said, "Look, here he is, sweetie."

He brushed by the two other people in the room, registering distantly that somehow they were his parents, and sat on the bed to pull Maggie into his arms. She buried her face against his chest, tears wetting his T-shirt.

"It's okay. I'm here. I'm sorry." Pulse thudding, he rubbed her back, staring at the rumpled sheets, aware of his parents' weighty gazes.

Sobbing, Maggie whined, "Where were you?"

The guilt intensified, and he despised himself. "I'm sorry, sweetheart." She'd needed him and he'd been *having sex*. He was unbearably selfish.

Everyone was right. I'm a horrible father.

A man spoke up, the hospital security guard who'd been watching the door to protect against the media since the FBI had left. His voice was low, bushy eyebrows drawn into one line. "I'm so sorry, Mr. Kellerman. They said they're your parents. Shelly and Robert Kellerman. I checked their ID."

Jason cleared his dry throat, still holding Maggie tightly. "They are." He looked his parents in the eye. "But they have no right to be here."

"Son, we only want to help." His father peered at him, his face craggier than Jason remembered, dark, neat hair receding past his forehead and shot through with gray.

"*Son*? Seriously?" He exhaled slowly. "Maggie needs her rest. Wait for me outside."

His mother nodded. "All right. We didn't mean to upset her. Or you."

They left, along with the guard and Karen, who gave him a sympathetic smile. Maggie's sobs had slowed, and she hiccupped and sniffed.

"Why did they come?" she asked. "I thought they didn't like us."

"Oh, honey. It's not that. It was never about not liking you. You're wonderful. We just disagreed on how to raise you. It was about me, not you. I know it's confusing." He'd rarely ever talked to Maggie about them. He'd answered any questions she'd had, but his family simply hadn't been part of their life.

She lifted her head, face red and wet, eyes puffy. "You're the greatest dad, and they're stupid."

He'd usually scold her for using that kind of language, but he only kissed her head and murmured, "We'll talk about this more tomorrow. It's time for bed."

Even though it was still early, Maggie didn't argue for once, and was asleep almost immediately after he tucked her in and caressed her hair until he was sure she was out. He turned down the lights, reluctant to go anywhere, but he had to deal with his parents.

Karen came in and spoke softly. "I'm so sorry. She was completely fine until they showed up. She really was. Don't beat yourself up, okay?"

He nodded, since there was no point in arguing. "Can you stay with Maggie while I talk to them?"

"Absolutely. It's quiet tonight. I put your parents in the empty room next door to wait. Just to the left. I'll come get you immediately if Maggie wakes up."

"Thank you." With a last kiss to Maggie's forehead, he left.

In the hall, he accepted another apology from the guard, then took a couple deep breaths before walking through the open door of the room where his parents waited, his mother pacing, his father standing by the window, the last beams of sunset glowing outside. Jason closed the door.

Under the fluorescent lights, the dark circles under his mother's eyes were stark, fine lines fanning out around her eyes and mouth. Her blond hair brushed her shoulders in waves, shorter than he remembered. She was still slim and fit, and diamonds glittered in her ears. Her slacks and blouse were surprisingly wrinkled.

"Jason. I… We…" She looked to his father, who cleared his throat and fiddled with the cuffs of his dress shirt, his tie hanging loose. He'd never seen his parents so dishevelled.

"First off, it's so good to see you, Jason." The low timber of his father's voice was exactly the same. "We've missed you more than we could ever say."

Missed didn't capture the instinctive need filling Jason. The need for their love and approval, simply for *them*. He'd convinced himself he'd excised them from his life cleanly, but the wound had been jagged and fanged after all.

Being in the same room with his parents after eight years, part of him wanted to rush into their arms despite the deep-seated resentment. But no, he had to be strong. He managed to keep his voice even. "How did you know we were here?"

"It's all over the news," his mother said. "We couldn't believe it when we heard your names. Maggie and Jason Kellerman." Her lips trembled. "You both could have been killed. We knew we had to come and try to make it right. Had to help you."

"I don't need your help. *We* don't. How dare you bust in and upset Maggie like that?"

She shook her head. "It wasn't our intention. We didn't expect her to react that way."

"How did you think she'd react? You're strangers! She doesn't know you." Anger whipped through him. "*I* don't know you anymore! And you're going to say that's my fault, right?"

"No," his father answered emphatically. "It's our fault. We realize that. We've known it for a long time, but we were stubborn. The first few years, we told ourselves you wouldn't be able to manage. That you'd see we were right. That you'd come back."

Jason breathed shallowly, his fingers clenching and unclenching. "You were wrong."

"We were." His mother's eyes glistened. "We were wrong and inflexible and didn't want to admit what an enormous mistake we'd made. We've wanted to reach out for so long, but we let our pride win." She gulped in a breath, wiping her cheeks. "When we saw you both on the news. The thought that you could have been killed without knowing how sorry we are—God, it was unbearable."

Robert swallowed thickly. "I don't know if you can ever forgive us. I don't know if you should. But we had to see you both. We had to try."

A mess of conflicting impulses battled. Jason wanted to scream and shout his bitterness and betrayal at the same time that he wanted to fix the fracture in his soul, fill the void. He rasped, "I don't know either."

"We're just so relieved you're all right." His mother pressed a hand to her chest. "Maggie's beautiful, Jason. And look at you! So big and tall. So grown-up. We've all missed you very much. Your brother too."

Bitterness boiled over. "Then why didn't he answer my texts when I moved out?"

"We took his phone away. Changed his number." Robert rubbed a hand over his face. "We were so angry. So convinced we were right. Please don't blame your brother for any of it."

"All these years, I haven't had a family. It's just me and Maggie. I can't—you can't fix this overnight."

Shelly nodded. "We realize that. But we want to help, honey. We've contacted a child psychologist, and she can see Maggie as early as Wednesday. There's a flight tomorrow morning—"

"Wait, what?" He held up his hands. "No! Stop! You can't just take over." He backed up, his brain buzzing. "I can't deal with you right now. I need to be with Maggie. She's the priority."

"Of course she is," his father soothed. "Both of you are our priorities. We're here to help you."

"I haven't seen you in eight years!" His chest tightened painfully. "I need to think. This is too much right now." Maggie kidnapped, sex with Ben, and now he was actually in the same room with his parents. They stood there a few feet away, flesh and blood—his and Maggie's.

"Darling, you look pale. Sit down and breathe. Robert, find a doctor."

"No! Stop!" Blood rushing in his ears, he blew out slowly. "I need to process. I need to be alone—with Maggie. Come back in the morning. Please."

They shared a long look, and his mother said, "Of course. As we told you, we only want to help. We have so much to make up for." Her eyes filled again. "You're a father. You can understand how much we've missed you. How much we want to be there for you."

He was drowning in the swirling flood of conflicting emotions, barely keeping his head above the surface. "I'll never understand how you turned your backs on me. On us."

"It was the biggest mistake of our lives." Tears shone in Robert's eyes too, and Jason realized he'd never seen his father cry. "Almost losing you both, it showed us once and for all what fools we've been. We want to make it up to you and Maggie. We don't expect you to forgive us. But we hope you'll let us be a part of your lives. We'll be back first thing tomorrow."

His mother took a step closer. "Jason, will you… Can I hug you? Please?"

Eyes burning, he nodded and let her wrap her thin arms around him. She felt so much smaller than he remembered, and she shook with a wretched sob. But she smelled the same, jasmine and sage, her perfume filling his senses as he fought tears.

"Come on, Shelly. Let's give him the space he wants."

She let go, and Jason almost reached out to draw her back and return the embrace. But he let them leave, waiting until the hall was clear to duck back into Maggie's room. Karen gave his shoulder a squeeze after vacating the chair by the bed and leaving, pulling the door halfway closed.

He turned off the low light, the only brightness now the diagonal beam from the hall. The cot was folded in the corner, but he wouldn't be able to sleep anyway. He dropped into the chair, wincing at the tenderness in his ass. Adrenaline spiked, a cocktail of excitement and confusion with a thread of panic.

I had sex.

He could hardly believe it had happened, but he could feel where Ben had pushed his cock inside, where their bodies had joined. Despite already coming twice, his groin tightened. He hadn't known sex could be like that. Hadn't known it could peel away every one of his layers of protection and leave him a nerve exposed at the root. Hadn't known something could be so incredible and terrifying at the same time.

Sweat prickled the back of his neck. Shit, he'd run out on Ben, who was good and kind and deserved better. And he'd been reckless, so selfish in leaving Maggie for even a minute. And now his parents were back, and, and, and—

"Jason?"

Heart hammering, he shot to his feet, barely catching the chair before it crashed. He stared at Ben, who stood in shadow, backlit in the shaft of light from the hall.

Ben came closer, that concern etched on his handsome face once again. He peered down at Maggie, who was still asleep. "Is she all right?"

Jason jerked out a nod.

"Then what's wrong?" he whispered. "You look like you're going to fly out of your skin." He reached out, but Jason staggered back, shaking his head. Ben lifted his hands in surrender. "I'm sorry. I just want to talk."

With a long look at Maggie, Jason led the way into the bathroom, both of them blinking in the sudden glare as he switched on the light. Ben pulled the door halfway shut and took a deep breath, his shoulders hitching.

"I realize you probably don't want to see me right now, but I just had to make sure Maggie was okay."

"She is now. She was freaking out wondering where I was."

"Shit."

Ben scrubbed a hand through his hair, and a thrill of excitement zipped through Jason as he remembered the sensation of those long fingers inside him. In the small bathroom, Ben's scent filled Jason's nose—clean like hotel soap, but still musky and tangy like pine. Jason wanted to rub against him at the same time he wished he could retreat and turn off these new feelings.

"I'm sorry about what happened. It's been a long time since I was with a virgin—or an almost-virgin—and I thought I went slowly enough. Was I too impatient? Did I hurt you?"

Jason studied the simple tile pattern under his sneakers. "No."

"Obviously I did something wrong. Will you please tell me?"

"It wasn't anything you did."

"You can't even look at me."

Jason raised his head then, wishing he knew the right thing to say as he looked into Ben's beseeching eyes. "You didn't do anything wrong. It was just…"

"Because I'm a man?"

"No. It's not that. I'm gay. I know that's the truth. It's all the other things. My parents want to take over, and I just got Maggie back, and everything is changing too fast."

"Wait, your parents?"

He could still hardly believe it was true. "They're here. They said they're sorry. That they want to help and were worried about us when they saw the news."

Ben's brows rose. "Wow. I wasn't expecting that. Obviously you weren't either."

"Or Maggie. They just showed up, like, 'Hey, it's Grandma and Grandpa! We're here to take care of everything!' And I wasn't here. She was with a room full of strangers, so upset and scared, and I was with you because I'm selfish."

Leaning forward, Ben implored, "You're not. Jason, you said Maggie told you to go. That she didn't want to be smothered. You weren't gone that long, and you had no way of knowing your parents would show up. You can't see the future. You can't be with her every second of every day. You're allowed to have time to yourself. To have your own feelings. Your own desires."

"But this is what happens!" Jason took a shuddery breath and lowered his voice again. "I was distracted with you on the trail. Attracted to you and flirting, and I gave that son of a bitch the chance to grab her."

"She was out of sight for maybe thirty seconds. And today…" His face creased. "I'm sorry if I pressured you. That was the last thing I wanted to do."

Jason's stomach clenched to see Ben's stricken expression. "No. You didn't, not at all."

"I feel sick to think that I took advantage or—"

"You really didn't. You asked me a bunch of times, and I said yes. When I left I was freaking, but you didn't talk me into anything. I wanted to be with you. I wanted to have sex. I made that choice. Just like I chose to be a father and dedicate my life to Maggie. I have to focus on her. I was selfish today, and I can't let that happen again."

"But you don't have to do it on your own. Let me help you. Let me take care of you. I can—"

"I'm not a kid!" Jason shouted, anger suddenly flaring white hot, his parents' overbearing voices ricocheting through his head. "Just because you're older... I don't—I can't..." He clenched his fists, a riot of emotions tangled on his tongue. "I don't need you to *take care of me*. I'm an adult."

"I didn't mean it like that." Ben lifted his hands, then dropped them. "I'm not saying anything right."

Jason's anger simmered into a stew of guilt, confusion, and fear that carved out a hollow calm and realization.

A resolution.

"I'm taking Maggie home tomorrow. She needs familiar surroundings. She needs normalcy. So do I. This has all been too much. My parents said there's a flight, and I'll let them take us. Then we're going home to our apartment, where we can be together, and everything will be okay again. Then I'll be able to think."

Ben looked as if he wanted to argue, but nodded instead. "What about you and me?"

"I don't know. I guess we have to be realistic. You live here. I live across the country. We barely know each other, right?"

"Is that really how you feel? That you don't know me?"

Jason fidgeted. Ben's steady, patient gaze bore into him. "I'm not sure what I feel. I need time to work this all out. It's too much. I have to get Maggie home. She's my priority. She always has been, and she always will be. You're not a father. You don't understand."

Sucking in a breath, Ben's spine straightened. He dropped his gaze, voice gravelly. "You're right. I'm not."

Damn it. "I'm sorry. I'm the one saying everything wrong. I'm not trying to hurt you. You've done so much for me and Maggie. Hurting you is the last thing I want." He yearned to close the distance between them, but he had to be strong. He couldn't let Maggie down again. He'd almost lost her, and he had to get her home safely and make everything the way it was.

"Can we still talk? Text, anything?"

"Of course." The idea of not talking to Ben again seemed impossible. "I just need some time right now."

Adam's apple bobbing, Ben asked in a rough voice, "Can I kiss you?"

Jason could only nod, the urge to melt into his arms overwhelming as their lips met, Ben's callused palm cupping his cheek. But it was only a moment of sweet pressure before Ben stepped back, dropping his hands.

"Call me if you need anything, Jason. *Anything.* If nothing else, I want to be friends."

Then he was gone.

Leaning back against the white tiles, Jason squeezed his eyes shut, a desperate need to call Ben back clawing up. But it was all too much—almost losing Maggie, discovering himself with Ben, his parents' sudden appearance after eight long years. Everything was changing too fast. He couldn't keep up. Couldn't breathe.

An inch at a time, Jason's lungs expanded, and he gasped for air until the threat of burning tears passed and he was in control again.

MAGGIE CLOSED HER EYES as Ben left the bathroom. She was pretty sure he was standing right by her bed, but she was afraid he'd be mad if he knew she was awake, so she didn't move until she heard his boots walk out of the room and down the hall.

She hadn't meant to spy.

But she'd woken up thirsty, and she'd seen Dad and Ben in the bathroom mirror through the half-open door. She didn't hear what they said, but she saw them kiss. It wasn't that long, but it was a grown-up kiss.

Was Dad gay like Mrs. Wexler? Why hadn't he said anything? And why did he and Ben look so sad? She loved Ben, and if he and Dad liked each other, why weren't they happy about it?

He was in there a long time, but he was out of sight of the mirror. Finally she heard the taps run and water splash, and the light went off. She closed her eyes, wondering if she should ask him about kissing Ben.

But she couldn't figure out the right words, and soon she was sleepy again, listening to him breathe in the chair beside her. She'd ask when it was a better time.

CHAPTER FIFTEEN

"AH, IT'S…LOVELY."

Jason bit back a sardonic laugh. His mother was trying, she really was. He peered out of the Town Car at the four-story apartment building where he and Maggie lived on the top floor. It certainly wasn't lovely, but it was safe and clean despite the aged, brown brick and dated seventies style, one of the white letters missing in the old sign over the front door proclaiming the building *The H velock* instead of Havelock.

The flight had been delayed, so it was after midnight when the driver pulled up at the curb. Maggie sat between Jason and his mother, his father in the front. Jason held Maggie's hand, and she still slept on his shoulder as the driver got out to unload their suitcases and take them into the vestibule.

"We'd love to have you over for dinner," Robert said, twisting around in his seat. "And please think about the therapist."

Jason nodded. "I will. I… Thank you for the flight and dropping us off. I appreciate it."

"Of course. We want to help in any way we can. Jason, there's so much—" Shelly broke off. "I don't want to push. I know we don't have the right. But if you need anything, please call." She gazed down at Maggie. "She's wonderful, you know. You've done so well, darling. We'd really like to know her. To know both of you."

"We just need some time. This has all been…a lot." He gently squeezed Maggie's hand before letting go to unbuckle her and give her a gentle shake. "Mags, we're home. Come on."

"Hmm? Okay." She blinked blearily at her grandparents. "Um, bye."

"Sleep well. We hope we'll see you soon." Shelly reached out and awkwardly patted Maggie's knee.

Walking back into their building after more strained good-byes, Jason dragged the suitcases and cooler and pressed the elevator call button. The cables groaned as it descended. He could see the Town Car still idling at the curb in the mirrored wall by the elevator. It was utterly surreal that he'd spent the day with his parents, full of stilted small talk about the weather and airplane food, although the fare in first class wasn't bad at all.

Utterly surreal that days ago he'd been in the middle of the wilderness, desperately searching for Maggie, and now they were home again. Everything looked the same, but he felt like imposters. When they'd left home, they'd had no idea what was coming. Their lives had been neat and orderly, and Jason wanted to escape back to that easier time. But there'd be no Ben, and that thought ached.

The back of his neck prickled with his parents' gaze as he and Maggie got on the elevator with their luggage. Jason jabbed the fourth floor, then the close-door button repeatedly. With a clunk and mechanical whine, they traveled up, safely alone again.

Alone. He'd told Ben he needed time, but how long would it take for Jason to get back to normal? To work through this thorny tangle of emotions?

Inside the apartment, he abandoned their stuff by the door, throwing the two extra bolts and turning on the main overhead light as Maggie shuffled to the bathroom, still half asleep. Her lung congestion had mostly cleared, but she was sleeping a lot, which Dr. Sharma had said to expect.

They'd only been gone less than two weeks, but the apartment felt stuffy and strange. He'd left the thin curtains closed against the heat, and pushed one aside now to slide open the window. The humid night air carried a hint of a cool breeze, and with the ceiling fan, it was usually enough for Jason to sleep.

He peered around the small apartment, imagining seeing it through his parents' eyes. A narrow galley kitchen to the left of the front door, the old fridge humming faithfully, magnets covering it haphazardly, some holding up Maggie's artwork from day camp.

Then a bathroom and hall closet where Jason kept his clothes, and the one bedroom, Maggie's secondhand wood-framed bed dominating the small space. Jason tugged off his shoes and took Maggie's suitcase in, opening her window and turning on her fan before unpacking and filling the laundry hamper in the corner.

Posters of animals and trees covered the walls. Would she still love nature after what happened? Or would forests frighten her now? Impotent rage at what Harlan Brown had stolen from her surged, and Jason gripped the wicker lid of the hamper, the hard fibers cracking.

"Dad?"

He forced out an exhalation and replaced the lid. "Ready for bed, sweetie?"

"Uh-huh."

He opened the second drawer in her yellow and purple dresser, pulling out a fresh set of light cotton PJs. "Here you go. Feels good to be home, doesn't it?"

"Yeah. Weird too. I wanted—" She stopped and bent to pull off her socks.

"What?" he asked softly.

She shook out her PJs. "I wanted so bad to be back here. You know, before."

"Me too." He hesitated. "When you were out there, without me, what else did you think about?" The psychiatrist in Kalispell had given him some suggestions for gentle questions.

Shrugging, Maggie changed and pulled down her thin summer bedspread, climbing in. Jason didn't press, instead asking, "Did you floss and brush?"

"*Yes.* Can I sleep now?"

"Okay, baby. I'll be in the living room if you need me."

"I know. You always are."

Choking down a swell of emotion, he kissed her forehead and turned off the light, leaving the door ajar.

His suitcase untouched, Jason pulled down the back of the futon in the living room and tossed his pillow and light blanket onto the lumpy surface. He stripped down to his boxers and turned off the lights, wandering restlessly to the kitchen to open the fridge.

He stared at the collection of condiments and half-full Brita filter. He dumped it out in the sink and refilled it with fresh water. He'd have to get groceries in the morning, and he wasn't even hungry, but he still poked through the cupboards and dug out an opened box of Ritz, the crackers gone soft in the humidity. But they were still buttery, so he stood there against the counter eating them.

What's Ben doing? Is he home in his cabin? What does it look like? Is he okay? Is he thinking about me?

The questions swirled endlessly, although Jason was the one who'd said he needed time. Yet he could feel the phantom touch of Ben's hands on his body, the wet press of his lips and slide of his tongue. Could smell the clean pine and hear Ben's puffs of breath, the warmth on his skin.

Grabbing his phone, he opened a text message to Ben, the previous one from the morning of the kidnapping, Ben saying he'd meet them if he could. Before Harlan Brown had ripped Maggie away, before their lives had changed in a blink. At least Ben had been there. At least one good thing had come out of it.

Guilt sliced through him with a serrated edge. How could he look at the bright side of his daughter being kidnapped?

Jamming the phone off with his finger, he shoved the box of crackers back in the cupboard and turned abruptly, kicking a shopping bag of recycling he hadn't had time to take out in the rush of leaving for vacation. Cans and plastic spilled out onto the checkered brown linoleum, rolling this way and that.

Biting back a curse, Jason stepped over the wreckage and tip-toed to Maggie's door to make sure she hadn't woken. She was sound asleep, breathing deeply and evenly. He went back and flicked on the overhead light, shoving everything in the bag and frowning at the dull flooring.

A stain he hadn't noticed splashed out by the fridge, and he wet a sponge to get at it. On his knees, he could see the edges of the floor under the counter needed a thorough clean as well, weekly mopping not picking up everything in the crevices.

With spray Comet in one hand and the sponge in the other, Jason scrubbed every inch of the floor, his knees sore by the time he moved on to the bathroom, getting into the grout with an old toothbrush. His hands were dry from the cleaner, and he probably should have worn gloves, but he kept going, attacking every surface of the apartment except Maggie's room.

On the wall by the couch, dust covered the IKEA picture frames hanging there. Jason sprayed Windex on a paper towel and carefully wiped the glass surfaces. Maggie's school pictures smiled back at him, and a selfie they'd taken last Christmas morning with crumpled wrapping paper around them and bows on their heads.

He hesitated at the pictures of Amy. There were two—one of Amy's school photo from junior year, taken before she was pregnant and their lives changed completely, the time in hers running out.

Her light, thick hair hung around her shoulders, her smile wide, eyes bright and mischievous, still laughing at the dumb joke

Jason had whispered to her in line while they tugged at their uniforms and she straightened his tie.

The other picture was the two of them at the pool, dripping water, arms slung around each other with medals hanging from their necks after a swim meet. Another lifetime, becoming more and more distant each year.

Throat tight, he cleaned the glass until it sparkled like Amy had. He wouldn't forget her, and he'd make sure Maggie knew her as well as she could. He'd always answered Maggie's questions about her mother, but he vowed to tell her more stories, knowing there was a finite number, that she'd never be more than an idea to Maggie.

Returning to the kitchen, Jason picked up his phone and unlocked it. Would Ben become a distant memory too? Perhaps they never would have gone beyond friendship if Maggie hadn't been taken, but she had. Staying in touch now wouldn't change anything that had happened.

Jason had no idea what he wanted from Ben, but it was only a text. It was something. He opened the app and stared at the empty narrow box, then typed and retyped and stared some more.

And some more.

Finally he hit the blue arrow and sent a message:

Hi. Just wanted to tell you we're home. Hope everything there is cool.

Cringing as he reread it, he wished he could reach into cyberspace and yank it back. "Cool"? Why had he said cool? He might as well have just called Ben "bro" or something equally lame.

Should he have included an emoticon? Maybe he should send a smiley face on its own? No. Too…something. Jesus, this man had been inside Jason's ass and Jason was going to send him a smiley face? No, definitely not the right message.

But what is the message? What am I trying to say? What do I want him to say?

His breath caught as the wavering three dots appeared on

screen, indicating Ben was typing. A moment later, he realized it was the middle of the night in Montana. "*Shit*," he muttered, waiting for the message to arrive. "He's probably telling me I'm an asshole for waking him up and—"

So glad to hear it. Are you okay?

Jason typed with clumsy thumbs.

Yep. Sorry to wake you. Guess I'm jet lagged or something.

He waited for the response. He should have used an emoticon this time. But which one? A wink? A plain smile? Or he could find a gif…

No prob. Glad you're okay. Keep me posted.

Hmm. What did that really mean? Was Ben just being polite? He was totally just being polite. Or maybe he was trying to be chill and not pressure him? That seemed like something Ben would do since Jason had told him he needed time.

There was so much Jason wanted to say, but he had to let Ben get back to sleep, so he typed:

Will do. Thanks.

He stared at his phone for a few minutes, but there was nothing else from Ben. Which made sense since it was the middle of the night. And maybe Ben was having second thoughts. They lived so far apart, and now that the adrenaline rush of what they'd shared was wearing off, maybe the reality that they'd only just met was setting in.

Maybe, maybe, maybe.

The pale light of dawn brightened the gleaming floors as Jason finished mopping and sat heavily on the side of the futon. His muscles ached, but as soon as he stopped moving and cleaning, his mind filled once more with endless questions and futile longing.

Should I let my parents help? What's Ben doing right now? Is he sleeping again? What does his bedroom look like? Is it right to make things as normal as possible for Maggie? What if I'm doing it all wrong? I don't know what I'm doing.

"You're awake already."

Jason jerked his head up from his hands to find Maggie outside her room. She rubbed her eyes and said, "You hardly ever get up before I do. You don't have to work today, do you?" Her voice rose slightly. "Am I going to the Y?"

He smiled, shoving everything else away. "No, not today. Work is letting me take a few sick days, so I don't have to go back until next week. I thought we could hang out and get settled back in. Then you can go to day camp Monday if you want."

What if it's too much for her? What if it's too much for me? I don't want her out of my sight. Who's going to look after her? I have to work, and I already paid the day camp fees. Can't afford a sitter. The utility bill is due, and my Visa will be way higher than normal, and she needs new clothes for school in September, and what if the insurance screws me on the hospital bills and—

"Okay. That sounds good." She padded into the bathroom and shut the door.

Jason rubbed his face, willing his brain to shut off. Sleep wasn't going to happen, so once Maggie was done, he turned on the coffee machine and had a long, hot shower. Not bothering to shave, he pulled on sweatpants and a T-shirt and grabbed the recycling and another couple bags of clutter he'd sorted through. There were always junk collectors coming by to grab stuff left by the garbage bins outside the building.

"Mags, I'm taking this stuff down. Be back soon. I took a loaf of bread out of the freezer for toast, and there's peanut butter in the cupboard."

Chirping birds greeted him, the day already hot. His flip-flops slapped on the concrete as he headed around the side of the building to where the garbage and recycling bins sat.

"Mr. Kellerman!" A tall woman, immaculately coifed and dressed in a power suit, strode toward him.

"Jesus!" He almost spilled the stupid recycling again, this time only a plastic bottle rolling out.

The woman smiled. "Sorry to startle you."

He eyed her warily as he dumped the cans and bottles into the bin with a crash. "It's fine. Can I help you?"

"You can. I'm Elizabeth Wheeler with *People Magazine*. America needs to hear your story, Mr. Kellerman. A story of bravery and courage and a father's love—"

"No. Look, we don't want to be interviewed. We don't want to be on TV, and we don't want to be in *People*. Please leave us alone."

"But yours is such an inspiring story." She was the picture of sympathy and understanding, her voice soothing. "Just think of the good you can do other families out there who've been in similar situations."

Jason barked out a laugh. "With all due respect, I think our situation was pretty unique. You'll have to find someone else to inspire the world."

She kept her calm tone as if speaking to a skittish animal. "You're turning down a lot of money, Jason. Money that could help send your daughter to college."

He couldn't deny the temptation and hated himself for it. He shoved away the thought of how much easier money would make things. "So I exploit her now for her own good later?"

Elizabeth Wheeler chuckled as if that was silly nonsense. "Our interview would be done with the utmost sensitivity, I assure you. How is Maggie? The public wants to know."

"The public will just have to mind their own business." He dumped the rest of the bags and tried to sidestep her.

Blocking his path, she sighed and lowered her voice conspiratorially. "Look, Jason. I'm trying to help you. The payment my editor has approved for an exclusive interview and photoshoot is extremely generous." She held up a folder. "I have the paperwork all signed and ready to go. You'd have a direct bank deposit in your account before noon. But this is a one-time offer. Maggie won't be a hot topic next week."

A hot flush of disgust filled him. He managed to keep his voice low and steady, over enunciating. "My daughter is not a *topic* to be dissected." He walked around Elizabeth Wheeler of *People Magazine*, scraping his arm on the brick wall as she tried to block his path again.

She called after him, her heels striking the concrete like a volley of gunshots. He ignored her, jamming his key in the lock of the outer door and yanking it shut in her face behind him. Her gentle façade cracked, sharp words clear through the glass door in the lobby.

"I'm sure Ben Hettler will be happy to take our money for an exclusive. Don't be a fool, Jason."

He resisted the urge to give her the finger and took the stairs, breathing hard and struggling to control his anger as he ran up the steps two at a time. On the landing of the top floor, he leaned against the wall and breathed deeply.

It was true—if he agreed, he wouldn't have to worry nearly so much about money or Maggie's future. But at what cost? Trotting Maggie out in some dog and pony show, making her relive the terror she'd suffered with Harlan Brown for the prurient reading pleasure of America?

No, he wouldn't do that to her. He wouldn't make her a spectacle.

And there was no way Ben would ever agree to an interview either. Jason didn't even have to wonder, the certainty as solid as the wall at his back. He'd trusted Ben with his and Maggie's lives, and he trusted him now.

Missing Ben was a visceral pang. Had it only been a day and a half since he'd seen him? It felt like an eternity even though he imagined he could still smell the sweat and sex on Ben's skin as they'd pressed together so close, before Jason had freaked out.

Pushing off the wall he gave his head a shake. Enough. He had to focus on Maggie. He realized he was clutching his keys so hard his palm was almost bleeding. He took another few breaths before going into the hallway.

"Hey, Jason. You guys are back." Joe Morton, his middle-aged neighbor two doors down stood by the elevator. "How are you doing? How's Maggie? We were really worried."

"She's good, thanks."

"Glad to hear it. Good to have you home." The elevator doors opened, and he stepped in, calling back, "Let me know if you need anything."

"We're fine, but thanks."

They were home, and everything would go back to normal. Jason just wished he knew if "normal" was what they really needed.

CHAPTER SIXTEEN

A S THE ENGINE drone grew louder, Ben braced himself, pushing to his feet, his dad's rocking chair creaking behind him. The old wood of the porch was starting to split, and he ran a bare toe along a crack. The whole cabin needed renovations, but he hadn't mustered the enthusiasm necessary since he'd moved in after his life with Brad blew up.

A jeep rounded the bend, and he exhaled in relief at the sight of Dee's vehicle. He was ready to get the shotgun out if reporters didn't stop pestering. At least he could block numbers on his phone, although the reporter from *People* had called four times from different numbers. Ben had thought it a good thing that the cabin was close enough to the main road into Kalispell to get cell service, but now he missed the days when the cabin was cut off from the world.

Granted, he was checking his phone every five minutes to make sure Jason hadn't called.

He hadn't.

The longing was barbed and vicious, and Ben hoped it wouldn't be too long before it faded into something manageable. It had only been three days, so he had to be patient, but he wished he could hibernate and wake up in the future where he didn't miss Jason and Maggie with every beat of his useless heart.

When Dee climbed out of the jeep, wearing her uniform pants

but having swapped her button-up shirt for a Grateful Dead concert tee, he pasted on a smile. "You lost? I have a map if you need it."

She pulled out several large Tupperware containers from the back seat and walked up onto the porch. "You need fattening up, Hettler." She passed him without waiting for an invitation.

"Come on in." Ben followed her into the kitchen of his cabin, the screen door bouncing shut behind him. "You know, I can feed myself."

Dee grunted and opened the fridge. "It would help to have some actual food then. With vegetables and everything."

"Okay, okay. Thank you. Have a beer and relax."

Already twisting the cap off a bottle, Dee smiled. "Don't mind if I do." She headed back onto the porch.

Ben shuffled around his impressive condiment collection and container of chili he'd defrosted and had only picked at. Beer took up most of the bottom shelf of the fridge. He neatly stacked the Tupperware containers and closed the door after grabbing himself a bottle.

The cabin was basically one room with a toilet and bedroom opening off to the side. His couch was worn and the old wildlife paintings faded. He really did need to spruce the place up, but…later. Maybe after the summer, when work wasn't as busy. Not that he was working at the moment, much to his chagrin.

He paused at the wobbly kitchen table, fingertips gliding over the heavy books he'd piled there, guilt and deep need battling. No, he wouldn't let himself look at what was underneath. Dee was waiting.

On the porch, Dee rocked in the other chair, which was newer and still had a gleaming polish on the dark wood. She pulled a bag of party mix out of a canvas tote by her feet and tore it open. "I didn't only bring healthy crap. I'm not a complete monster."

Chuckling, Ben eased into his rocker and reached into the bag for a handful of cheese twists, nacho chips, and pretzels. "Thanks."

He gazed out at the trees. The sun was still high in the early evening sky, the air calm and warm. But before they knew it, the long summer days would pass and temperatures would drop. The thought of another lonely winter in the cabin constricted his chest.

"How are you holding up?" Dee asked.

"Fine. I'd be better if I could get back to work. This leave of absence Brad ordered is ridiculous."

She sipped her beer. "Well, I don't agree with the schmuck on a lot of things, but he's right on this one. I know you don't want to hear it, but you need some time to get your ducks in a row after what you went through. You're getting paid to relax. So relax already. You'll be back in no time."

"I don't need to relax!" He realized he was almost shouting, and took a deep breath.

Dee pushed up her round glasses on her nose. "Clearly."

Ben had to laugh, the pressure easing. "Okay, so I'm a bit tense. I'm going stir crazy sitting around doing nothing. Any exciting gossip from the office?"

"You mean since the psycho killer kidnapped a little girl and you and her father heroically—if somewhat foolishly—went on a rescue mission?"

He laughed. "Nothing's happened to top it?"

"The guard rail on route twelve needs repairs and we had to give a camper a stern talking-to for playing loud music over at the Nettle Creek site."

"These are crazy times we live in."

They drank and munched, watching a chipmunk scurry across the small lawn to scratch at something by a tree stump. Then Dee asked, "Have you spoken to Jason?"

He shrugged, going for careless and probably landing on spastic. "Not really. Just a few texts." *Stilted, awkward texts that made him cringe every time he looked at them, which was too often.*

"So you're going to pretend you're fine with that?"

"That's the plan."

Dee pulled the elastic off her ponytail and let her graying hair hang loose. "Fake it 'til you make it, huh?"

"Something like that. It shouldn't even bother me. I only knew him and Maggie a week."

"Hell of a week, though. It's okay to care."

He peeled off a strip from the damp label of his beer bottle. "You know what they say about relationships based on intense experiences. They don't last."

Dee smirked. "Yeah, I saw *Speed*. I think Sandra suggests they base it on sex instead. He's a handsome young man. That could work out."

Ben's laugh was hollow. "I don't know. I think I scared him off. Besides, Jason and Maggie live on the other side of the country. They have their life, and I have mine."

"Mmm."

"Jason has to put Maggie first. I understand that."

You're not a father.

Jason's words echoed through Ben's mind, and he wished they didn't hurt so much.

"Well, of course. But you're great with kids. I bet she adores you. I don't see why it has to be one or the other. Have you tried to reach out again?"

"He said he needs time. I don't want to pressure him. Things got…intimate, and I think he regrets it. So if he wants time, I'm giving it to him." He had to be patient. If he pushed too hard, that could be the end of it.

Tensing, he rocked to his feet, reaching for Dee's empty bottle. "Refill?" Not waiting for an answer, he strode inside, twisting off the caps of two fresh beers and taking a calming gulp of his before returning.

Dee was leafing through a glossy parks brochure, and Ben

craned his neck to read the cover. "Yosemite? Planning a trip with Paul and the kids?"

"Was thinking about it, although the kids are probably too busy with college now to vacation with Mom and Dad. I hear they've got great programs down there and they want to be even more progressive. They're hiring a new head ranger."

"Are they?" He snorted. "Subtle, Dee. Real subtle."

"I thought so." She put the brochure on the table between them and popped a pretzel into her mouth.

Ben thumbed through the glossy pages. Unsurprisingly, Yosemite looked like one of the most gorgeous places on earth. He peered at a picture of a crystal-clear lake, mountains rising above it into blue sky. Similar to what he enjoyed in Montana, but new and different. Maybe it was just what he needed.

What about Jason? Yosemite isn't any closer to Philadelphia. Maybe I should wait and see what happens with him first.

Dee said, "Change isn't easy, but it can't hurt to look into the position. I know a few people in the main office down there. I could make some inquiries."

He took another gulp of beer. "Okay." Butterflies flapped in his belly. Hell, he probably wouldn't even get the job, but he'd apply for it. It wasn't a commitment to simply send his resume. He'd been putting off too many things for too long. It would be too easy to stay in his rut and let another opportunity pass by.

"And if you want to know what I think—"

"Have I ever had a choice?"

Dee grinned. "Nope." Her smile faded. "I think if you and Jason Kellerman have something special, you should go for it. You've got nothing to lose."

He picked up a pretzel and toyed with it. "I don't have the right to pressure him. He was overwhelmed. It's understandable."

"Sure it is. It was a lot to process. But you can help him. Help that sweet little girl. Help yourself while you're at it. I'm sure you can list a whole bunch of excuses about why you shouldn't even try. He's younger, he lives far away—"

"I have to respect his wishes. I asked him to keep me posted."

Dee screwed up her face. "Gee, that sounds romantic."

"What was I supposed to say? 'My life is empty without you, my sweet flower glowing with morning dew'?"

She swigged her beer. "You can't do much worse than 'keep me posted.' I'm just saying." Dee dropped the teasing tone. "I hate seeing you give up."

He picked up the brochure. "I'm going to apply for this job. That's something."

"Okay. One step at a time. I'll drink to that." She raised her bottle, and Ben clinked it with his own. It had to be enough for now.

AFTER COUNTING THE BEAMS in the ceiling four times, turning onto one side and then the other, and resolutely closing his eyes only to be haunted by images of Jason in bed—breathy moans and delighted gasps, sweat-sweet skin under Ben's tongue, warmth all around—Ben gave up and threw back the covers.

In his underwear, shivering in the cool air, he opened the curtains to let in the moonlight and wandered from the kitchen to the living room and back again, a ghost in his own home.

Nothing in the cabin was his aside from the TV. Not the furniture or decorations, nor the dusty round clock high on the wall ticking errantly, off by a few more minutes each year. The fridge was ancient and clanging.

He'd left Brad and their house with only his clothes. No CDs or knickknacks or artwork. He'd abandoned it all, despite Brad's repeated attempts to split their belongings. He told himself he'd redecorate the cabin and make it his own, but here he stood surrounded by his father's choices, and the odd remnant from his mother, like the stained glass butterfly stuck to the kitchen window with a suction cup.

The Yosemite brochure sat on the kitchen table, and he found himself flipping through it. In the silver moonlight, the pictures were pale and beautiful, like Ansel Adams's famous black and white shots of the park.

Ben thought about how much Maggie would love it there, hoping fervently that Harlan Brown hadn't tainted her passion for the wild. A hard spear of a thought filled his mind.

I'm glad he's dead.

Maybe it was wrong, but he wouldn't deny it.

Flipping the brochure shut, his gaze drifted to the pile of books. With a sigh, he moved them over one by one. The last was an ancient atlas that likely still featured the USSR and colonial names like "Bombay" instead of Mumbai. He ran his fingers over the pages and put it aside.

Ben stared at the sketchbook. He'd forgotten he had it, and then it had been too late to return it to Jason. It was battered and ripping at the edges, some pages torn out completely. He'd flattened it under the books to try and smooth away the creases and make it whole again.

He opened it to the middle and gently pulled out the loose drawing of him and Maggie on the Road to the Sun. The remnants of wrinkles and crumpling lined the page, but in the pale gleam through the window, he could see the image of himself and Maggie clearly.

A fat tear plopped on to the paper, and he swore under his breath. It was absurd to miss two people he'd only just met. Absolutely ridiculous. Jason was too young for him. It would probably never work out. They barely knew each other.

"I'll meet someone else. I only feel this way because of the intense experience we shared. This isn't real." His flat voice seemed loud in the stillness. Utterly unconvinced, he closed the sketchbook and stacked the books back on top.

If it wasn't real, how did it hurt so damn much?

CHAPTER SEVENTEEN

GO TO SLEEP. You're tired. Sleep.

Shifting on the lumpy futon, Jason exhaled loudly in the stillness. Even with the curtains drawn, the streetlights were too bright, the odd car engine piercing. The occasional rumble of the elevator, something he never noticed during the day, was thunderous.

Why aren't you sleeping?!

Opening his eyes, Jason sighed. He usually fell into bed at night and was reluctant to drag himself out in the mornings. What was his problem? It must have been because he wasn't working his usual shifts on his feet for hours at a time at the factory, sorting fresh cookies on a conveyor belt, the air permanently sweet.

Yes, when he went back to work in a few days, everything would finally be normal. It had to be. Sure, some things had changed, like the fact that he was gay, but he supposed that wasn't so much a change as a revelation.

He wondered if it was strange that he'd accepted it so completely, but he had. There was no shame or discomfort when he rolled the words around in his head: *I'm gay.* He'd considered whether he was bi, but he really didn't think so.

I'm gay.

There was no panic, only...rightness, a deep relief to have solved a problem he hadn't even realized he'd had. He'd taken charge of it and there was no sense in denying the truth. Maybe his parents wouldn't like it, but that was their problem.

A fresh wave of anxiety washed over him, his neck tensing. He still had to deal with his parents and couldn't keep avoiding their calls.

Coming home hadn't magically hit a big red reset button. When he closed his eyes, he saw miles of green and Maggie disappearing right in front of him, gone, gone, gone. He still had to deal with what had happened to her.

How was he going to leave her at the Y on Monday for day camp? There was no way he could go to work and pretend everything was perfectly fine. She'd always been safe there, but what if something happened? Some psycho could sneak in and grab her and——

"Stop it," he muttered to himself. What-ifs led to a spiral of panic, and then he'd really never get to sleep.

As a white glow appeared, he turned his head, automatically reaching for his silenced cell phone on the coffee table, heart in his throat. He'd blocked a dozen media numbers, and was considering changing his number if they kept calling, although this was awfully late, so maybe...

Focusing on the screen, he came back down to earth. It was only one of his monthly reminders, this one to pay the utility bill in the morning. He tossed the phone back down, and after a few moments, it went dark.

Stupid. Go to sleep and stop it.

Why would Ben be contacting him? He'd told Jason to keep him posted, but there hadn't been anything new to say, so Jason had typed out and erased a dozen messages and sent none of them.

Kicking at the sheet, the fan not enough in the dog days of summer, he tried to get comfortable on his stomach. He was shirtless, his pajama bottoms only light cotton, but he was hot all over.

It was more than the humidity and lack of air conditioning.

When he closed his eyes and tried to drift away, he was grateful not to see the forest. But instead, his traitorous mind replayed images and sensations of sex with Ben—wet friction and baritone moans, tensed muscles and the burning stretch as Jason was exposed. Desire that had lain dormant and ignored for so many years was awakened, a low hum he could ignore during the day with welcome distractions.

But now it vibrated through every pore, the craving refusing to be denied. Jerking his hips despite himself, he humped the mattress pathetically, trying not to think about Ben. Maybe if he just thought about other men, it would be better. Less messy somehow. Less emotional.

Yet he couldn't imagine trusting anyone else. In Ben's hands, he'd been safe even when he'd felt defenseless, his skin too thin like tissue paper, his whole self flayed open. What would it be like to have sex with Ben again? Now that Jason knew what to expect when he had a cock in his ass, could he handle it all better?

Memories of the hotel room seemed imprinted on his flesh, indelible. Ben had been gentle and patient, but he'd gone hard too when he fucked him.

I've actually been fucked.

A thrill zipped through him. Pandora's box had been thrown wide open, his body and soul awakened. It sang in his veins, his dick rock hard at the thought of doing it again with Ben. Doing *everything.*

Because there had to be so much more, wasn't there?

He remembered the sensation of Ben's cock inside him, splitting him open, the burning pain worth the tidal wave of pleasure in the end. Then it had all been too much for him to handle, but now he was ready for more. He was going to explode if he didn't come.

With a furtive glance toward Maggie's room, he jumped up and hurried to the bathroom, locking the door and leaning against it, blinking into the glare when he flipped on the light. In the large mirror over the sink, he stared at himself, lips parted and chest rising too fast, nipples hard.

Before he could think, his hands lifted to circle them, teasing and squeezing, the tent in his PJs just visible at the bottom of the mirror. Sparks showered his skin, his belly rippling as he caressed his chest down to his waistband.

Jason stared at his flushed skin and light muscles. He didn't have anything close to washboard abs, but...he wasn't bad. He'd never looked at himself like that before. Like something sexual. Desirable.

His hair was a mess, and he imagined Ben's fingers tangling in it. The sensation of Ben's tongue and hot, wet mouth on Jason's dick had been incredible. What would it be like to drop to his knees and suck Ben's cock?

Biting back a groan, he shoved down his pajamas and kicked them off before squirting lotion into his hand from the Costco bottle under the sink. Naked, he watched in the mirror as he stroked himself, his shaft heavy and curving slightly to the left, the tip glistening.

Jason swiped his finger over the head and tasted his pre-cum, the tang tightening his balls. After sucking his finger, he reached back between his cheeks, poking experimentally into his hole. It was dry and tight, but he liked the burn.

Spreading his legs, he braced, fucking himself and stroking his shaft with his other hand, watching in the mirror. It wasn't as smooth jerking off with his left hand as it would be with his right, but he was so close it didn't matter, and he loved the feeling of his finger inside him. It wasn't Ben's cock, but it would have to do.

Then he imagined Ben was there watching. Jason pressed his lips together hard to prevent a cry from escaping as he pictured Ben's broad, hairy chest, his big cock and heavy balls. Ben would jerk himself as well, and he'd come all over Jason—

Spurting on the sink and counter, even splashing the mirror, Jason trembled through his orgasm, watching himself and imagining Ben's cum mixing with his.

Head back, he finally closed his eyes, slipping his finger out of his ass, panting. If Ben was there, he'd draw Jason into his arms and hold him close, whisper kisses and praise against his skin. Jason longed to feel Ben's body against him again. He could see it so clearly...

Jolting, he grabbed a paper towel from under the sink and mopped up his mess before washing his hands and tugging on his pajamas. The sketchbook he'd brought to Montana was lost, and he hadn't even thought about picking up his pencils since they'd been back.

But now need filled him, urgent and unrelenting. He grabbed a pad and pencils from a drawer in the living room and turned on the kitchen light, standing at the counter and drawing furiously, fueled by the sudden despair that he'd forget what Ben looked like.

Page after page, he drew Ben—smiling, standing, sitting, hiking, naked in bed. Blushing and tingling, he drew Ben's cock in its nest of dark hair, capturing every angle. Breathing hard when he was done, he flipped through the pages, not sure what to feel.

A sound from Maggie's room had him jumping a mile high, and he shoved the sketchbook to the back of the top shelf in the hall closet holding his clothes, well out of reach and sight.

Maggie cried again plaintively as he reached her side and turned on the lamp on the bedside table. She twitched, sweet face screwed up, and he shook her gently.

"Baby, wake up. It's okay. Everything's okay."

Gasping, her eyes flew open, and she burst into wrenching tears that tore into Jason's heart. He rocked her, rubbing her back and murmuring as she sobbed against his bare chest.

There was no magic reset button.

They couldn't pretend everything would just go back to normal. As Jason comforted Maggie, assuring her it was only a nightmare and she was safe, he knew he had to swallow his pride and take his parents' offer to pay for therapy. Anything that could help.

Gulping as her sobs subsided, Maggie asked, "Can I sleep with you?"

"Of course. Come on." Jason scooped her into his arms, cradling her close as he carried her into the living room. He settled her on the futon, tucking the sheet around her.

"Will you read me a book?"

"Sure. Which one?" He'd read to her all night if it would take her nightmares away.

She sniffled. "Hospital."

His heart clenched as he kissed her forehead before returning to her room to scan the bookcase for the thin, faded yellow spine. The top corner of the cover had already been torn off when he'd picked up the book at a second-hand shop for fifty cents. The pages inside were worn now too after the hundreds of times Maggie had read it.

He turned on the lamp beside the futon and propped up a few pillows at the end before stretching out. She cuddled into the burrow of his arm as he cleared his throat and began by announcing the title, as he'd always done when reading to her.

"*Curious George Goes to the Hospital.*"

He hadn't read it in a couple years, Maggie long since moved on to books with more words and fewer pictures. But he still knew the tale of the mischievous monkey, his owner—the man with the yellow hat—and a swallowed puzzle piece that lands George in the hospital almost by heart.

He savored each word as he read with Maggie warm at his side, wishing his daughter could have stayed innocent forever.

CHAPTER EIGHTEEN

L IGHTSABERS CLASHED, CARTOON CHARACTERS battling in
The Clone Wars. Maggie watched avidly, scraping her cereal
bowl for every bit of sugary milk remaining. Jason usually only
kept bran and granola cereals in the apartment, but had added a
box of Frosted Flakes to the grocery delivery.

He hadn't bothered hauling up the back of the futon into
couch form, and sat cross-legged beside Maggie on the mattress,
his own cereal barely touched and soggy. He never normally
ordered groceries online, but he didn't want to deal with people
recognizing them. He'd have to face the world on Monday when
he went back to work, but he hoped the attention would fade by
then. Surely there were more interesting things happening in the
world. Another *hot topic.*

The episode ended, and Jason watched the credits, the Netflix
auto-play announcement appearing in the corner of the screen. It
would be easy to just let another play, sit there and put it off for
another twenty minutes.

He picked up the remote and hit stop. Time to deal with it.

Maggie's spoon clattered in her empty bowl. "We can't watch
another one?"

"We can. I just want to talk for a few minutes."

Her shoulders slumped, and she stared down into her bowl.
"About what?"

"About going to see someone you can talk to about what happened."

"But that will cost money. I'm fine, Dad. Really. It was just a stupid dream last night." She lifted her head, eyes gleaming. "I'm sorry."

"Sweetie, you have nothing to be sorry for." He put their bowls on the low coffee table and scooted closer, wrapping an arm around her slim shoulders. "There's nothing wrong with having nightmares or being afraid. Especially after what happened in Montana. It was really scary and upsetting, and I don't want you to pretend everything is fine when it's not."

Hypocrite.

Jason ignored the little voice in his head. Yes, maybe he was a hypocrite, but he'd deal with his own shit later. Maggie came first.

She huffed. "But I don't want to talk about it all the time! I had a stupid dream about being cold in the river, but I'm fine now. I just want everything to be okay again. The way it was."

"I know. And we don't have to talk about it constantly. Just sometimes. Grandma and Grandpa offered to pay so you can see a nice doctor who knows all about this stuff. It's not healthy to bottle everything up inside you and not talk about it."

"What about you? What about the stuff you don't talk about?"

"I..." *Busted.* "Okay, you're right. I should see someone to talk about Montana as well."

"I don't mean just Montana." She fidgeted, bouncing her foot. "Was Mom your girlfriend?"

His heart skipped. "Uh, no. Your mom was my best friend and I loved her very much, but she wasn't my girlfriend. We were curious, so we had sex to see what it was like." When Maggie had started asking a myriad of questions earlier that year, he'd bitten the bullet and borrowed a few books from the library on sex ed that they'd read through together. He didn't want her to have any hang-ups, so he tried to discuss it as openly as possible using straightforward language.

"Why don't you have a girlfriend? Or even go out on any dates? Ever?"

His mouth went dry. "Well, I just haven't met the right...person."

She echoed, "'The right person.' Dad, are you gay?"

"I..." He had to be honest. He had to tell her the truth, but no words squeezed out through his closed throat.

"I saw you and Ben kissing at the hospital. I was supposed to be asleep, but I woke up and I could see you in the mirror."

"Oh." *Say something! Say the right thing!*

"I still love you just as much if you like boys." She stared at him solemnly. "You know that, right?"

A weight lifted from Jason's chest, and he exhaled. "I know, baby. Yes, I'm gay. I didn't actually realize it for a long time, or I would have told you sooner."

"Is Ben your boyfriend?"

"Uh..." Trust Maggie to cut right to the chase. "I'm not sure."

She frowned. "Why not? Ben's awesome. What's there not to be sure about?"

"It's just not that easy."

"You like each other, right? Why does it have to be hard?"

"We live thousands of miles apart. There's a lot to figure out."

"Are we never going to see him again? Why didn't he say goodbye to me?" Hurt was clear in Maggie's plaintive whine. "Why didn't he come see me before we went to the airport? Is he mad?"

"No, baby. It all just happened quickly when we left, and Ben had to get back to work."

"But he was there, and he didn't say goodbye. What if I never get to see him again? Don't you want to see him?"

Memories of Ben's smile and low laughter echoed, the sensation of his rough stubble on Jason's skin, the caress of lips and hands. A tangle of contradiction suffocated Jason. One minute he was firm—he didn't need anyone to take care of him. Yet in the next breath, he longed for the strength of Ben's arms. Ben had seen Jason with every defense stripped away and wanted him nonetheless.

Maggie asked, "Do you still like him?"

Jason's heart clenched as his brain answered clearly: *I love him.* Digging his fingers into the futon, he got out, "Uh-huh."

Do I love him?

"Don't you want to see him? Why are you scared?"

Jason didn't have a good answer. "I don't know."

She sprang to her feet. "I think you're being dumb."

"Maggie! Don't talk to me like that." *Even if you're right.*

"I'm going to play with Max."

"What? No. I don't want you going out."

She huffed. "It's not *out*. He lives right downstairs. I want to see him. I want to play."

Jason opened his mouth to argue, but snapped it shut. Having her out of his sight for more than a few minutes made him squirmy, but it was good that she wanted to play with her friend and do normal things. He'd be back at work soon to pay the mounting bills, and he couldn't bring her with him. He had to deal with the reality that he couldn't watch her every minute and that Maggie didn't want him to.

He stood. "Okay. Let's get dressed and I'll walk you down and say hi to Mrs. Lane."

Still in pajamas, Max's mother greeted Maggie with a big hug, her curly dark hair hanging loose over her shoulders. Jason stood stiffly as she hugged him next, the kids already breathlessly planning what kind of fort to build.

He tried to smile. "Hi, Christy. You're sure it's okay for Maggie to invade?"

Christy grinned. "Are you kidding? She'll keep Max and Madison entertained for hours with her imagination, even though Madison barely understands." Her smile faded. "How are you holding up?"

"Fine. I'm great."

Eyebrow popping dubiously, Christy said, "Look, I know we've never really talked about anything but the weather or the kids, but I'm here if you need an ear. I know you went through hell."

Jason's throat tightened. "Yeah. Thanks." Christy was right that they'd never talked about anything serious, although she'd invited him to have drinks with her and her husband or dinner with the family more than once. He'd always said no. What had he been afraid of?

That they'd see I wasn't good enough, that I could barely manage, that I'm a bad father.

He said, "Can you call me to come get her when she's ready? I know it's only one floor and I'm being paranoid, but…"

Christy squeezed his arm. "I get it. I'll walk her up."

Jason's cell buzzed in his pocket, his childhood phone number appearing on the screen, instantly recognizable. "Thanks, Christy. I have to…"

She waved him off, and he took the stairs two at a time back to his apartment. Inside, he wanted nothing more than to close the curtains, go back to bed, and not have to think about anything at all.

The phone buzzed again in his hand, and he almost dropped it. His mother had always done that—called twice before leaving a message. He could let this one go unanswered as well. Could pretend that nothing had changed and go years again without acknowledging his family, could stay in control and make everything normal.

Taking a deep breath, Jason swiped the screen, jumping off the ledge. "Hello?"

HE PULLED UP to a red light, asking himself for the hundredth time if he was nuts for agreeing to dinner at his parents' house. But his mom had been so eager on the phone, and considering they were paying for Maggie to see a therapist, dinner was a reasonable request.

The radio played a noisy pop hit, and he turned down the volume, glancing at Maggie in the back seat. "How do you feel about tonight?"

In the rearview, Maggie shrugged. "Fine."

She'd avoided him most of the day and he'd let her, but it was time to deal with it. "Come on, that's not a real answer."

She rolled her eyes, but after a few moments, said, "Why do they even want us to come? I thought they hated us."

"*Maggie*. We talked about this. They don't *hate* us at all. I thought you understood what happened when you were a baby? They just thought you'd be better off if they raised you."

"Because they're stupid."

"Hey! No name-calling. They thought they knew best, and they were stubborn."

"They were wrong."

"Yes. They were, and they realize that now." He wanted to believe them—wanted so badly to trust them, but he wasn't sure he could. Not completely. Not after they got lawyers and a judge involved to try and take his baby away.

But he'd try.

For the first time since he was a teenager, he drove the streets of his old neighborhood. Some houses looked the same, and he made the turns from memory, barely glancing at the signs. The tennis court that had been weirdly squeezed in the front of Carson Whitmer's house was gone, replaced by a stretch of lush lawn and sculpted flowerbeds.

The man-made bump of a hill in the park had seemed huge when he was a kid. He and Tim had tobogganed on it, and now it looked ridiculously tiny. Had it always been so small?

Jason's stomach tightened as he turned onto his old street, twilight descending. He turned left into the driveway and parked behind a gleaming black SUV that was a massive vehicle for people who rarely left the city. At least they hadn't driven many back roads while he was growing up.

"Is this it?" Maggie asked, ducking her head to peer up. "It's a *mansion*."

Jason killed the engine and took in the house. Two long stories in a Tudor design—beige brick, brown wooden slats on white walls—with a double car garage. Perfectly designed flowerbeds curved along the flagstone walkway, and the lawn stretched out quite a ways before the next house.

"Yeah. I guess it is. I never thought of it like that."

"You really lived here?"

He realized all over again how much he'd taken for granted. "I did. It was just my house. It was normal."

The door had been painted red at some point, a pop of color amid the earth tones. Then that door opened, and a young man stepped out.

"Who's that?" Maggie asked.

It took Jason a few frozen heartbeats to realize it was his brother. He spoke hoarsely. "That's your Uncle Tim."

"Seriously? I thought he was way younger than you."

"He is. Seven years. He's eighteen now." Jason had seen Tim's pictures on Instagram, so it shouldn't have been such a surprise, but somehow it was as Tim filled the doorway, his jeans and button-up shirt tight on a toned, lanky body. His sandy hair was curlier than Jason's, and it was cropped short aside from a couple inches on top.

"Are we going in?"

For a moment, Jason wanted to turn the key, throw the rusty old Chevy in reverse, and not look back. But he took a deep breath, and the panic eased. "We are."

Maggie clung to his hand as they walked to the door. Tim waited, an unreadable expression on his face. He nodded to Jason. "Hey."

"Hey. Um, this is Maggie."

"Yeah, I figured." His face softened as he offered her his hand. "Hi, Maggie. Nice to meet you again."

She glanced at Jason before shaking Tim's hand. "You too." She fidgeted with the collar of her favorite purple sundress.

"Oh, you're here! We didn't hear the car." Robert appeared, his dress shirt sharply pressed and cufflinks shining. Jason was glad he'd worn his best slacks and button-up shirt, although he'd rebelliously considered sweatpants and flip-flops. His father said, "Your mother's just putting the finishing touches on some carrot roulades and caramelized onion tartlets. Come in, come in."

Robert ushered them inside and awkwardly shook Jason's hand and patted Maggie's shoulder. He rubbed his palms together. "What can I get you? Maggie, we squeezed some fresh juice for you. Do you like juice?"

She looked to Jason before nodding mutely.

"Great!" Robert said too loudly. "Jason, are you a beer man? Wine? Spirits?"

In the surrealness of his father offering him a drink, Jason realized he hadn't brought a bottle of wine, which was what grown-ups did when they went to someone's house for dinner. "Uh, whatever you're having. Beer, I guess?"

"Beer it is. Stella okay?"

"Uh-huh."

Tim stood nearby, and Jason ached to pull him into a hug. But he didn't know how to make that happen, so he followed his father into the sitting room, where his mother soon appeared with trays of appetizers, including macaroni and cheese bites, clearly geared for Maggie's taste buds. Shelly wore a knee-length floral dress, her golden hair done up in a fancy swirl.

After uncomfortable chitchat about the weather, the Phillies, and Maggie's favorite subjects at school, they moved into the dining room. The beef and roasted potatoes filled Jason's nose, a hint of rosemary bringing back bittersweet memories.

Shelly passed a china dish to Jason. "Your favorite kind of potatoes. Remember? The rosemary and sage are growing so well in the garden this year."

Nodding, Jason spooned a bit of everything onto Maggie's plate. His mother sat at the head of the table to the left beyond Maggie, Tim across from them, and Robert at the other end to the right. The chandelier over the table was different than Jason remembered, sleeker and more modern in a horizontal design.

They ate quietly for a few minutes, everyone complimenting the food a little too zealously, even though it really was delicious. Maggie picked at her plate, eating little bites. Jason had always tried his best to make her a variety of food with lots of vegetables, but rarely anything as fancy as this. The tenderloin was wrapped with a strip of perfectly crisp bacon.

His mother sliced neatly into her meat. "So, Jason. Do you have a girlfriend?"

Ugh. Just the conversation he wanted to have. "No. I haven't had time to date."

"Oh." Her smile was strained. "No girls your age at the, uh, factory?" She said *factory* the way she would *dirty sock* while pinching it between two fingers and asking whose it was.

"No." Jason chewed a brussels sprout and tried to decide if he should just tell them and get it over with. What was the point of all this if he wasn't going to tell them who he really was?

Before he could say anything, Maggie spoke, her eyes flinty. "Why should he only want to date girls? Maybe he likes boys.

There's nothing wrong with boys liking other boys, you know."

In the silence following Maggie's declaration, his parents blinked, then Tim laughed triumphantly. "I knew it."

Perhaps Jason should have been angry with Maggie for outing him, but he exhaled in relief. At least it was in the open. He smiled at her as his father said, "Oh."

His mother still held her knife and fork above her plate. "Well. We—"

"Think it's wrong? Disgusting? A sin?" Jason finished for her, tapping his foot restlessly. He should just take Maggie and go. This had been a mistake.

"*No.*" His mother frowned, her sculpted brows drawn close. "May I please finish my sentence?" After a moment of silence, she said, "When you were in high school, your father and I questioned whether you were gay, but then everything happened and we assumed you weren't. No, we don't think it's wrong, or disgusting, or a sin."

His father added, "The Breslins' boy is homosexual. Captain of the rowing team at Yale. He just graduated, actually. We could introduce you."

Jason swallowed a burst of hysterical laughter. He had to be dreaming. Things were actually going all right with his family. "Uh, thanks, but that's okay." He glanced at Tim. "You knew?"

Shoveling a forkful of food into his mouth, Tim shrugged. "I figured probably. Dunno why. Just something, I guess. It's not like I care. It's cool."

Shelly sighed. "Please don't talk with your mouth full." To Jason, she said, "So, are there any boys you're interested in? Stephen Breslin really is handsome, you know."

"No! He's going to be with Ben. Not anyone else." Maggie glared, as if daring anyone to argue, including Jason.

"Ben?" Shelly smiled encouragingly. "Who's this Ben?"

"Ben Hettler," Maggie answered. "He's a park ranger, and he's smart and funny, and he saved me."

Jason's parents blinked and shared a glance. His mother said, "That...*man?*"

Robert added, "He's a fair bit older than you, isn't he?"

Jason gritted his teeth, all the old resentment surging. "*I'm* a man too. Yes, Ben's older, but I'm not a teenager. A lot has changed in the last eight years, and you don't get to sit there judging me. You don't get to tell me who I should date." He tossed his napkin on his plate. "This was a bad idea. We should go."

"Just like that?" Tim scoffed. "Of course. Run away again. That's what you do."

"What?" Jason scoffed back, self-righteous indignation straightening his spine. "That's not true."

"Sure," Tim bit out. "Did you run away from this Ben dude too? I bet you did."

He wanted to scream, "*I did not!*" but snapped his jaw shut. He breathed shallowly, guilt stinging with every inhalation. He couldn't think about Ben. Not now.

He had to deal with this first. It was long overdue.

After another long breath, he said, "Maggie, come with me." He pushed his chair back.

"Are you really going to leave?" his father asked incredulously.

"Of course he is." Tim crossed his arms, jaw tight.

Maggie looked at him with wide eyes, and Jason tried to smile reassuringly at her. He kept his tone even. "I'm just going to take Maggie into the den. Mags, you can watch TV while you finish your dinner, okay?"

"I'm not hungry."

"Okay. Let's just take your plate and milk in case you change your mind. We're going to talk in here. We won't be too long."

"But I want to stay!"

He used his "that's enough, young lady" tone. "*Maggie.* Please do as you're told."

Huffing, she carried her glass and napkin as Jason took her plate and utensils and led her out of the dining room and down the hall to the den. The TV was bigger than he remembered, and the wraparound couch was velvety leather, a change from the suede he and Tim had scuffed up.

The art was the same, brass rubbings from churches in England on black backgrounds, Arthurian soldiers with swords and pious ladies in long, flowing gowns. He was struck by a memory of curling up with his father on the suede couch, Dad telling him stories of knights and maidens.

"Dad?"

"Uh-huh." He shook himself and settled Maggie on the couch with a lap tray, flicking on the TV and starting an episode of a David Attenborough nature show on Netflix. As chimpanzees hooted and climbed trees, Jason kissed Maggie's head. "I'll be back soon. I need to talk some stuff out with them."

She nodded. "Okay. I won't eavesdrop. Even though I really want to."

He had to laugh, a tiny bit of the pressure in his chest easing. "Thank you. You're a good girl. I love you."

"Love you too."

He closed the door to the den behind him. In the dining room, he found his family still sitting where he'd left them, tension simmering in the air and food untouched. He took his seat, Tim glaring at his plate across the table.

Jason said, "I can imagine it must have seemed that way to you—that I ran away."

His mother exhaled sharply. "Oh no. No, it didn't just *seem* that way, Jason." Tears shimmered in her eyes. "You just left! Ran away! We woke up, and you and Maggie were simply *gone*. Do you have any idea how frightening that was? No note. Nothing! You drained your bank account, and that was it. You were gone.

We didn't know if you were alive or dead."

Jason snorted. "Don't be so melodramatic."

"I'm not." She swiped at her eyes. "It's terrifying, not knowing where your child is. Not knowing if they're safe. You should understand that now, especially after what happened in Montana."

His stomach clenched. "It's not the same thing."

"Night after night, we laid awake, praying you were all right." She gulped from her wine glass, red liquid sloshing. "I kept imagining all the unspeakable things that could happen. By the time we tracked you down, we were frantic."

His father spoke up. "We were afraid, Jason. We were afraid for you and that sweet baby. You were making rash decisions, and even though you'd turned eighteen, we didn't think you were old enough to be a responsible parent. So yes, then we pursued legal action because we didn't feel you left us any choice."

"No. No, don't turn this around on me. You were already talking about taking Maggie away." He glared at his mother. "I heard you. On the phone. 'We'd have to have Jason declared an unfit father,' you said."

She opened and closed her mouth. "But that was just discussion. We wanted to know the options. We were frustrated. Angry. We were wrong, and we realize that. At the time, we truly thought it was best for you and Maggie if we had custody. But we had no intention of actually taking you to court. It was the last thing we wanted."

"But it's exactly what happened," Tim said. He looked from their parents to Jason and back again. "How did you all let this get so fucked up?"

"*Timothy.*"

Tim barked out a laugh. "What, Mom? 'Language?' I think we're all fucking old enough to handle it. So come on, let's get it all out. You guys screwed up. Big time. And Jay shouldn't have run away without at least calling to say he and Maggie were okay."

To Jason, he added, "That really sucked, man. You didn't even call me. I get why you were pissed at them. But what did I do?"

"You didn't do anything, I swear." Jason hated the pain etched on his brother's face.

"I was a kid, and you just took off. Didn't you care about me? I know I was annoying, and I swiped your video games and hogged the bathroom and ate the last cookies—"

"No! It wasn't anything you did. You didn't do anything wrong." Jason raked a hand through his hair, trying to find the right words. "I texted you, but they changed your number."

"That wasn't until after the court case," Robert said.

"I just… I didn't want to involve you." Jason cringed at his lame excuse.

"Like I wasn't *involved?*" Tim shook his head. "Dude, I was involved. Trust me. I couldn't do anything. I couldn't go anywhere. They were so paranoid something would happen to me too. Not only was my brother gone without a word, I was stuck here without you. And then after you got custody, they put all their focus on me." He looked between their parents. "I know you guys didn't mean to smother me. It was just intense sometimes."

Their father nodded. "I can understand that."

Tim said, "But the real problem is that none of you tried to fix this."

The words hung in the thick silence as they stared at each other. They'd been a family once upon a time—flawed and imperfect, but a family nonetheless. Now they were strangers, and in that moment, Jason truly realized how much he'd lost. How much they'd all lost.

Pointing, Tim accused Jason. "You wanted so damn badly to prove you were a grown-up, and clearly you've worked your ass off raising Maggie. But aren't adults supposed to be mature and not hold grudges? And okay, my phone number changed. So that was it? You just gave up? There was no other way to get in touch? It's not like you didn't know where I lived."

Fidgeting with hot shame, Jason whispered, "You're right. I'm sorry. I was too wrapped up in my own pain. I was determined not to need anyone and to prove everyone wrong. I didn't think about how you felt." Saying it out loud was like swallowing shards of glass. "I told myself you'd contact me if you wanted to. I put the ball in your court. It wasn't fair."

Tim swallowed hard. "I realize I'm being a hypocrite because I didn't contact you when I got older. But I was too afraid you'd hang up or shut the door in my face. So I didn't try either."

Jason looked at his brother and parents, the three people he'd once been closest to in the world. "It doesn't matter whose fault it is, or what any of us did or didn't do. Let's just fix it now and move forward. What do you say?"

In unison, they said, "Yes."

His mother got dessert—Jason's favorite from childhood, a strawberry shortcake with fresh cream—and they joined Maggie in the den, balancing their bowls on their knees and watching chimps dig for termites. His life had become one surreal moment after the next.

Thoughts of Ben circled like a shark, guilt building. Tim was right. Jason had absolutely run away. After everything that had happened—both terrible and amazing—he'd retreated desperately, grasping at some semblance of normalcy. Any bit of control he could cling to after losing Maggie and barely getting her back.

Even now, he wished he could curl up and go to sleep just for a little while so he didn't have to think.

"Aren't they clever, using sticks like that," Shelly said.

Jason refocused on the TV as Maggie offered, "No one knew they used tools until Jane Goodall saw them. I did a project on her."

"Oh, how interesting!" Mom smiled. "We'd love to see your project sometime."

There was still so much to hash out with his family, and it was awkward, eggshells everywhere underfoot. But surrounded by his parents and brother for the first time in years, Maggie tucked into his side, it was a start.

CHAPTER NINETEEN

"U M, HEY. TIM?" Pressing the phone too tightly to his ear, Jason reminded himself to breathe. *Sit down and chill out.* "Jay?"

Adjusting his sunglasses in the morning glare, Jason sat on the bench and kicked off his flip-flops, freshly mown grass soft under his feet. Maggie and Max swung from the monkey bars in the playground. "Yeah. Are you busy? We didn't get a chance to talk last night, just the two of us."

Tim hesitated, then asked warily, "What do you want to talk about?"

Great question. "Uh, what have you been up to?"

"Since last night, or my entire teenage existence? Preteen too, actually."

Jason shifted uncomfortably, picking up leftover dried grass with his toes. "I'm sorry."

Tim sighed. "No, don't be. I have to let it go. My girlfriend Regan says I need to release the past or I'll miss creating beautiful memories for tomorrow. She's into yoga and meditation and all that. Drinks a lot of smoothies. Burns a lot of incense."

The name rang a bell. "Oh, right. The redhead you went to prom with? She's really pretty. How long have you been together?"

"Since junior year. She's going to UC Santa Cruz and I'm heading to Harvard, so I guess we'll see what happens. How did you know we went to prom?"

He picked up more dead grass with his toes. "Your Instagram. I've followed it for a while now."

"Huh. Okay."

As silence stretched out, Jason searched for something to say. "What's your major going to be?"

"No clue. Not business or law, but Mom and Dad are actually okay with it. They say I can do whatever makes me happy."

"Whoa. Times have changed."

Tim was silent a moment, then quietly said, "They really have."

"I'm glad." Another silence descended as words tangled on Jason's tongue. *Say the right thing! Okay, just say* something *at this point. Talk!* He blurted, "Hey, maybe I can get your advice."

There was a pause. "Really? Yeah, sure."

"Cool." Jason tried to find the right way to ask, his mind spinning uselessly.

"Uh, Jay? This is the part where you talk."

He laughed nervously. "I know. Sorry. I suck at this."

Tim laughed too. "No shit, bro. Hey, where are you? I hear shrieking."

"At the park with Maggie and her friend." They were on the swings now, little legs pumping as they tried to fly higher and higher, egging each other on.

"Are the paparazzi hiding in the bushes?"

Jason scoffed, but glanced around. "I don't see any. It's not like I'm Brad Pitt. I think they've moved on."

"Guess you'll find out. That's cool Maggie's okay with going outside. I'd probably be hiding under the covers."

"That's pretty tempting to me too, not gonna lie. But my—" He cleared his throat. It had been so long since he'd called them anything but "my parents" in awkward conversations if anyone asked about his family. "Well, Mom and Dad are going to pay for a shrink for her, which will be good."

"What about for you? No offense, but I think you could use some time on the couch too."

He laughed. "None taken. You're probably right. I'll look into it."

"Mom and Dad would pay for you too."

"I know. I think I need to start with talking to my friends and stuff. Like you, maybe? I mean, you're my brother, but... I'd really like it if we could be friends too." His heart thumped dully.

"Same here."

Exhaling, Jason said, "Thanks. My neighbor offered to listen to my shit, and she's really nice, but it would be weird to go from 'Yes, this is an unseasonably cold spring' and 'Has the super told you about the new recycling bins?' to unloading all this stuff in my head."

Tim laughed softly. "Yeah, I get that. So go ahead. Unload."

"Yeah?"

"Just spit it out, dude."

"Hold on." To the kids, Jason yelled, "Maggie! No jumping off the swing at the top! I don't care if Max just did it! And Max, don't do that again! You know the rules." The last thing they needed was a trip to the ER. "Tim? Sorry."

Tim just laughed. "Man, it is trippy that you're a *dad*. You sound all grown-up and shit."

"Well, I try." He wriggled his feet in the grass. "So... Okay, you were right about Ben—the park ranger we met out there? I totally ran away from him. It was like... He got too close, I guess. So much had happened in only a few days with Maggie missing and us going after her. Things got...intense with Ben. Then Mom and Dad suddenly appeared, and it was like..."

"Circuit overload?"

Jason smiled. "Yeah."

"I don't blame you. How did you leave things with Ben?"

"I told him I needed time, and we've sent a few excruciatingly lame texts. I don't know. Maybe he doesn't even want to be with me anymore. We barely know each other."

"Dude, what you guys went through? That's the express version of getting to know someone. It's like you went on fifty dates. Stressful, crappy, life-threatening dates."

He laughed. "I guess that's one way of looking at it."

"So when was your last boyfriend? Have you been serious about anyone before? Assuming you're serious about Ben now."

"I am. I definitely am." A flock of birds squawked, and he watched them soar in perfect unison. "I've never actually had a serious relationship. Or, um, any relationship. Or dates. Or anything. At all. I'm in way over my head here."

Tim whistled. "Whoa. Okay, that's cool. You've been busy being super dad. I get it. So wow, if you haven't even had close friends all this time, let alone a boyfriend… Have you ever trusted someone? Like with Regan, I don't know if she's 'The One,' but I trust her. I could tell her anything. She's solid, you know? Sometimes her head's in the clouds with all her love and peace stuff, but she's strong. I can depend on her. What about you? Have you ever trusted someone like that?"

Memories crescendoed—Ben's eyes crinkling as he sang along with Will Smith on the Road to the Sun; his bulky warmth holding Jason close during that endless black night in the woods, sheltering him from the worst of the wind; his sweet, desperate kisses as he brought Jason's body to life.

"Yes," he croaked, his throat thick.

"I assume it's Ben since you sound like you're going to cry?"

Exhaling a little laugh, Jason said, "Yes. He… He was so kind to us, and then after everything happened, he was a rock. I can't imagine what I would have done without him." He swallowed, mouth dry. "I don't know what to do anymore without him. I got by for years on my own, and now I feel so weak." He shivered in the bright sunlight.

"It's not weak to need someone. You just have to be strong enough to trust this guy. Put yourself out there. Lay it on the line, man. If you hide behind excuses and let the opportunity with him pass, you'll always wonder what if. Stop running away. Who can say how shit will turn out, but at least you'll *know*."

"You're right. You're so right." A calm, deep sense of hope filled Jason. He wasn't going to give up Ben without a fight. He was done standing in his own way.

Blinking, he realized Maggie was standing by the bench giving him a quizzical look. Into the phone, he said, "Hold on," then asked Maggie, "You okay, sweetie?"

"Uh-huh. Why are you grinning like that?"

"Because your uncle's grown up to be really smart."

"Is that him? Hi, Uncle Tim! We're getting ice cream!"

Tim laughed in Jason's ear. "Tell her hi back and that Rocky Road's my fave for future reference."

"I will. Talk to you soon, okay?"

They hung up, and Jason fixed Maggie with a faux stern look as Max raced up, practically doing cartwheels as the musical tinkling of the ice cream truck filled the air. Somehow kids always heard it a mile away. "Who says we're getting ice cream?"

Clasping her hands, Maggie begged, "Pleeeease?" as Max chimed in.

Jason bought them dipped vanilla cones, along with one for himself, getting almost as much chocolate on his face as they did.

He buzzed as they walked home, tempted to do a cartwheel of his own. He was going to call Ben and tell him how he felt.

As soon as he figured out how to say it.

THIS WAS A *huge mistake.*

A bus rumbled by, a distant horn honking as Ben stood on the sidewalk in front of the building. He stepped onto the grass to make way for an enormous baby stroller and stared up at the brown brick, wondering which unit was Jason and Maggie's.

Unable to stomach another lonely night at the cabin, he'd made the biggest impulse purchase of his life with a stupidly expensive plane ticket. It had taken a red-eye and two connections, but now he was actually looking at Jason's home.

Finding the address had been alarmingly easy online. Ben knew he should at least call before showing up, but he kept telling himself he'd do it at the next airport. Then in the cab. But now he was on the narrow strip of lawn between the sidewalk and a row of bushes, phone in his damp palm.

It was late afternoon. Storm clouds darkened the sky in the distance, the humid air thick with promise. Sweat dripped down Ben's spine, the sleeves of his thin plaid shirt rolled to his elbows. This had all made sense when he'd hatched his plan. Not that it had been a *plan* per se. The idea was basically to beg Jason to give him a chance. Give *them* a chance.

Jason was young and scared and overwhelmed. Ben had to fight for the future they could have together. He'd plead his case one more time, and if Jason said no, that would truly be the end of it. But at least Ben wouldn't have to wonder what if and live with the regret of having not even tried.

Rolling back his shoulders, he pocketed his phone and took one step. Then another and another, rounding the bushes with his duffel in one hand, squeezing the straps. Inside the foyer, he scanned a list of surnames with buttons beside them. There it was. His finger hovered in the air.

Kellerman 404

Just then, someone pushed open the locked door and left the building, and Ben caught it, slipping inside. He could still turn around and leave. Jason would never know he'd been there. Ugh. At this point he was feeling like a creepy stalker. No, he was here, and he'd talk to Jason, and then what would be, would be.

Resolved, he rode the groaning elevator to the fourth floor. Marching up to 404, he knocked before he could chicken out. His heart pounded as footsteps approached, a shadow falling over the peephole.

The door sprang open, Jason standing in the threshold, jaw on the floor. "Ben? Are you... You're here?"

He dropped his duffel, shaky hands motioning as he spoke. "If you kick me out I'll totally understand. I just had to see you in person. I couldn't let this go without trying. Couldn't let *us* go."

When Jason simply stared, Ben kept going. "I think about you and Maggie all the time. I realize we only knew each other a few days, but I've never felt anything this strong in my life. You're not a kid—you're a brave and beautiful and wonderful man. But I do want to take care of you. I want to protect you from anyone who would hurt you. I want to hold you at night and know you're safe. I want to make sure you're happy and laughing, and that you have everything you could ever want."

Jason still stared soundlessly.

Mouth dry, Ben barreled on. "And it's not because I think you're weak. You had to grow up so young. Most people wouldn't have had the balls to keep Maggie. To raise her and sacrifice everything else. You're one of the strongest people I've ever met, but I still want to take care of you. Maybe that's wrong, but it's how I feel." He thumped a hand on his chest. "I feel it so deeply. I want to take care of you both. I want to share my life with you. You and Maggie came along when I least expected it and filled up the hole inside me that had been empty for so long."

Jason still wasn't saying a word. He stood frozen, chest rising and falling rapidly.

"I think we could be so good together. You make me excited

about life again. Excited to explore and share and really *live*. We meet hundreds of people—thousands—and they come in and out of our lives. But when I met you there was a spark, and I don't know if it's chemistry or pure dumb luck, but I don't want to let you go. I know it was wrong to just show up here—"

Choking down a sob, Jason launched himself, locking his arms around Ben as Ben staggered. He grabbed Jason back, squeezing with all the love in his heart.

Jason gulped in a breath. "I can't believe you're standing here. I was working up the nerve to finally call you and try to tell you how I feel, and now you're *here*." He gripped Ben harder. "God, I want that too," Jason whispered as he lifted his head, eyes bright and gleaming. "What you just said."

Ben's impassioned speech was a blur now. "Which part?"

Jason laughed, and it was glorious. "All of it."

Lightheaded, he laughed too. "With me? This is all new for you, and you might find someone else. Someone closer to your age. Someone… I don't know. Better."

"Better than you?" Jason shook his head vigorously. "Not possible. You're brave and loyal, and you don't make fun of me for liking Will Smith. You, you… You're patient with Maggie's million questions, and you're so sexy I just want to climb you like a tree and rub myself all over you. You're everything I never knew I wanted. Never even imagined I could have."

"You've got me. All of me."

Jason clutched Ben's sides. "I thought if I didn't do it on my own I was a failure. I was wrong. I don't want to be alone anymore. I want to be with you. The three of us together."

With a shudder, Ben pulled him into another hug, pressing his face against Jason's neck. "I don't want to be alone anymore either," he murmured. "God, Jason. I missed you so much. Both of you. I didn't think I could fall in love that fast."

Jason leaned back, searching Ben's face. "Love?"

"Absolutely." It shone in Ben so strongly he was sure it had to be visible. "Yes."

"I love you too. I do." He laughed disbelievingly. "I really do, Ben."

"Do I get to kiss you now?"

Jason nodded vigorously, tugging him over the threshold. "All the kisses. Everything."

Ben caught Jason's lips as they came together hungrily. He managed to close the door, pressing him back against it, roaming his hands over Jason's chest, skimming up under his clothes, eager for warm skin.

Jason spread his legs, and Ben shoved his thigh between them. They were both hard already, and he squeezed Jason through his jeans, anticipation flooding his senses. Then Ben jolted with a thought, pulling back.

"Where's Maggie?"

Panting, Jason got out, "Downstairs. Her friend's place. Don't stop."

"You're sure?" *Please be sure.*

"I know I freaked out in the hotel, but yes. I'm a hundred percent sure. A hundred and ten if we want to get into sports clichés."

"I'm disappointed it's not a hundred and twenty."

They laughed and kissed and rubbed, all needy gasps and moans, devouring each other. Jason bucked into Ben's hand, groaning low in his throat. Ben wanted to climb into Jason's skin, frantic emotion drumming through him like the rain that had begun to pelt the windows.

They had too many clothes on, and Ben didn't have time to peel them off. His fingers made fast work of their buttons and zippers, and they groaned in unison when he shoved down their underwear enough to take their cocks in hand. He spit on his palm and stroked in concert with his thrusting hips, gripping their dicks together.

"Oh, God. This is too good to be true." Jason moaned, his eyes squeezed shut. Ben jerked their hot, straining cocks as he kissed Jason again, sucking his tongue into his mouth.

Ben leaned back, panting. "I'm here. We're together. Open your eyes."

Jason did, and with a soft gasp he came, gaze still locked with Ben's. Ben sped up the pace of his strokes, and a few seconds later he shuddered with his own release. He rested his face in the crook of Jason's neck as he came down, pulse still racing, milking them through their aftershocks.

He licked at the beads of sweat in the hollow of Jason's throat, then lifted his sticky hand, their seed mixed together on his skin. Ben licked his fingers clean, his balls twitching with the salty, musky combination, Jason watching, his pupils still blown, lips kiss-red, stubble burns on his face.

When Ben had gotten the last drop, Jason cupped his face and kissed him long and slow, licking into his mouth. Ben breathlessly shared their taste with him, and it felt like nothing less than a promise.

CHAPTER TWENTY

"BYE, MRS. LANE!" Maggie's voice rang out as the front door opened.

In the bathroom, Ben and Jason sprang apart, laughing. They'd cleaned up and had been kissing each other for Ben didn't know how long, all lips and spit and whispers of breath, quiet and perfect. It was like oxygen, the need to kiss Jason and have him close. He was giddy with it.

"Dad? There's a bag in the hall."

Ben realized they'd totally forgotten it as Jason squeezed his hand and led him from the bathroom. Maggie stood in the open doorway in shorts and a T-shirt, frowning down at his old duffel. She said, "Why would someone just leave it out here?"

"Sorry, I forgot it," Ben said. "Scatterbrained today."

Her head shot up, and she stared at Ben wordlessly. His gut clenched with sudden uncertainty. What if Maggie didn't want him there? Montana had been one thing—would she want him to become a permanent part of her life? He and Jason hadn't even had time to talk about logistics or *anything*, really.

He ran a hand through his hair, straightening it. "Hey, Maggie. How are you? I... I'm here," he finished lamely.

Blinking, she looked between Ben and Jason, then zeroed in on Ben. "You're here?" Her round face alight with pure joy, she raced over and threw her arms around his waist. "I missed you!"

Hugging her tightly, Ben swallowed the lump in his throat and kissed her head. "I missed you too, sweetheart."

"You're not mad at me?"

"What?" He jerked, glancing at Jason, then crouching and holding Maggie's arms. "Why would I be mad?"

"Because I saw you and Dad kissing at the hospital. I pretended to be asleep, and then you didn't say goodbye, and I thought maybe you knew and you were mad at me."

"No, no, no. I'm so sorry I didn't say goodbye. You didn't do a single thing wrong. Okay?"

"Okay." She smiled tentatively, glancing up at Jason and then back down to meet Ben's gaze. "So are you and Dad kissing again?"

Ben's grin felt like it glowed out of every inch of him. "We are. And if it's okay with you, we want to keep on kissing."

She bounced and clapped. "Yes, yes! Does this mean you're moving here?"

"Uh…" Jason smiled uneasily. "Good question. We still have to talk about that. About everything."

Ben stood. "We do. I actually have an idea I wanted to run by you guys." He retrieved his duffel and they settled on the couch with Maggie between them, beaming. He cleared his throat, nerves jangling. What if they hated it?

Then we'll figure out something else. It doesn't matter where we live as long as we're together.

He exhaled slowly. "First off, I have this for you, Jason." He unzipped his bag and carefully pulled out the sketchbook, which he'd kept flat by hauling the atlas along too. "I meant to give this to you before you left."

Sucking in a breath, Jason took it, reverently running his hand over the battered cover. "Thank you. I thought these were lost forever."

"A little worse for wear, but no." Ben gazed at him over Maggie. "Not lost."

Jason met his eyes, smiling tremulously.

"Are you going to kiss, like, right now?"

Laughter bubbled up, and Ben pecked Jason's lips, Maggie giggling between them. Jason gently laid the sketchbook on the coffee table and asked, "So what's your idea?"

He pulled out the Yosemite brochure next, and Maggie eyed it excitedly, squirming. "Are we going there?"

"Well, I want to know how you'd feel about that," Ben said. "After what happened, I wasn't sure if you'd still want to go to the woods."

"I do! I love it away from the city." She grimaced. "I'm not going to let that bad man wreck everything. There are bad men everywhere anyway. Hopefully we'll only meet good ones from now on."

Jason leaned over and rapped his knuckles on the table. "I hope so too." To Ben, he said, "Okay, Yosemite. Are you talking about a vacation?"

"No, not a vacation." Butterflies flapped, Ben's skin tingling. Would they want to share this future together? "They're looking for a new head ranger at Yosemite. I asked Brad about it, and he thinks I have a great chance. He's talking to the people down there."

Maggie wrinkled her nose. "I don't like Brad."

Ben laughed. "I didn't like him much myself the past few years, but he's really trying to help. I want to make peace between us. He was a big part of my life for a very long time, and I hate to think it was all for nothing."

She seemed to ponder it. "That makes sense. Okay. I'll try to like him more."

"Thank you. So, if I get this job, I'd move down to California. And I want you both to come with me. If that's something you'd want to do."

Maggie sat up straighter, eyes bright. "We could live by Yosemite? Instead of in the smelly city?"

"You could," Ben answered, excitement rippling. *Don't get ahead of yourself. You might not even get the job.*

Jason was quiet for a few moments. "I'm not sure. It would be a huge change."

"It would," Ben agreed, wiping his sweaty palms on his jeans. "I came up with a plan, and I could just tell you and see what you think?"

Maggie and Jason shared a glance, then nodded, Maggie kicking her feet rhythmically.

He exhaled. "Jason, there's a new CalArts satellite campus in Fresno. Do you still want to go to art school?"

"I think so?" A little smile tugged on Jason's lips. "Wow, CalArts? I dreamed of that."

"Of course he wants to go to art school!" Maggie motioned with her hand. "What else, what else?"

They might say yes. Holy shit. "We could live around Oakhurst, on the outskirts of the park. It's about an hour from Fresno, and you could commute to classes, Jason. Maybe do it part-time? It would be doable." Ben realized he was talking too quickly and stopped to take a breath.

Jason licked his lips. "Yeah. That could work."

Maggie shook Jason's leg, bouncing the whole futon. "Daddy, it would be perfect!"

"But what about the tuition?" Jason asked. "I don't want to get into huge debt."

"We'll figure it all out. I can sell the cabin in Montana. I was looking at houses while I was waiting for my connection in Chicago, and the prices aren't bad. There's one in particular..." He fished out his phone and tapped. "It's outside of town, but still close to the schools and stores. It's at the end of a street, nice and secluded, can only glimpse one neighbor's place through the trees." He gave the phone to Maggie.

She and Jason scrolled through the pictures, Maggie swiping with her finger, an excited tension zinging through the air.

Ben said, "Big porch at the front and back. The estimated mortgage is twelve hundred a month. It's totally doable. Brad bought me out of our house in Kalispell, and the money's just been sitting in my account. I really should reinvest it. This house has been on the market a while too. Might be able to bargain them down." He added, "And I know this is putting the cart in front of the horse. But I wanted to give you an idea of what it could be like. What we could have out there together."

As Maggie scrolled through the pictures again, glued to the phone, Jason looked at Ben and said, "It does sound amazing, but…"

He held up his hands. "I know this is probably too much. I'd have to get the job first, and maybe you guys don't want to move at all. I'm sure I could find a job here."

Maggie whipped her head up, eyes wide in horror. "*Here?* Instead of being a ranger in the mountains? No way! That would be so dumb!" She snapped around to face Jason. "Right, Dad? Can we go? Can we move to Yosemite? You can go to art school and we could have a *house!*"

Jason was apparently at a loss for words. He finally said, "But where would I work? I have to make money."

"I'm sure you could find something part-time," Ben answered, heart hammering. "I have savings and a good salary. If money were no object, what would your dream life be? What would you change about this plan? I don't want to come in here and dictate. We need to decide together. This is a jumping-off point. You know, just a start and…" He was babbling, and he stopped.

Jason stared into space. "What would I do differently?"

Maggie's brows drew together. "You know you don't have to do something different just for the sake of it. You don't have to be a control freak all the time."

Jason's cheek dimpled with an incredulous smile. "You know what? I don't think I would do anything differently. You could still work in a national park, Maggie would live in nature, and I could go to art school. It really is perfect if we can pull it off."

Ben's throat was dry, and he was going to come out of his skin with nervous optimism. "I know this is happening crazy fast, but if it will make us all happy, I think we should grab it. At least try, and if this plan won't work, we'll come up with another one. What do you say?"

Vibrating, Maggie clutched their hands, and Ben wanted to make her smile that widely for the rest of his life. He waited for Jason to answer. Jason looked at them, taking a shuddering breath before he asked, "Can we really do this?" Then he answered his own question. "I think we can. I trust you. I trust you, Ben. Let's go for it."

Maggie flew off the couch, literally jumping for joy, and Ben pulled Jason close. It was time for another kiss.

HOW IS THIS my life?

The last time he'd wondered that, Jason had been shivering in the black of night, miles and miles in the middle of the Montana wilderness, Maggie gone. But Ben had been there, strong and dependable and good.

And here he was again.

Jason's arm was numb, but he didn't want to move an inch as the first rays of dawn brightened the living room. Ben's steady breath gusted over the back of Jason's neck, Ben spooned up close behind him, arm slung over Jason's waist. It had been too hot for T-shirts over their pajama bottoms, which they wore for Maggie's sake. Their heated skin pressed together.

Jason grinned to himself in the stillness.

They'd stayed up late making tentative plans that depended on Ben getting the job, and backup plans in case he didn't. Without a proper bedroom, they'd only kissed softly and held each other as they fell asleep, content simply to be in each other's arms.

Maybe it was crazy and impetuous for them to plan to move to California, uprooting both their lives to make a new one together with Maggie. But only one other thing in Jason's life had ever felt so right, so destined and true—keeping his daughter when everyone said it was a mistake.

Ben stirred, his dry lips nuzzling Jason's neck. "I can't wait to wake up with you in our own bed," he whispered.

A dizzy thrill sparked. "Me either." Feeling Ben's morning hardness pressing against him through their pajama bottoms, he boldly added, "Can't wait to do so many things in that bed."

"Hmm, tell me more." Ben scraped his teeth over the back of Jason's neck, then kissed the spot, trailing his hand down Jason's chest. Then the teasing tone was gone, and he flattened his palm over Jason's heart. "We can take it slow. I know what happened at the hotel was a lot to take in."

A snort of laughter escaped Jason's lips. "You could say that."

Ben shook. "Oh my God, I did not mean it that way. I swear." His laughter trailed away. "But seriously, I want to make sure you're comfortable with everything we do. Or don't do."

Jason covered Ben's hand on his chest with his own. "I know. It was intense—I guess more than I thought it would be. I'd never really let myself think about sex, so maybe that played a role. It was like…"

Ben nuzzled Jason's neck. "What, baby?" Then he went rigid. "Shit, sorry. You didn't like it when I called you that."

"No, it's okay." He rolled it around in his head. "Say it again?"

"Baby," Ben whispered before kissing Jason's neck behind his ear.

A shiver skimmed over his skin. "I think I like it, actually. When we're like this." Now that he could relax, feeling taken care of—protected and safe—settled him and let him breathe easier. He turned his head so they could kiss briefly, slow and sweet, then rolled onto his back. Ben propped his head on his hand, waiting, his palm returning to Jason's chest, patient and steady.

"The thing is…" Jason cast about.

"You don't need the 'right' words. Just talk." He smiled encouragingly.

"Okay. The thing is that sex was really…vulnerable, I guess. I was scared. Overwhelmed at how close I felt to you. I've never had that with anyone. Never trusted someone that much. Giving up control like that? It wasn't easy."

"I understand." Ben's blue eyes shone with warmth and love. "Like I said, we can go slowly. It's not a sprint—it's a marathon. Or something. That was supposed to sound deep."

Jason kissed his chin and gave him a wink. "Super deep. And mmm, a sex marathon sounds pretty good now that I've had a chance to process everything." He dropped his voice lower although they were already talking softly. "Now that I know what to expect, I want more. In every position possible."

His whole body went hot as Ben rolled on top of him with delicious pressure, staring hungrily. "We don't have our own bed yet, but let's see what we can do in a bathroom."

Quite a lot, as it turned out.

Flipping the lock and pressing Ben against the door, Jason whispered, "I want to suck you."

Eyes flickering, Ben moaned softly as he tossed a condom and bottle of lube on the counter. "You have no idea how hot it is hearing that come out of your mouth."

Jason was determined to use his mouth to get Ben a whole lot hotter, and he dropped to his knees, the fuzzy blue bathmat cushioning him as he tugged down Ben's pajama bottoms. The head of Ben's cock was stained a deep red, and he licked at it like he would a cherry popsicle before sucking fully.

Ben's hands tangled in Jason's hair, not pushing or pulling, but heavy and good. Grounding. To have Ben's cock throbbing in his mouth and filling his senses, hearing the little pants and moans, was pure heaven.

Jason sucked greedily, sloppy and probably doing it all wrong. But Ben wasn't complaining, his thighs quivering as he hoarsely whispered, "That's it."

Experimentally, Jason ran his tongue up and down the ridge on Ben's dick. Breathing through his nose, he slid down farther, but gagged. Ben's gentle hands guided him back. "Not too much the first time," he murmured.

Jason swirled his tongue around the way Ben had done to him in the hotel, and bobbed his head up and down, sucking firmly. He thought of what always got him off when he masturbated, and cupped Ben's balls in his hand, rolling them together in his palm. Ben moaned loudly and his hips thrust up sharply. Jason followed his lead and sucked faster and harder.

Then Ben urged him to his feet, kissing him deeply and moaning into his mouth. "Going to make me come already." Breaking their kiss, he kicked off his PJs and got rid of Jason's too. "Need to fuck you again. You still want that?"

Jason laughed, his whole body electric. "Is that a trick question?"

Ben leaned in, his lips at Jason's ear, hands sliding down to palm Jason's ass cheeks. "You want me to fuck you?"

Cock jumping, Jason nodded.

"Can you say it? Can you tell me what you want?"

Even after everything, Jason's face went hot. "I want you. Please, I...I want you to fuck me."

Ben groaned, rutting against Jason. "Want my cock in your ass?"

It clearly turned Ben on to hear things out loud, and a frisson of power snaked down Jason's spine. "Yes. Fuck me, Ben. I want your cock in me. Stretching me, filling me. I want all of it. All of you."

Ben practically growled, and Jason found himself bent over the counter, Ben on his knees behind him, spreading his ass. *Licking* the crease. Gasping, he thought, *Good thing I had a shower last night.*

Ben's laughter huffed against his tender flesh, and he realized he'd said it out loud. Then Ben's tongue found his hole. He coated it with saliva, licking and kissing and poking inside as Jason clung to the counter and tried not to moan too loudly, incredible sensations pulsating through his body. He pressed his forehead to the mirror, glimpsing his red face and wet lips, desire-dark eyes.

He inhaled sharply as Ben's slick finger slid inside him. The pressure burned beautifully, and Ben added a second finger. Jason's whole body was on fire. "Fuck me."

Standing, Ben's teeth grazed Jason's earlobe. "How about you fuck yourself?"

"Huh?"

His ears rushed with so much thick, heavy want that he wasn't sure he'd heard right. But he understood when Ben stretched back on the bathmat on the floor and urged Jason to straddle him.

Ben rolled on the condom and slicked it, then guided Jason to sit and press down. "Take only as much as you want."

Inch by glorious inch, Jason impaled himself on Ben's cock, controlling his descent, his body flushed and alive, muscles flexing. He leaned over to kiss Ben messily, their tongues seeking.

Having Ben inside him was the sweetest pain he'd ever experienced, and soon he was fully impaled, pubes brushing his ass. "Ben," he moaned.

"You're beautiful," Ben whispered. "This is what you've wanted all these years, isn't it? What you've denied yourself."

Jason could only nod, throwing his head back as he rolled his hips, experimenting with different angles before lifting a few inches up and back down, fucking himself, his hard cock leaking, Ben's fingers digging into his hips.

He met Ben's dark, lustful gaze again. Jason was open and vulnerable, Ben so deep inside him, seeing him laid bare. But this time he felt wild and *free*. He didn't fight his emotions—love and trust and pure primal pleasure vibrating through him as he found just the right spot.

Jason wasn't going to last, and he took hold of his shaft. "Want me to come on you?"

A flush spread all the way down Ben's chest as he bit back a cry, ramming up forcefully, bending his knees and digging in his heels as he fucked up into Jason. "Yes. Give me your cum. Want it all."

Jason stroked himself roughly, meeting Ben's thrusts. He wanted to yell, but the walls were thin, and there was something strangely intimate and powerful about their whispers and hushed moans, the air thick with sex.

Pain and pleasure truly became one, and Jason came with a strangled moan, turned inside out as he splashed over Ben's chest, the thrill of giving Ben what he craved adding an extra dimension to the power of Jason's orgasm. Ben thrust frantically, shaking and groaning as he emptied himself into the condom.

Head back on the mat, mouth open, Ben smeared Jason's semen over himself, and Jason helped with the dirty finger painting before dropping his head to Ben's collarbone, panting. They had to move and clean up, but not yet.

A minute turned to five, giving way to lazy kisses. Bumping and laughing in the small tub, they showered, then wrapped themselves in towels. Jason brushed his teeth, then looked at himself in the mirror. He liked what he saw. Who he saw. Behind him, Ben kissed his shoulder, wrapping his arms around Jason's middle.

"Dad?" Maggie knocked at the door. "Are you suddenly becoming a morning person? I always get to pee first. Hurry up, I have to goooo."

They laughed, and Ben squeezed Jason tighter. "We're getting our own bedroom *and* our own bathroom." When he moved to step away, Jason threaded their fingers together, just for another heartbeat.

Ben was right. Jason was grabbing happiness, and he was never, ever letting go.

EPILOGUE

"Mmm." Ben shifted and stretched his legs, smiling at the sensation of Jason's soft lips and light stubble brushing over his shoulder.

"Happy birthday," Jason murmured, pressing up behind him, his erection poking Ben, hot and hard against his bare ass.

"*Now* it is." Grinding his hips back, he reached down and stroked himself. "Do you think we can squeeze it in? Pun entirely intended."

Jason pulled Ben onto his back and slid on top, both of them moaning as they kissed slowly, waking up their bodies and waking up to the day, the soft glow of sunshine through the half-open blinds already warm on Ben's skin.

Tongues exploring, they rubbed together, legs tangled, breathing faster. Ben cupped Jason's head, running his fingers through Jason's mess of hair. He pushed up with his hips and whispered, "Want to play cowboy and go for a ride, baby?"

From the hallway, Maggie called, "Are you guys up? Come *on*. I have to get to school eventually, and there are presents to open!"

Ben groaned. "This tradition of opening gifts at the crack of dawn needs to be revisited." He called back, "Coming!" before grumbling under his breath, "Or not, as the case may be."

"Oh, you will. It'll be worth the wait, I promise." Jason nipped Ben's ear, his breath hot. "I'll ride you so hard you'll—"

Dylan's wail pierced the dawn stillness, echoing in stereo over the baby monitor. Ben sighed. "Hold that thought, because I'm going to hold you to it tonight. As God is my witness, we are going to have sex."

Dylan cried louder, and Jason rolled out of bed and stepped into track pants before tugging on a tee. "How about you *hold me to it* this afternoon? Mrs. Leung down the street agreed to babysit. I'll come out to the park, and you can take a break. Out in the woods." He waggled his eyebrows.

"Why, Jason Kellerman. Are you suggesting we go off the trail?"

He opened the door and winked over his shoulder. "I know I'll be in good hands."

Ben stretched back on the mattress, arms over his head and toes pointed. Dylan's cries tapered off, and Jason's low lullaby murmured over the monitor, his voice as bad as ever as he warbled the campfire song about barges Ben had taught him and Maggie years ago.

After pulling on a tank top and flannel pajama bottoms, Ben headed downstairs, hardwood smooth under his bare feet. At the bottom of the stairs, he paused at the framed picture Jason had drawn of him and Maggie that day on the Road to the Sun. The crinkles still showed in the faded paper, but Jason's pencil strokes were strong and true.

He couldn't imagine what his life would be without Jason and Maggie. A terrible ordeal had cemented their bond, but they'd survived it. Not simply survived—thrived and grown stronger together.

He swallowed thickly and laughed at himself. He always got a little emotional on birthdays. With a tap of his fingers on the wooden picture frame, he walked on. Maggie still saw a local therapist every month, and was one of the most remarkably well-adjusted people Ben knew. They'd never forget Harlan Brown, but he was a speck in the rearview mirror.

Ben walked into the open-concept kitchen and squeezed Maggie's shoulder on his way to the coffee machine. "Morning." A bigger dining room spread out beyond the granite-topped peninsula, along with sliding doors to the wide verandah, where Ben's rocking chairs sat, dew glistening on the faded wood.

At the little round kitchen table where they usually ate, Maggie had gathered a few gifts and cards, the rising sun highlighting her long, golden hair. "Hey. Happy birthday!" She held up a box with an artful eye-roll. "From Brad and Tyson. Probably something super pretentious and 'zen' or whatever now that they've discovered Buddhism. They're so enlightened, don't you know."

Ben laughed. "Oh, I know. They mean well."

Holding Dylan, Jason appeared and strapped him into his high chair at the kitchen table. "Just as long as we never have to chant at dinner again. A simple grace will do me."

"And me. Good thing we only see them about once a year." Ben poured a cup of coffee from the pot that brewed automatically every morning, inhaling the rich, bitter scent deeply. "Next time they come through they'll probably be wearing those red string bracelets Madonna used to."

"Who?" Maggie asked.

Ben pulled out his chair beside hers. "Ha, ha. You were singing along to her new song on the way home from junior rangers last night."

She held up a cream-colored envelope. "This one's from Grandma and Grandpa. Probably money. Nothing from Uncle Tim, but he'll send a text just before midnight when he remembers at the last second."

Jason sat and sipped a mug of coffee. "But we love him anyway." He screwed the lid on a sippy cup and helped Dylan slurp. "Should we start with cards?"

Maggie thrust a brightly wrapped box toward Ben, her eyes

bright. "No, open mine first." Biting her lip, she tucked a long leg under herself and fidgeted, toying with the fraying hem of her pajama top. Ben still couldn't believe how much she'd grown. She was almost thirteen and a real teenager, as she liked to remind them.

He shook the surprisingly light box, which didn't seem to have much inside. Was probably a gift card under a pile of tissue paper. "Hmm. Is it that new super-super-super high-def TV?"

Maggie tilted her head and gave him a look. "Ha, ha."

"Lawn mower? Oh, come on. You know I'm funny. Dylan thinks I'm funny, don't you, buddy?" He reached over and tickled his little feet.

Dylan gurgled with delight and kicked, slapping his palms on the tray of his high chair. His dark hair stood up on end the way it always did, bedhead or not. After a two-year adoption process, they'd picked him up at the agency in Brazil six weeks before, and Ben still had to pinch himself.

He ripped the paper to reveal an old Amazon box. "Okay, what do we have here…" He opened the cardboard folds, and inside there was indeed a pile of tissue paper. He pulled it out, throwing it up in the air so it drifted down, Dylan clapping his pudgy hands.

There was a letter-sized piece of paper at the bottom, probably a printout of a gift card, as he'd guessed. He pulled it out, realizing it was several pages and stapled. Reading the words printed on top, his heart skipped.

"I mean, if you want." Maggie watched anxiously.

Ben hoarsely read out loud, "State of California, application for adoption of a child." He didn't try to stop the tears that flooded his eyes as he looked between Maggie and Jason, who blinked away tears of his own. Ben was so full of love he could barely breathe. "Yes. Yes, I want this so much. Are you sure, sweetheart?"

Maggie nodded and sprang forward to hug him. He held her so tightly, and they cried as Dylan watched in puzzlement, Jason wiping his cheeks.

When Maggie sat back, rubbing her eyes and sniffling, she said, "You're already my dad in every way that counts, so I want it to be official. And I want to call you that too. Dad, I mean. Or will that be weird?"

"Weird?" Ben could only laugh, joy shining in him like the sun through the oaks in the backyard. "Maggie, it would be the greatest thing I've ever heard."

"Okay. Dad." She laughed too, and Jason joined in, Dylan drumming his heels.

Ben reached over the table for Jason's hand. "I can't believe I have a husband, a daughter, and a son. Thank you."

Jason squeezed, their gold bands digging into their skin. "You haven't opened my present yet." He passed over a slim package. "It's going to pale in comparison, but…"

"Nonsense." Ben tore away the wrapping. "I'm sure it's—" He stared at the title of the storybook. The words *Road to the Sun* arched over a drawing of… "It's us," he breathed. "Our family."

He recognized Jason's smooth lines and soulful artistic expression in the mountains soaring into blue sky behind them—Jason, Ben, Maggie, and baby Dylan cradled in Ben's arms. With trembling fingers, he opened the book.

"Maggie helped me write it," Jason said. "It's our story, but in a magic kingdom."

Grinning like a fool, Ben turned the pages, reading the tale of Prince Jason, Princess Maggie, brave knight Ben, and Dylan, the little lord. On one page was a recreation of the picture at the foot of the stairs, only this time he and Maggie wore old-fashioned garb. In the end, they all slayed the evil dragon and built a beautiful castle deep in the forest.

Ben traced the pages with his fingertips. "This is gorgeous.

These drawings are exquisite."

Cheeks flushed, Jason shrugged, beaming. "Professor Atherton had one of his friends at a publisher print it as a one-off. He said they really liked it. They do kids' books, and they want to talk to me about an internship. Part-time, so I can still be here with Dylan most days."

"Really?" Maggie bounced in her chair. "You're almost done with school, so that would be perfect!"

Jason held up a hand. "We'll see what happens. I still have two credits, and it'll take a while doing them only at night. We don't want to get ahead of ourselves."

"Fair enough," Ben agreed. "But that's a very encouraging sign. Right, Dylan?" He tickled those pudgy, squirmy feet again. "Now who's hungry? Do I get birthday pancakes?"

The smell of sizzling bacon soon filled the air, Jason at the stove as Maggie stirred the batter, telling them excitedly about her idea for a school project on butterfly conservation. She detailed her plans to track the alpine butterflies in Yosemite as Ben spooned steel cut oatmeal and pureed peaches into Dylan's mouth, the vast majority of it seeming to drip down his chin and get all over his sticky hands.

Jason was right—they shouldn't get ahead of themselves. Because they were in the most perfect, beautiful place.

The End

About the Author

Keira aims for the perfect mix of character, plot, and heat in her M/M romances. She writes everything from swashbuckling pirates to heartwarming holiday escapism. Her fave tropes are enemies to lovers, age gaps, forced proximity, and passionate virgins. Although she loves delicious angst along the way, Keira guarantees happy endings!

Find out more at: www.keiraandrews.com

Made in the USA
Las Vegas, NV
09 March 2024